'I should thin[illegible] you do owe m[illegible]

'Who knows *what* name you use, or *who* your family are? You could be anyone, changing your name, changing your appearance, fooling people. My father should never have employed you. Never have sent me here. It's . . . it's despicable!'

Isabella was aware that her voice had quivered, and she clenched her fists furiously. 'Despicable!' she repeated.

Glancing indignantly up at him, she almost felt that he was stifling a smile, and she seethed that he could dare, but when he spoke his voice was passably contrite.

'I said I owed you an explanation, and I dare say you have reason to be angry, though I can assure you that your father knew precisely who I was when he employed me. He has never been in ignorance. And I indeed *was* Mr D'Estine when I came to tutor your brothers, and that remained my correct title up until ten months ago... But perhaps I had better begin at the beginning?'

'Yes,' Isabella retorted sharply, 'perhaps you had.'

'My father,' he began, and her mind flew contemptuously to the little man with the wheelbarrow, 'is Cuthbert Oswald Wilfred D'Estine, Seventh Earl of Kintrove, Third Viscount of Neame, Baron D'Estine of Nore, of Alladay and of Kifford.'

For Tim, Simon, Cathy and Sam.

Janet Grace was born in Kent and educated in Staffordshire and at the University of Kent where she studied English and American literature.

Since then she has taught English in schools and to foreign students, supervised a playgroup, fostered disturbed adolescents and taught craft, child development and sex education at a Technical College, before turning to writing.

She is happily married and now lives in a large ramshackle farmhouse in Nottinghamshire with her husband, three children and a menagerie of animals, including dogs, cats, three rats and a parrot.

Previous Titles

FOOL'S HEAVEN
A MOST UNUSUAL LADY

ISABELLA

Janet Grace

First published in Great Britain 1990
by Mills & Boon Limited

This edition 1991

ISBN 0 263 77136 9

Masquerade is a trademark published by
Mills & Boon Limited, Eton House,
18–24 Paradise Road, Richmond, Surrey, TW9 1SR.

Set in Times Roman 10 on 10¼ pt.
04-9101-83930 C

Made and printed in Great Britain

CHAPTER ONE

'PAPA! No! How can you say this?'

Fists clenched, chest heaving, Isabella glared at her father. His look of wearied irritation was tinged, not with guilt at his treatment of her, but with impatience.

'Aunt Caroline promised I would stay with her. She promised! All the dances and picnics and visits were planned. I had chosen everything I wanted to do. It was going to be a perfect summer! And now you tell me this!'

She quivered, almost unable to speak for the fury and disappointment that shook her. As always, her thoughts flew immediately to Harry Exton. As soon as her father had left the country they would have been able to meet every day. Aunt Caroline would not have objected. And they had made such plans, such promises...

'Why must I stay with my brothers and their tedious tutor? I hate that dreary man and the way the boys hang on his every drop of wisdom.' Had she dared, she would have stamped her foot. 'Surely, Papa, surely, there is somewhere else I can go?'

Her father turned with annoyance from a contemplation of the road below his study window, where the driver of a high-perch phaeton was endeavouring to disentangle his equipage from a train of donkeys laden with fresh vegetables for sale on the London streets. He regarded his daughter's flushed face with distaste.

'It is too late for these unseemly tantrums, Isabella. Kindly endeavour to control yourself. All Caroline's children have the measles. Naturally she doesn't want you making extra work for the household at such a time. As for other arrangements, I have no time to be bothering my head over such trifles now. Mr D'Estine took my suggestion that you accompany your brothers to his home very civilly, very civilly indeed, just as he should; and the arrangements are made. As for not liking the poor crippled fellow, no one expects you to like him. But you'll keep a decent tongue in your head while you are at Long Trovers, my girl, and, though things may not be as you have been accustomed to expect at home, none the less you will act as befits my daughter. The family are doing us a kindness by taking you all...though I dare say the sum I'll be paying them will be welcome enough.'

His face lightened momentarily into self-satisfaction. The thought of his own bulging coffers always pleased him; consequently he thought of them frequently.

'Papa.' There were tears on Isabella's cheeks, but she spoke without any real hope. 'Papa, I could come with you to Europe. It would be a fine thing for my education...'

Her voice tailed away at the look on her father's face.

'A diplomatic mission with an ill-tempered child in tow! Don't be ridiculous, Isabella. I shall have far too weighty things on my mind to be bothered with female trivia. Now, I have listened to enough of this nonsense. You will stay where you are told.'

'For how long will it be, Father?' Her voice was heavy with despair.

'Good grief, I can't tell that. Who knows how long delicate negotiations of this importance will take? I will send to you when I return home. Go now, and tell that fool of a maid to organise your packing, then give her notice. She has never been worth the wage I pay her, and at the rates I am paying D'Estine's family they can provide their own staff.'

Mr Horatio Larkham turned back to his desk, preparing to forget the inconvenience of providing for his daughter and fill his mind with matters of state, when a final thought occurred to him.

'You should also know, Isabella, that you will no longer be troubled by the attentions of that young pup, the Exton boy, so you can dry your tears and forget him, and his impertinent verses. Which, I trust, are all now burned, as I ordered?'

Eyebrows raised, he glared the sudden angry query at her, and, resentfully, hating his calm assurance that Harry would desert her without a word, she crossed her fingers and nodded.

He talked impatiently on, taking her obedience for granted.

'I arranged with his father that he be removed from your circle of acquaintances. Mr Exton agreed to my suggestion that it would be most beneficial for the boy to travel out with his older brother to assist in the overseeing of their sugar plantations in Jamaica. I believe they sailed yesterday.'

He was fingering papers on his desk, and missed her small, stifled gasp of disbelief.

'However, in view of your unsuitable behaviour in accepting his letters, and the fact that I have no female relative available to leave you with, I have this morning finalised, very satisfactorily, the details of Lord Carlton Crue's offer for your hand. I decided that it would be preferable to leave you more formally under his protection during my absence, and he was in complete agreement. I have already sent the notices to *The Times* and the *Morning Post*, apprising them of your engagement. I dare say you will see them tomorrow, and you must prepare yourself to be congratulated. It is an excellent match. It is good of him that he is happy to concern himself with your well-being while I am away, and I expect you to be appreciative of any trouble he takes on your behalf.'

Blue eyes very wide, again brimming with tears, Isabella stared at him in amazement and struggled against shock and disbelief to hold her voice steady.

'Papa!' Her voice shook, and she began again. 'Papa, *I* have not been consulted. Yes, I knew you had plans, but... but... not yet! Not without taking my feelings into account...' She paced the room in little agitated steps. 'Lord Carlton Crue has yet to speak to *me*. He has not asked *me* for my hand. *I* have not accepted his offer—and my affections... Harry...Mr Exton...we had hoped——'

'You were still in your bed when he answered my note this morning,' her father interrupted irritably. 'You would hardly have had me send him up to your room, now, would you? As for your affections, they are an irrelevance. Young Exton has no part in your life. He has been forbidden to contact you again, as you are forbidden to contact him. No more of this absurdity. I am a busy man. The matter is closed. You may go.'

Lips quivering, despair in her heart, Isabella went.

The lanes had become narrower and more rutted as they plunged further from the main highway into the burgeoning tangle of the English May countryside. Queen Anne's lace frothed festively along the banks, pushing through the open windows of the carriage as it jolted and rocked, and scattering the dark velvet squabs with a starburst of creamy specks. The scents were not sweet, but rich, rank and earthy.

Isabella scowled at the intrusive flowers and irritably flicked two small black creeping things and a ladybird from the skirts of her sprigged muslin dress. At least here the lane was damp, overhung with elm trees and hollowed into the hillside. The dust that had plagued the rest of their journey had cleared, allowing Isabella to fling the windows down to cool the stifling air within the coach. Just remembering the choking dust clouds made Isabella cough again, and blow her nose.

The journey had seemed a nightmare, but then, everything had seemed a nightmare since that interview with her father. Isabella's fingers curled and clenched in her lap as she brooded yet again on his cold, callous dismissal of herself and her wishes. Not that they had ever been close, but she had expected more than this. She had always thought he cared for her. She reflected bitterly on his past indulgences, and, with sudden painful clarity and a spurt of hurt fury, saw for the first time the emptiness of her relationship with her father.

Having lost her mother twelve years ago, when Thomas was born, Isabella knew she had been indulged with every wish and whim that money could buy, for Mr Larkham loved to flaunt his wealth. She had quickly learnt how to please him. It was necessary only to look charming, speak feminine nothings, ensure she never unnecessarily disturbed him, and unquestioningly obey his wishes. This had brought her countless treats and presents, but never time or love.

She had been forced to live a life without affection, apart from that of her young brothers. They were all she had had to love.

Up until now Isabella had been grateful to her father, and had seen as paternal protection the way he had ruthlessly rejected all the offers of marriage that had come her way during her London season. Until Harry, she had not met a single man who had awoken her heart. But Harry... He had no title, he was a younger son, but he had a respectable income, was of excellent family, and Isabella loved him. She loved his shy letters, his long, laboured verses, and his soft, stolen kisses. She had hoped for her father's eventual consent.

She had allowed herself to forget the time when he had casually mentioned that he considered that a marriage between herself and Lord Carlton Crue might be to the advantage of both men, and help to further her father's diplomatic career.

She scowled unseeingly out of the window.

With the carelessness of her nineteen years she had always dismissed the possibility from her mind. She hardly knew Lord Carlton. He was one of her father's friends, but the men dined together at White's, never at home. She had never, in her darkest fears, anticipated an engagement forced unknowingly upon her. Indeed, naïvely, she had never seriously doubted but that she would marry where she chose, until the day Mr Larkham had discovered one of her letters from Harry Exton, containing several verses which he had written in rapturous tribute to her beauty.

She had not burnt the verses. His letters, his poems and a lock of his soft, curled black hair lay treasured in between the pages of her diary, hidden in her portmanteau. He might have been forced to sail with his brother, but he would write. She had been expecting a note each day. Soon the longed-for words would come, explaining all, reassuring her of his love. She had defied her father and sent a letter each day winging its way after him across the ocean. No parental ban could quell their love. Nothing could change it. Of that she was certain.

The coach swayed around a corner, brushing the hawthorn hedges and filling the window with petals of May flowers. She could hear her brothers on the roof of the coach, catching at the branches to shower each other with blossom. A large bee flew in, making Ellie, hitherto quiet in her corner, scream and flap her apron.

'I'm right glad I'm not staying down 'ere with you, miss,' she remarked, grinning cheerfully. 'I never took to all this Nature. Give me the London cobbles any day o' the week.'

The maid, so disparaged by Mr Larkham, had taken the news of her dismissal cheerfully, informing her mistress that she had sisters and cousins in half the houses in London, any of whom would speak for her. She would have no problem in finding another place. Isabella, who had not been brought up to consider her maid as a person who might have a family, and had hoped for a flattering show of sorrow, had been surprised, and a little irritated.

'Well, you need not think I shall be unhappy to see you returning in the coach,' she rejoined petulantly. 'I dare say I could manage better alone than with your cack-handed attentions, and, besides, Papa is to pay for a maid to be provided.'

'Yes, miss.' Ellie's demure words did not quite compensate for the flicker of a grin, however quickly it had been suppressed. Ellie well knew her mistress's opinion of life in the country.

Isabella sighed, martyred, and shut her eyes. One of her brothers had once again begun to absent-mindedly drum his heels on the front of the carriage. They and Mr D'Estine were noisily enjoying riding outside in the sunshine, but she lacked the energy to lean out and complain once more. That tutor seemed to do nothing to control the boys, and to care not at all for her pulsing headache. She screwed her eyes tighter shut and clutched the strap as she was flung heavily against the side squabs. Dust billowed in at the window again.

'Nearly over that time, sir,' she heard Thomas shout, and Mr D'Estine, inconsiderate, callous Mr D'Estine, merely laughed. Without opening her eyes she reached out and flung the window shut.

She did not open her eyes again until the carriage drew up, and she knew they must have arrived at Long Trovers. She was reluctant to open them. She had been told nothing, she realised despondently, of Mr D'Estine's family or circumstances, and dreaded what she might see when she looked out.

Her father never concerned himself with his staff. If they worked well he paid them; if they did not, then he sacked them. As people, they were of no interest to him at all. Isabella had always considered his attitude to be normal and proper, but now she resented it. Surely she had a right to know what she might expect to find in this benighted backwater? What sort of family did men who became tutors have?

She never nowadays accorded Mr D'Estine more than a frosty nod of acknowledgement, never considered the possibility of engaging him in conversation. She resented the affection and loyalty he received from her brothers, was even a little jealous of the closeness between them. She disliked the man. Unaccountably, she frequently felt uncomfortable in his presence; indeed, she had on occasion half suspected that he was amused by her, if such a thought had not been incredible. She avoided him whenever possible, with his limping tread, and the way he invariably seemed to stoop whenever she or her father approached, pushing on his spectacles, and peering over them as he spoke to Thomas or William. He was, she thought angrily, no more than an object for pity, or contempt.

The enormity of what her father had inflicted upon her this summer threatened to overwhelm her in tears of self-pity, but at that moment in her thoughts the carriage door was flung wide, and Mr D'Estine himself was looking in at her. He had removed the customary spectacles and, standing unexpectedly straight, was watching her from very bright hazel eyes, his expression faintly, infuriatingly, amused.

'We have arrived at Long Trovers, Miss Larkham. May I hand you down?' he asked.

With a scowl she handed him a bandbox to carry, then blinked in surprise as she noticed the grey-haired butler who was hovering anxiously just behind the tutor, wearing an immaculate but threadbare uniform, and who now hurried forward, tutting in disapproval, to take the bandbox and hand it back to a young footman who stood behind. She stood poised in astonishment, half out of her father's familiar, luxurious coach, her hand on the glossy black paintwork of the doorframe, and stared beyond the footman.

Long Trovers was not, as she had half imagined in the gloomy moments of the journey when she gave it thought, a cramped and odiferous rustic hamlet; all jumbled cottages, pigs and chickens, with Mr D'Estine's father the impoverished curate eking out his days in a draughty vicarage crammed with the tutor's noisy younger brothers and dreary unmarried sisters. It was not like that at all.

Long Trovers was not even a village, though it could have housed all the inhabitants of one, and still had rooms empty and unexplored. It was a vast, sprawling house, stretching from the ruined, tumbled stones of a great tower on a mound at one extreme of her vision, through a sprawling growth of stone and brick, tilting roofs and twisted chimneys, windows blinking in the sunlight, to a seemingly random series of extensions, whose functions defied guesswork and had probably long been forgotten, that vanished into encroaching trees and undergrowth somewhere in the distance.

The coach had stopped before a huge oak door which stood flung wide to the sunshine, and all the staff of the house seemed to have appeared to welcome them, not in the starched lines that met with her father's approval, but with wide grins, chatter and fluster. Her brothers, she saw, had already discovered the round, aproned, rosily beaming woman with a giveaway smudge of flour on her cheek, who was, amazingly, already producing cakes from her apron pocket.

Utterly disconcerted, resenting her brothers' ready acceptance, Isabella looked back at Mr D'Estine. He was still waiting patiently, offering his arm to help her from the carriage. Stiffly, she accepted the unavoidable, and climbed down.

'Come,' he said, his tones impeccably polite, but his eyes dancing with a sharp amusement. 'I would like you to meet my parents.'

Their advance to the door was slow, for the tutor greeted everybody with interest and affection. Isabella, rigid with embarrassment under the scrutiny of these forward, intrusive servants, hardly noticed what they said, according each only her most repressive nod. She had never known such unrestrained behaviour among her inferiors. It was unsettling. It was not such a large staff, she noted with relief, as might have been expected from the size of the house, and most of their uniforms were deplorably faded and worn, even occasionally patched. Had her father seen them, she thought crossly, he would certainly never have sent her. And the worst was not over. A little wizened old woman was clutching the tutor's hand, and he was calling her 'Noosey', which made her laugh and cry all at once, then he actually bent and kissed her cheek before introducing her to Isabella.

'Miss Larkham, I would like to introduce Nurse Pusey, affectionately known to everyone as Noosey.'

To Isabella's horror the aged crone took her hand and clutched it.

'You will be very happy here, my dear,' she smiled, nodding. Isabella kept her doubts to herself, and disentangled her hand.

'And my parents,' Mr D'Estine was saying.

The couple who stood at the top of the steps to welcome them defied Isabella's powers of classification. They smiled at her with a gentle dignity which somehow commanded deference, yet the lady of the house wore a faded dress of printed calico that could have belonged to any working woman, and her cap, not lacy and beribboned, was of plain white linen. Her face was lined, weatherworn, kindly and surprisingly shrewd and amused as she took Isabella's hand to welcome her.

'Yes, my dear, I am Anthony's mother. I trust he did everything he could to make the journey pleasant for you. These lanes can make a very rough ride when the dirt bakes hard, almost worse than the winter muds, don't you think? And the dust can be appalling. But Wilfred will want to greet you. Wilfred!'

The old man, who had been fondly greeting his son, turned to Isabella with a sweet smile. His wispy white hair blew lightly about his head, and his blue eyes had a wide, child-like gaze. His jacket, of what had once been an excellent brown broadcloth and stylish, if old-fashioned, cut, now hung loosely off his shoulders, over the incongruous working man's corduroy breeches.

'It is good to welcome you,' he said gently, 'and your young brothers. It will be good to have the sound of young people in the house again. Very good.' He beamed, and turned to shake the hands of William and Thomas, who had finished their cakes and remembered their manners. 'Welcome, all of you, to Long Trovers. So good for Anthony to have the company. Welcome.'

Smiling and nodding, the old man led them into the house. With a small, ironic bow the tutor offered Isabella his arm again to escort her in. Sharply she tossed her head and, ignoring him, crossed the threshold alone.

CHAPTER TWO

THE sound of her bedroom door creaking open, on the following morning, did nothing to cheer Isabella's spirits. She had woken early in this strange house, and had dozed fitfully through the sunlight and birdsong, thoughts and fretting dreams of Harry adrift on the ocean intertwining with the dreary tedium of the calls of pigeons on the roof above her room.

How she hated the very sound of them, and the crowing of cockerels, squawking of hens, and lowing of cattle. She would have given anything for the familiar rattle, clatter and rumble of iron-bound carriage wheels on cobbles.

She kept her eyes closed, the sheet pulled up around her face. There was the hopeful clink of china, then a sudden wonderful smell of toast. Also, a curious clicking and scuffling sound, impossible to identify. Isabella turned over and sat up.

Nurse Pusey was pulling back the curtains, pushing wide the window to let in the morning air.

'There's many as are afraid to let in a bit of air,' she remarked cheerfully, 'but when the good Lord gives us a morning like this, why, it can only do you good. Let me plump up your pillows.'

As Isabella reluctantly leant forward, she realised the origin of the puzzling sounds. Half a dozen dogs had accompanied Nurse Pusey into the room and were wandering about, sniffing at Isabella's clothes and bandboxes. They were curiously speckled in brown, white and black, soft-eared, with gentle brown eyes, and as they moved about the room their claws clicked and scuffed on the polished wooden floor. One of them, greying about the muzzle, sat leaning against the side of the bed, gazing up at Isabella soulfully.

'Go away!' Isabella flapped an irritated hand at it. 'I am not accustomed to a bedroom full of farm animals,' she snapped, as Nurse Pusey brought over the breakfast tray, and placed it on her lap.

'Well, they have certainly taken a liking to you, my dear,' the old woman responded comfortably, with infuriating satisfaction. 'There's not many visitors get this sort of attention. See how fond they are of you already.'

Indeed, several of the dogs were now leaning against the bed and regarding her with adoration.

'Fond of my toast and chocolate, more probably,' Isabella muttered, but the nurse only shook her head knowingly, and smiled.

'I hope you are all recovered from your headache? These journeys can be so exhausting—no wonder we get nervous spasms. But you have all your pretty colour back in your cheeks now.'

Isabella shrugged ungraciously. She had excused herself, and retired to her room, almost immediately on arrival the previous day, using her headache as an excuse to escape the horrible necessity of speaking to these people, and particularly of speaking to Mr D'Estine, with his disconcerting smile. She had refused offers of food, sulkily aware of her own petulance, and had insisted that only complete quiet and rest would effect a cure.

To her outraged fury, they had taken her at her word. She had been left alone: left, and utterly neglected. Accustomed, at home, to a similar request for solitude resulting in a train of anxious but discreetly silent servants bringing hot bricks, tisanes, powders, and tiny portions of cold boiled chicken breast to tempt her appetite, Isabella, without even the attentions of the irritating Ellie, had spent the evening lonely, furious, mortified and resentful.

'I'm sure no one in this house cares how I feel,' she muttered, but Nurse Pusey was shaking out the clothes Isabella had left scattered on the floor, and made no response. The old dog edged closer, and thumped its tail quietly on the floor. Isabella glared at it.

'If you would like to come down when you are ready, one of the family will show you round. 'Tis a big place, easy to get lost in if you don't know the way of it. Those brothers of yours,' Nurse Pusey's lined face creased yet more into a fond smile, 'why, they are out already with paper and pens, all set to make a map of it all! That will keep them busy for a while! Now, there is water in the ewer, and a towel ready——'

'But surely the maid will bring up hot water!' Isabella interrupted pettishly.

'Why, no, my dear. There are no maids to run up regular to these floors, and Mrs Stoke can't be sparing girls from the kitchen to be running about on such errands. No one has hot water upstairs, not even her ladyship. Everyone uses the scullery if they want hot water. I shall be off, for I have work to do. Remember, turn right from your bedroom door, and follow on this corridor, without turning off it, until you reach the main staircase. Somebody will find you in the hall to show you around. Goodbye, my dear.'

Isabella, her cup suspended midway to her open mouth, gazed at the closing door in astonishment, outrage and bewilderment. No maids? No hot water? Her ladyship? Scullery? What could the old fool mean? No one who was not of the servant class washed in a scullery. And as for any persons of distinction... The nurse was talking nonsense.

But then, what sort of family might own a house as vast as this? Although Mr Larkham was wealthy, his money had come from manufacturing, and he was not entirely accepted in the most aristocratic of circles, despite his diplomatic ambitions. Isabella's acquaintance with life in the great English stately homes, whether wealthy or impoverished, was thus gleaned second-hand from better-connected friends.

She pondered on Mr D'Estine and his home. Were these improbable people the owners? Or were they some sort of impoverished tenants? Just who were Mr D'Estine's family? Once again Isabella dwelt resentfully on her father's casual disposal of her into this unknown world. The only reflection that perversely cheered her was the utter certainty that had her father met these people he would have profoundly disapproved of them. This gave her a sulky satisfaction.

She surprised herself by finishing her toast and hot chocolate quickly. She felt unusually hungry. But eating was one thing; dressing herself was another matter altogether. It was not a task she had ever attempted alone before, and it was plain that she could expect no assistance in this uncivilised and under-staffed household. Stepping warily round the dogs who, despite Nurse Pusey's departure, and the disappearance of the toast, showed no inclination to leave her, she spurned the cold water, and examined her wardrobe.

It was necessary for her to regretfully reject several dresses in the latest styles which would have done much to reassure her of her hopeful superiority over these rustics; they had elaborate buttoning up the back, and would be quite impossible to manage alone. Eventually she decided on another muslin, a plain pale primrose, sprigged with white, which, despite its simplicity, complemented her blonde curls admirably, and had the great advantage of tying at the front, with a bow under the bosom. Isabella struggled awkwardly with the bow for some time until she despaired of perfection and, angry and frustrated at her own helplessness, decided it would have to do.

Her hair also presented problems. No longer could she command Ellie to produce the style of her choice, or order Madame Lallay to visit to try out the latest modes. After vainly trying to achieve the style '*à la* Madonna', which had been a favourite with Harry, leading to compliments on her divine purity, and heavenly, angelic beauty, she dwelt miserably on his departure, and dragged the ribbon out.

Peering into the yellowing mirror, she pushed her long blonde tresses roughly back and tied them as best she could, hoping that the curls fell into something approaching the antique Roman style.

She scowled at her reflection, at her face, so often praised. Her deep blue eyes, thickly fringed with honey-gold lashes, her clear, pale skin with a hint of rose-pink across the cheekbones, and her curved lips, too often rounded in petulance, were all as beautiful as ever. She grimaced. But what use was beauty here? Whom was she to impress? The poor, crippled tutor? And how was she to impress anyone, with no maid, no one to pay her any attention?

Never had she felt less prepared for venturing out to meet strangers. But there was nothing to remain in her room for. Isabella pulled open the bedroom door and, as instructed, turned right.

The way was not as straightforward as might have been imagined from Nurse Pusey's directions, for the corridor meandered around the various projections along the front of the house, reaching unexpected corners and traversing long galleries without obvious exits. Isabella peered down side passages and into doorways, looking with amazement at mildewed hangings, worm-eaten furniture and moth-eaten carpets, and a regular procession of buckets standing under black stained patches on the ceilings and cracks in the plaster, mute witnesses to the state of the Long Trovers roofs.

The portraits in the galleries showed long lines of ancestors, some ruffed, some bewigged, all blackened by dirt and age. Their still faces watched her venture past, until she felt she was the only living soul in all this great sleeping house. Everywhere was quiet, except for the buzzing of a bumble bee against the sun-drenched window at the end of a gallery. The sunlight streamed in bands of bright gold across the worn oak planks, each so broad that it was the width of a vast tree. Specks of dust drifted drowsily before her, then settled gently downwards as her footsteps slowed.

She paused. Here she stood, Isabella Larkham, very nearly twenty years of age, and for perhaps the first time in her life she was utterly alone. She could do anything she liked, go anywhere she liked. Nobody knew where she was standing, and probably nobody cared. She had managed to dress herself, alone, without any help. This sudden sense of independence was frightening, but also exciting. Isabella ran over to the window and, having struggled with the catch, flung it wide, releasing the trapped bumble bee out into the golden morning.

She watched its flight until she lost it in the distance, then gazed out across the rolling green fields and copses that spread beyond the immediate park. Walking across a nearby field, approaching a small rustic gate, was the elderly man she had been introduced to yesterday; Mr D'Estine's father. Wearing a white shirt with the sleeves rolled up to the elbow, and the same coarse corduroy breeches, but now tied about the knees with string, or so it appeared to Isabella, his peasant look was underlined by the wheelbarrow full of stones that he was labouring to push before him across the field. Isabella smiled pityingly as she watched. Poor Mr D'Estine. How embarrassed he must be by his family. No wonder he had never spoken of them. What a good thing Papa was not here to see this. She could imagine his comments.

Just then the old man paused to rest. He straightened his back and drew out a white handkerchief to wipe his forehead. As he did so he turned to survey the front of the vast house and caught sight of Isabella leaning on the sill. Even at this distance she could see the beaming, kindly smile as he waved to her. Unexpectedly a little ashamed of her thoughts, she waved half-heartedly and hastily shut the window.

She reached the main stair at last, and walked slowly down, trailing her hand along the great oak banister, smooth and dark from the fingers of centuries. She lingered to touch each of the massive acorns decorating every turn of the rail. She was reluctant to reach the hall, reluctant to meet the family again.

As she paused a door below her opened, and Mr D'Estine walked out across the stone-flagged floor. She stared in surprise, uncertain at first that it was indeed he.

He stood perfectly straight, a tall, slim, young man with sunlight from a high window catching in hair almost as fair as her own. His clothes were quite different from the drab black coats and breeches, plain white stockings and buckled shoes that her father deemed suitable wear for a tutor in his employment, that she had always thought of as a part of this man. Now he was wearing comfortable buckskin breeches, top boots, and a waist-coat of blue-striped jean over a spotless white linen shirt. He was gazing out of the open front door, gazing without need for any spectacles, shading his eyes with his hand. As he moved away from her she realised that his limp, so pronounced whenever he had called at her father's study to discuss the boys' work, was barely noticeable.

Puzzled, she moved a little forward to watch him as he walked out of the door, and the stair beneath her gave a betraying creak just as the dogs, who had followed her spasmodically but persistently since she left her room, came clattering down behind her, all tails wagging.

Mr D'Estine turned abruptly and, seeing her, sauntered to the foot of the stair, his face lit up in a welcoming smile, though whether it was for her or the dogs she remained unsure. He bent to caress the animals who wove affectionately about his legs, and spoke looking up at her, his eyes very bright, the lashes unexpectedly dark.

'Miss Larkham, good morning. I trust you slept well and are recovered from your headache. I had been hoping you would soon be down. My mother wished me to show you something of the house and grounds, if you would care to see them.'

Isabella descended the last few stairs and stood beside him, then regretted it, uncomfortably aware of how tall he was. Infuriatingly, it crossed her mind how untidy she must look.

'My headache is unlikely to be cured by neglect,' she snapped, 'and doubtless I would have been down here early enough to suit your convenience had a maid been provided for my assistance as my father required, and hot water been made available in my room.'

She wanted him to look ashamed, hurt or even angry, but he merely regarded her somewhat quizzically, making her more than aware of her ill manners. She glared back at him, and ignored the arm he offered as they walked out into the sunlight.

'I am sure we are all deeply sorry if you have felt in any way inconvenienced,' he said, with an inscrutable sideways look that made the colour rise in her cheeks. 'My parents thought to welcome you, as they had planned to welcome your brothers, entirely as one of the family, to live as the family do. You will find our life here somewhat different from your life in town.'

'That much is immediately obvious,' Isabella interjected bitterly.

'Certainly, your father mentioned nothing to me of obtaining a maid for you,' the man carried on as if she had not spoken, 'or I would have explained the near impossibility of finding anyone trained in these parts. I had no idea until we began the journey that Ellie was not to remain with us. I can make enquiries about finding a willing girl in one of the villages, but you would find her quite unskilled, I'm afraid.' He smiled. 'My mother believes very strongly that each of us should be able to care for ourselves, and, instead of demanding the services of others, should contribute in his or her own way to the running of the estate. She has refused the attentions of a lady's maid for as long as I can remember.'

'I see!' Isabella remarked, with chilly disapproval. She just managed to bite back her immediate thought that this lack was painfully obvious. 'So, I suppose, Mr D'Estine, that I will be forced to dispense with their attentions also, though I can assure you that is not what my father intended. But I have better things to do with my time than to train your country bumpkins!'

'Really?' Mr D'Estine commented, with a slight but perceptible drawl, one eyebrow raised as he glanced down at her.

Isabella, her mind flashing over her empty days, flushed angrily, and vented her feelings by pushing roughly away the old dog whose nose nuzzled gently at her hand.

How dared this man, a mere servant of her father's, deliberately make her feel in the wrong? She gazed frostily away from him, and searched her mind for an excuse to leave him.

They were walking, trailed by a straggling of dogs, along the front of the great house, following a flagged pathway that led through the lawns beneath the windows, towards the jumble of extensions to the main building. They rounded a large stone buttress, skirted what appeared to be disused estate offices of warm red brick with red pantiled roofs, ignored two archways into cobbled courtyards, then entered the third.

'The hot water should be a possibility, though,' Mr D'Estine cheerfully remarked, when Isabella had just concluded that she was to be relieved of the burden of conversation with this man; that she had daunted his impertinence with her icy silence. The smile he gave her was friendly, peace-making. 'Mama should have known it would be what you would expect. She has been so long out of the ways of town life and entertaining people other than her friends. I'll speak to Mrs Stoke and see what can be done.'

'Oh, no, Mr D'Estine. I would *hate* you to put anyone to a little trouble on my account,' Isabella responded icily, resenting the friendliness in his tones. 'Naturally I can always follow Nurse Pusey's advice. *She* recommended me to the scullery.'

Infuriatingly, he laughed. 'Oh, she would. She is a keen follower of all my mother's ideas, and my mother does not believe the girls from the kitchen should waste their time carrying water to able-bodied people. But Noosey will do anything I ask, don't worry. I'll organise your hot water for you.' He chuckled. 'You don't need to lower yourself by joining the rest of us riff-raff down in the scullery!'

Outraged at his laughter, bewildered by this strange household, she felt quite unable to thank him.

They were crossing a wide yard surrounded by stables. It was plain that much of it had fallen into disuse; many of the stalls stood empty, and weeds grew up through the cobbles, but several horses nodded over their wooden doors, and one whickered softly as it saw them. With a smile the tutor walked over towards it.

'Come and meet Captain,' he said, over his shoulder, his tones casually friendly as if he had not just deeply offended her. 'He was my brother's horse and we have not had the heart to get rid of him, although he has had no work to do while I have been away. Now I will have to exercise you, won't I, you old brute?'

He was stroking the black horse affectionately, whilst Captain nudged and nuzzled at his chest. Isabella, whose acquaintance with horses was limited to escorted trots in Hyde Park on the plump, docile mare her father kept for her convenience, kept her distance.

'I think . . .' The tutor turned to lean his back against the stable door, facing her, while with one hand he continued to caress the long black nose that blew gustily down his neck. He stared at the toe of his top boot for a moment, then looked up to meet her eye with something of a wry grin.

'I am uncertain what your father told you, but I think perhaps I owe you some sort of an explanation, Miss Larkham——' the tutor was beginning reluctantly, when suddenly a little wizened old man, brown with uncounted years of stable grime, ducked out of a doorway further down and came hurrying towards them, his face split by a beaming grin that boasted one fine yellow tooth.

'Mr Anthony, or m'lud, I should say now, though it's hard to get into the way of it, as I think we all find. I thought and hoped my ears were not tricking me when I heard your voice, for I knew you'd be down to see this old boy. Looking in fine fettle, isn't he, and eating his head off? If you'll not be wanting him today I'll be taking him out to Top Meadow just now. Well, now, but it's good to see you back where you belong, and not hankering off for a life in that London town. Captain now, he'll be that pleased at the sight of you...'

Isabella hastily put some distance between herself and Mr D'Estine with his garrulous ancient. She peered dubiously into stalls as she ventured down the yard. A couple of ponies looked less daunting than Captain, if somewhat shaggier, and she tentatively stroked the nose of one, while the dogs pushed about in some straw, sniffing for mice.

What did the man mean, 'an explanation'? Isabella looked back at...who was he? Mr D'Estine? Mr Anthony? M'lud? *My Lord?* She thought of the garbled words of the old nurse, talking of 'my lady.' Impossible! Unthinkable! This despised tutor who, following her father's lead, she had so cuttingly ignored for years, treated as a nobody. A servant. Who was he?

She stared. Yes, he certainly did owe an explanation to her! And to her father, it would seem. Had he truly been working for them all those years under false pretences? With a false name? Even a false appearance! This change in him was more than just his change of clothes! His stoop and his spectacles had gone, and he looked a different man now, much younger, handsome... She stared at him, then looked abruptly away, angry, hating the feeling she might have been fooled.

He still limped a little, she thought with spiteful satisfaction. He had been unable to cheat that away.

He had detached himself from the old man now and was coming after her. She deliberately turned her back on him and walked briskly out of the yard, through the arch at the far end. A little further, and she stopped, impressed despite herself.

Gardens and lawns and shrubs stretched in a pleasing disarray of winding paths down to a great lake, rippling and lily-clad in the sunshine. On the far side meadows sloped gently to the water's edge, and a few creamy brown cows were standing knee deep in the cool shallows. On the nearer bank, down the slope from where she stood, a ramshackle boathouse and landing stage perched precariously over the water, and just beyond them, equally precarious, were Thomas and William, endeavouring, with much splashing and no skill, to manoeuvre an antiquated rowing boat out into the lake.

'Oh, Lord,' remarked their tutor unconcernedly from beside her, 'I might have known they'd find their way in there.'

Isabella turned on him as if he had not spoken.

'I should think you *do* owe me an explanation,' she burst out angrily, her blue eyes bright with indignation. 'Me and my father, and my brothers too, no doubt, Mr D'Estine, or whatever it is you like to call yourself! Who knows *what* name you use, or *who* your family are? You could be anyone, changing your name, changing your appearance, fooling people. My father should never have employed you. Never have sent me here. It's...it's despicable!'

She was aware that her voice had quivered, and she clenched her fists furiously. 'Despicable!' she repeated.

Glancing indignantly up at him, she almost felt that he was stifling a smile, and she seethed that he could dare, but when he spoke his voice was passably contrite.

'I said I owed you an explanation, and I dare say you have reason to be angry, though I can assure you that your father knew precisely who I was when he employed me. He has never been in ignorance. And indeed, I *was* Mr D'Estine when I came to tutor your brothers, and that remained my correct title up until ten months ago... But perhaps I had better begin at the beginning?'

'Yes,' Isabella retorted sharply, 'perhaps you had.'

They were wandering down a winding walk between low box hedges in need of clipping, past clumps of Portugal laurel, yew and holly that formed an edging to the more formal beds directly in front of the house. Isabella kept her eyes on her brothers and the lake, careful not to appear too interested or impressed by anything this man might say.

'My father,' he began, and her mind flew contemptuously to the little man with the wheelbarrow, 'is Cuthbert Oswald Wilfred D'Estine, Seventh Earl of Kintrove, Third Viscount of Neame, Baron D'Estine of Nore, of Alladay and of Kifford.'

His voice was flatly factual, and it was hard to disbelieve him. Fighting to keep her shocked astonishment from her face, she risked a glance at him to see if he was smiling, joking, but he was standing casually, his thumbs tucked into the waist of his breeches, staring sombrely out across the water. He was paying no attention to her at all.

'The family title of Viscount, Lord Alladay,' he continued, without moving, 'has for some reason now obscured to us always been held by the heir to the Earldom. It was held by my eldest brother Jasper until his death three years ago in a riding accident, then by my brother Bardolph, who was in the military. We all tried to persuade Bardolph to resign his commission on Jasper's death, but he refused.'

Here Mr D'Estine paused, and the shouts and splashing of the two boys came loudly to them over the water. The dogs paddled in the mud, drinking.

'He died in the Peninsula ten months ago . . . and then, of course, the title became mine.'

He turned towards her, his face closed and hard. His hazel eyes seemed darker suddenly, brooding, his chin jutting firm beneath the narrowed lips. A cloud passed over the sun, draining all the brightness from his cropped fair hair, smudging the dark shadows from his face. Isabella shivered.

'I had no immediate desire to leave my post with your family. It is, whatever I might wish, foolish to try to hide from you that my family is impoverished. After my grandfather's disastrous gambling, and my father's unworldly nature, extremely impoverished. I thought it was of more use for me to continue in employment, and besides,' he gave a small shrug, 'I have a considerable fondness for your brothers. There was no necessity for insisting on changing my title, and, indeed, your father requested that I did not.'

'He knew?' Isabella burst in, indignantly.

She put aside any response to his other revelations. She did not want to react to his new status, or to the pain she had glimpsed in his face when he spoke of his brothers. Least of all to the possibility of friendship that his confidences had offered.

Sulkily, she continued, 'And I suppose my brothers knew too? That I was the only one kept in ignorance?'

'I believe your father preferred it that way,' the man she must now think of as Lord Alladay said quietly.

'But why——?' she was beginning indignantly, when a great splash and a scream from the lake took all their attention, and they spun round to see Thomas floundering in the water.

'He can barely swim!' Isabella gasped, her hand to her mouth. 'He might drown! Oh, do something!'

Fear for her brother held her rigid, all indignation forgotten.

Lord Alladay was already pulling off his top boots.

'William! Hold the oar out for him to hold!' he shouted, but it became obvious that William had managed to drop both oars in the confusion, and they had floated away from the boat. Stripping off his waistcoat, their tutor handed his things hastily to Isabella.

'Hold these, would you? Don't worry. I'll save the little beast!'

And he was gone, running swiftly through the muddy shallows then diving forward to swim in long leisurely strokes that carried him with surprising speed towards the boat. Isabella watched, taut with anxiety, the clenched fingers that held his waistcoat pressed against her mouth. She watched as he reached Thomas, grabbed him by the shoulders and pulled him over to the boat. She saw Thomas cling to him, panicking, until Alladay gave him a quick shake, and she heard his voice, calm and authoritative.

'Hold the side of the boat, Thomas, not me, but don't try to climb in until I say. Are you all right? Good. William, sit still, in the centre of the boat. I will swim to the far side and steady it for you.'

Thomas, coughing hard, was helped back into the rowing boat, and Alladay, water streaming from his linen shirt so that it clung to his chest, pulled himself aboard. Isabella relaxed, and her hand dropped to her side. She watched Alladay pull Thomas's shirt off over his head and wring it out over the side of the boat. She heard the boys beginning to explain. Then, just as her mind was filled with relief and gratitude, she heard laughter from the boat, and saw Thomas and Alladay scooping handfuls of water to fling at the still-dry William. He, naturally, began to retaliate.

Forgotten on the shore, her anguish of a few moments ago an irrelevance to the trio in the boat, Isabella stood alone and coldly furious. She stared for a moment in outraged surprise at the waistcoat and top boots she found herself clutching in either hand. Deliberately, distastefully, she held them at arm's length.

Before turning her back on the silly, childish games on the lake and returning, accompanied by dogs, to the house, she dropped his things disdainfully into the mud.

CHAPTER THREE

'MY DEAR!'

A voice spoke from behind Isabella, and she froze briefly, warily, over her sketching block, before turning her head. Lady Kintrove stood there, a half-smile quirking her lips. Her approach had been silent over the lush grass to where Isabella had retreated to seat herself on a fallen stone and attempt a view of the ruined tower.

'My dear, I am sorry, I did not intend to startle you. It asks to be treated in the Gothic manner, does it not, all tumbled stones and ivy? Perhaps you should attempt a night scene, with moonlight and shadows, even an owl! There are owls nesting at the top of the tower, my husband tells me, beneath those two surviving turrets. How the sight of you takes me back. I used to spend many hours sketching, once upon a time. Too busy nowadays!'

She was carrying a large flat basket filled with small bulbs. Isabella regarded them without interest. Her acquaintance with plants was limited to sniffing the flowers the housekeeper arranged in her father's house, and checking they matched the colour schemes. Her only emotion was an initial surprise that Lady Kintrove should carry the things herself. But then, a Lady who washed in the scullery...! Her ladyship, however, had caught the direction of the girl's glance.

'Grew them myself!' she remarked with a certain pride. 'Brought them on over winter and been planting them out in succession. Gives us a good steady crop. Mrs Stoke is very pleased.'

'What are they?' Isabella asked, her tone barely hiding her lack of interest.

'White Spanish this end, and James's Long Keeping that end,' she began enthusiastically, then, seeing the girl's complete bewilderment, she laughed. 'What a town child! They are onions, of course. I don't suppose you have seen my vegetable gardens yet?'

Isabella shook her head, regarding this strange woman dubiously.

'No. No, I'm afraid not.'

'Where is Anthony? Has he been neglecting you? I thought he was to show you round.'

'Oh, he left me when he joined my brothers,' she said bitterly, hoping this woman would condemn her son's lack of manners.

Her only response was a cheery, 'Well, at least you know how to entertain yourself.' Then, more briskly, she added, 'But none of this is what I came over to say. A neighbour of ours has just brought over his copy of the *Morning Post*. He always drops his copies by when he has finished with them. And I see that we are to congratulate you. I had no idea your engagement had just been agreed. I wish you very happy, my dear, very happy.'

Isabella had almost forgotten the involvement of Lord Carlton Crue in the nightmare muddle her life suddenly seemed to have become. She flushed in embarrassment and anger. A memory of Lord Carlton's swarthy face and heavy black hair, and his casual, confident smile, forgotten until now along with her own indignant reaction when he had once flicked her cheek in a brief touch of ownership and appreciation, was superseded by a vision of Harry's handsome open face, his promises, his kisses, their dreams.

She remembered her father's contemptuous ability to dispose of Harry, to dispose of her life, to arrange everything to suit his convenience. She shrugged gracelessly.

'Thank you, your ladyship,' she muttered.

Lady Kintrove regarded her keenly.

'Are you happy with the arrangement, Isabella? Is it of your own choice?'

Her voice was earnest, friendly. Isabella bridled, resenting the familiarity and the intrusion.

'Naturally,' she replied, coldly. 'How could it be otherwise? Lord Carlton Crue is an old family friend.'

She began to shade the outline of the tower on her sketching block, slowly and deliberately. Lady Kintrove waited for a moment or two, as if hoping the girl would speak again, but she did not.

'We have a light luncheon in about an hour,' she said quietly. 'I do hope you will join us. In the morning-room.' Then she moved away and vanished through a doorway in a high brick wall.

Isabella flung her pencil down. Her lip was quivering, and she felt tears start in her eyes. Damn her father! Damn Lord Carlton Crue, and damn Harry for being so far away. Damn the oh, so kind Lady Kintrove, and damn her miserable, penny-grubbing tutor son. The words, impossible ever to be spoken aloud, ran gnawing races inside her head.

While no one had known of it, she had been able to pretend, even to herself, that this engagement to a man she barely knew had never happened. Now, the knowledge was spread, and each congratulation she received would nail her more firmly into this unsought, uncharted future. She shivered, then a horrible thought crept into her mind.

Did Mr D'Estine, this Lord Alladay—did he know of her feelings for Harry? He had certainly seen them together, riding, meeting while she shopped, walking in the park. Her colour rose again as she remembered how casually she had dismissed the tutor as a mere servant, of no account, barely aware of his existence. She had flirted and giggled with Harry just behind him while they walked out with her brothers, even exchanged quick kisses half hidden by bushes or an ornate statue. They had not cared.

Did he know what her father had done? How he had dismissed Harry, and arranged this engagement for his own advancement? She shuddered to think how Lord Alladay must be laughing at her, or, still worse, pitying her. She could not tolerate pity from such a man, or any of his family. To be forced to endure their company was bad enough, whatever their titles and position.

The sketching block followed the pencil down into the grass as Isabella leaned forward, miserably huddled, her hands over her face.

'Oh Harry, Harry,' she whispered. 'Why can't you be here? Why don't you write to me?'

Slow tears of frustration, loneliness and despair trickled out between her fingers and dripped into her lap.

Lord Alladay, emerging through the doorway in the garden wall, paused and frowned. Although her hair fell forward, golden in the sunlight, and hid her face, her misery was quivering in every line of her body.

Indecision held him immobile. His instincts were to go on, to offer comfort, but, aware of his probable reception, Alladay shrugged impatiently and stepped back inside the garden out of sight. He stood, his brows knit angrily, as he glared at the morello cherry tree trained along the wall beside him.

Isabella pushed herself upright and drew a deep breath. She had learned very young that tears brought you nothing. Her father could not abide women who cried. She fumbled for a handkerchief, found she had forgotten to bring one out with her, and sniffed crossly, rubbing her face furtively on the hem of her dress. She would somehow have to find a way to live with this situation, she thought, and sniffed again.

There *was* only one realistic solution, of course. To make the best of the life her father had mapped out for her. To forget Harry, and accept that she would become the wife of Lord Carlton Crue. Could she do that? Every aching beat of her heart said not, but if she was to avoid the pity of Lady Kintrove, or, worse, of her son, she would have to convince them all that the engagement was to her total delight and satisfaction.

Certainly, Lord Carlton Crue was thought to be a very handsome man, and a good catch on the marriage mart. Women had been setting their caps at him for years. With sudden bitter satisfaction, Isabella forced a grim smile. Well, let them all know it had taken Isabella Larkham to capture him! She choked back a sob.

Alladay came out through the doorway once more, and glanced across to where Isabella sat. The movement caught her eye and she looked up. Wretched man, that he had to come and find her now, she fumed inwardly. She looked into the screening trees beyond the tower, but she could hardly turn and run away. Full of resentment, she bent forward and retrieved the sketching pad and pencil, then continued her assiduous shading, hoping he would go away.

'Miss Larkham! I have been looking for you. I am sorry I had to leave you so abruptly. Thomas is now a little wiser about the limitations of his swimming, and we are going to hold regular lessons. Other than that he was merely wet and chilly, no harm done.'

He did not sound sorry, she thought. His tone was offhand, almost indifferent.

'There was no need to trouble yourself over coming to find me just to inform me of that. That no harm was done was quite obvious from your childish behaviour in the boat,' she said coldly, keeping her gaze averted, afraid that tears still smudged her cheeks.

He laughed. 'Ah, well, it is too much to have to be sensible all of the time, don't you agree?'

Uncertain how to answer, she shrugged. Then she remembered her earlier grievance.

'So I suppose the fancy dress you assumed while working for my father was just your inability to be sensible, was it? There was no other good reason for that little deception?'

It was surprising how angry it made her, this feeling that she had been tricked by him, deceived as to who he really was. She had thought him only a servant, whose opinions, had he dared to hold any, were utterly irrelevant to her. She had behaved before him as if he did not exist. Somehow this seemed now to give him some obscure and unfair advantage over her. She turned to face him. He had changed into dry buckskins and shirt. His blue striped waistcoat had a smear of mud on the front, she noted with satisfaction.

He frowned, studying her face.

'I would hardly have called my clothes fancy dress,' he said coolly. 'Nothing could have been less fancy! And they were not of my choice. Your father dictated exactly what he wanted me to wear, and the clothes were supplied, just as they were for the rest of the staff.'

'He didn't supply the limp and the stoop and the spectacles,' she retorted.

'No.' His voice held a hint of bitterness. 'The limp was supplied by that walnut tree.' He gestured towards a large tree in the field in front of the house. 'I fell out of it when I was fifteen. My leg was broken in three places, and it mended badly. But the stoop and the spectacles...well, yes...' He smiled, a private smile, not for her '...there I must confess to a certain degree of deception, though it started innocently enough.'

She raised her eyebrows in what she hoped portrayed disdainful disbelief, then pointedly returned to her drawing.

He stretched out on the ground a little distance from her, leaning back against the great bole of a long-fallen beech tree. He tilted his head back to catch the sun on his face, and closed his eyes. Isabella, irritated, shifted fractionally further away from him without raising her eyes from her paper.

There was a pause. Isabella determined to ignore him; she studied the tower, and put pencil to paper in a fury of silence. He merely heaved a contented sigh and settled himself more comfortably in the grass. Isabella glared at him. Could the oaf not tell she wished to be alone? She thought wistfully of Harry's gentle sensitivity.

'So,' she began sharply, wanting to disturb his peaceful repose, 'what was this innocent deception?' The last two words were a sneer.

He spoke without even bothering to open his eyes. His lashes lay very dark on the fine cheekbones, and the bright sunlight showed up a dusting of pale freckles across nose and cheeks. One hand moved idly, pulling at the grasses. His fingers were long, strong. Isabella concentrated her attention on the tower.

'When I determined that I was not cut out for the Church as had been intended,' he began, and he sounded impatient, offhand, 'and yet must still earn my way, I decided my only option was tutoring. My brother Bardolph was, predictably, horrified. He had a great deal of family pride, and a lot of face to keep up in the regiment. When he realised I was serious about gaining a position he swore that I was too young and too...well, too young to gain a position.'

Eyes still closed, the tutor was once again smiling that private reminiscent smile.

'He found me the spectacles, and we spent several hilarious afternoons perfecting a character who looked dull, earnest, studious, and totally inoffensive, no matter how many hopeful daughters there were in the household where I applied for a post! He maintained that not only did I need to look unprepossessing enough to gain the job in the first place, but also to escape unwanted attentions later! It did not seem important then, when, as Bardolph said, we were only practising to deceive some family of...'

He broke off, seeming to recall to whom he spoke, and shrugged, opening his eyes and sitting up.

'Then Bardolph dared me to act out that character when I went to be interviewed by your father.' He paused. 'It worked to perfection, of course. We were cock-a-hoop. It all seems so long ago now. It was just a silly bit of boyish fun. But it rounded back on me. I took the job, and had to live the part.'

'It sounds very childish.'

She was aware of sounding petulantly childish herself, and that knowledge perversely made her feel more spiteful. This tutor and his disconcerting revelations were beginning to seem, illogically, responsible for all her miseries by bringing her to this place.

'And what *did* he say, this brother Bardolph who was apparently the only one of you with any ideas of his own, even if those ideas were ridiculous? What *did* this "wonderful" brother say about our family?'

She was angry and upset by his vision of what had occurred. She wanted to hurt the man, and it seemed she had succeeded. He looked coldly across at her, eyes narrowed. He spoke with deliberate clarity.

'He said it was hardly important, practising to deceive some family of ignorant, uncultured Cits!' He glared at her. 'To which I agreed.'

She started as if she had been struck.

'How dare you?' Isabella's face had flushed and she gasped out the words. 'How dare you? You were just our drudging servant! A nobody! How dare you speak so?'

He gave a short laugh.

'I merely told you what you asked to know. Your father may have employed me, but he did not buy my soul. Just as he is free to think me a drudging servant, I am free to think him an ignorant Cit. A privilege, dear Miss Larkham, of our free society.

'I don't regret having taken the employment, however. I learned, among other things, to mitigate my prejudices. I enjoyed working with your brothers. Your father has every reason to be proud of his *sons*.'

She was not deaf to his omission, and secretly knew that she deserved more than just a hint of reproof. In her welter of unhappiness she had not always been proud of her behaviour recently. But from him the knowledge only made her angry.

'But not of their tutor!' she retorted. 'Not if he had known you were indulging in such childish deceptions, and holding such opinions of him!' She frowned as a new thought struck her. 'And I cannot imagine why he wished you to hide the fact that you had come into the title. I would have thought him only too keen to show the world who he could afford to buy to educate his sons.' Her voice was bitter.

'I think that...' He stopped.

'What do you think, Lord Alladay?'

He gave a small shrug.

'I think that, despite my elaborate precautions, he did not wish me to appear in any way...in any way *interesting* in your eyes. In fact he told me as much.'

She gave a bitter, mocking laugh.

'Well, he could have saved himself that petty little decision. I am surprised he even considered it a vague possibility. He certainly had nothing to worry about on *that* score. Nothing at all.'

'Precisely how I reassured him myself,' Alladay said, coolly.

She glared.

'Well, all his worries are at rest now, as yours can be. My engagement is now official.'

'Your engagement?'

She was pleased to see she had startled him, and gave a little toss of her head, shaking her curls in the sunlight.

'Why, yes, had you not heard? Your mother saw the announcement in the *Morning Post* today. I am to marry Lord Carlton Crue as soon as my father returns from Europe. I shall be the envy of every girl in London. Lord knows how many hearts he has broken!'

'Carlton Crue? You and Carlton Crue?'

There was no mistaking the disdain and dislike in his tones.

'Yes, sir,' she retorted, becoming angry. 'It is customary to offer congratulations, you know, or has your time as our tutor allowed you to forget these niceties?'

'Congratulations, Miss Larkham.' He stood up. 'I trust you will be very happy. I am certain you and Lord Carlton Crue will be *ideally* suited.'

'Oh, we shall be, Lord Alladay. We shall be very happy indeed. Lord Carlton Crue has everything a girl could wish for. Looks, lineage, sophistication, fortune.' She closed her sketch pad and stood up. 'How can you doubt my delight?'

He made no reply to that, and they walked in to partake of the cold luncheon in a chilly silence.

At the meal Isabella was introduced to a Miss Pickering, who lived, it appeared, as one of the family.

'They met me in Italy twenty years ago,' she confided to Isabella, after she had, with Lord Kintrove, offered her congratulations. William's exclamation of disgust at hearing the news of the engagement was adroitly stifled by a look and a word from Alladay.

'They met me there, brought me back, and here I have lived ever since,' Miss Pickering was continuing, her smile wide and friendly. 'I'm in the east wing. Come over and visit me some time. I'll show you how I spend my days!'

She was a lady with a scrubbed red face, white hair dragged back but escaping untidily from its pins, and clothing made up of voluminous swathes of brightly coloured cottons wrapped randomly around her to form skirts, bodices, shawls or scarves, depending on where the multitude of pins held them. This odd garb was liberally splashed and smeared with some white substance, paint or plaster.

Isabella was much tempted to laugh at such a figure of fun, and thought wistfully of her best friend, Jane, with whom she would have whispered and giggled and enjoyed the absurdity. But Jane was spending the summer with an aunt in Bath, and the family here treated this clown of a woman with respect and affection. Isabella sighed, and thought again of the comments her father would have made.

The talk became general, though largely between Miss Pickering and Lady Kintrove, discussing the life and writing of some woman called Mary Wollstonecraft. Isabella had never heard of her, and was prepared to be thoroughly bored, except that, from what she could gather of the lively discussion, this woman had led the sort of life her father would have condemned out of hand, and certainly considered as unfit for the ears of his daughter.

It was extraordinary, she reflected, that this family, with titles and lineage her father must regard with awe and envy, should be everything he would despise, and seemed to have no idea at all of the correct way to behave. She did not understand them at all. Perhaps, she thought, it was being so poor that made the difference.

During a lull in the talk Isabella pronounced herself to be much enamoured of sketching, and keen to be allowed to explore the environs alone and undisturbed, looking for suitable subjects for her pencil. She had no wish, she assured them all coolly, to be a trouble to anyone, and was more than happy to entertain herself.

'Of course,' Miss Pickering agreed soulfully. 'When the artistic muse is upon us nothing should be allowed to interfere. Have no apprehensions, my dear. Your desire for solitude will be respected. This is a household that well understands the demon that drives the creative artist...' here she dropped her eyes modestly '...however slight her skills may be.'

Isabella stared at her.

'Really?' she said.

CHAPTER FOUR

A FEW days passed. Drearily miserable, Isabella spent long hours dreaming of Harry. She would have written him lengthy screeds pouring out her heart, but she could not bring herself to face the looks that would doubtless result if she were to put letters addressed to him with the other post to be franked. Instead, she wrote all her unhappiness into her diary, and watched for the post to arrive each day, hoping for a letter from him. Surely soon...

She avoided company, even that of her brothers, and she and Lord Alladay maintained the icy distance of mutual dislike. She would give no time to a man who thought her an ignorant Cit.

A small high point in Isabella's life had been the arrival, one morning, of a young girl at her bedroom door, labouring with a vast pail of steaming water, and professing, with desperate enthusiasm, a desire to care for Miss Larkham's clothes, and to help her to dress.

'Please, miss, it is all I have ever dreamed of doing, miss, oh, please, give me the chance. I'm not trained like a proper London maid, miss, but I'd learn ever so fast if only you'd let me, miss!'

Isabella was sorely tempted to turn the girl away, just to show Lord Alladay how little she needed his attentions. But, in her loneliness, she was not proof against such eagerness, much as she hated to be beholden to the hateful man. She comforted herself, as she accepted the girl's services with a show of reluctance, with the knowledge that her father had paid for the provision of a maid.

Thus Ruth, with her irrepressible grin, her flattering admiration, and endlessly wagging tongue, willingly abandoned her kitchen work for Mrs Stoke, and became a part of Isabella's days, along with regular hot water.

The dogs, too, had become a familiar part of her routine. On her first sketching attempt at the old tower she had eluded their pursuit by deliberately slipping out of her bedroom after fetching her pad and pencil, then closing the door on them, leaving them whining and scratching in frustration. This, she had discovered later, had been a petty triumph holding little satisfaction, for they had all used the enforced idleness to doze on her bed, and their feet were far from clean.

Now she was resigned to their company, even beginning to be a little disappointed if they did not all join her as she set off with her pad, pencils and cushion. Sometimes the younger dogs would desert her to join Alladay and the boys. She would see them in the distance, the dogs milling about excitedly, as they went swimming, rowing, shooting at wood pigeons in the trees around the gardens, or simply walking off into the fields and over the estate, Alladay with his gun, and returning with rabbits, hares, various birds, anything in fact that Mrs Stoke could convert into a good meal. Isabella would listen resentfully to their cheerful shouts fading into the distance, Alladay's deeper voice beneath her brothers' treble calls.

Bess, however, the oldest of the dogs, never left her, and her greying muzzle was invariably nudging at Isabella's hand for a caress, or stretched resignedly on to the skirts of her dress while she sat drawing. Isabella even found herself on occasion talking to Bess, and felt foolish, though the dog gave the appearance of understanding every word and sympathising deeply.

Conversations with the family were restricted to mealtimes, and Isabella found them difficult. She had read none of the books that came up for discussion and criticism, she cared nothing for gardening, and had avoided exploring the vegetable plots. She had yet to discover what Lord Kintrove did with the stones in the wheelbarrow that she regularly saw him pushing about, or what Miss Pickering spent her time doing in the east wing, and did not want to ask.

Her brothers talked only of their own activities, and everyone seemed to share their interest, asking affectionately how far each had swum, what creatures they had bagged, and continuing to tease William about a chicken he had shot when it had been misguided enough to roost in a tree nearby him and cunningly disguise itself as a pigeon. Alladay seemed to have stolen all her brothers' interest and affection, and, forgetting how she had ignored them all the months she was with Harry, she was sulkily jealous and ignored their talk.

She was asked about her sketching, but she could not bring herself to be more than coolly monosyllabic, and the talk would move away from her.

When Isabella emerged into the sunshine on this particular morning it gave no promise of holding any change or excitement. She stopped and surveyed the gardens sloping away from her down to the lake, yawned, and wondered which way to venture today.

Her initial urge to escape the house and its occupants at all costs was dwindling. Her sketch pad was filling up. She had embarked upon these excursions largely as a defiant statement of her separateness from all the Kintrove family, and to have these long, lonely sessions viewed as a deeply satisfying communion with her artistic muse was irritating. She also had an unsettling suspicion that Lord Alladay was aware of this fact, even amused by it. She frowned across the lake at the cows standing drowsing in the cool of their own reflections, and chewed on the end of her pencil. Bess, sitting beside her, wagged her tail hopefully.

On a sudden impulse Isabella turned her footsteps towards the sound of her brothers' voices. Their shouts were coming from the side of the house, beyond the stable blocks. She nonchalantly turned the corner that would bring them in sight, persuading herself that she would pointedly walk past, and vanish into the fields beyond. But it was immediately obvious that Alladay was not with them.

The boys were lugging a heavy straw archery target out of an old store. They had a wooden frame on which to balance it already set up on a clear stretch of grass, and assorted bows, arrows and quivers leaning up against the stone of the storehouse wall. They had managed, with much puffing and mutual insult, to set the target to their satisfaction, before they noticed Isabella and Bess.

'Izzie!' William shouted. 'Come on and show us how it should be done. I know you are good at archery. Jane told me about how you learned at the Hollings's house, and beat them all. Come and show us the proper way.'

It was true that, during a stay with mutual friends at their out-of-town house in Hampstead, she and Jane had been taught the skills of archery, and, although Jane had had problems in reaching the target at all, and had preferred the time spent in getting themselves dressed up as Greek goddesses in order to take part in the sport, Isabella had discovered in herself a ready ability and a good eye. By the end of their stay she had been regularly finding the bull's eye, and had beaten all the Hollings girls when they organised a tournament.

'I would have thought Lord Alladay would be helping you,' she said, advancing dubiously.

'No, he has to work in the estate office all day today, and we must entertain ourselves, he says. He says he will have to do more and more work in the office now, because his father is not well enough to manage the estate any more.' Thomas sounded disgruntled. 'But it is all right. We are allowed to use these things. He told us.'

With an impulsive smile, and the first twinge of enthusiasm since that interview with her father that had tipped her world upside-down, Isabella put down her sketching equipment, took off her straw chip bonnet, and picked up a bow. She tested it out, pulling at the string, and hoped her reputation had not been raised impossibly high by Jane's chatter.

'I was not as good as all that,' she said, 'and I believe these bows could do with restringing, but I will try.'

She took the bow and a few arrows and settled herself before the target.

'Watch what I do for a couple of shots,' she said, 'then I will help you.'

It was good to hold a bow again, to feel the spring in the wood, and the twang of the string. Her first shot fell short of the target altogether, and Thomas groaned, but her next found the straw, and the following two were inching nearer the bull's eye.

'Good shooting, Izzie,' William said, with a judicious respect. 'Can you show us how to do it?'

She spent an unexpectedly contented hour demonstrating, watching their efforts, then correcting their stance, how they pulled back their arms and sighted their shots. The boys were keen as their skills increased, running tirelessly back and forth retrieving arrows and shouting at dogs to keep clear of the target area. Eventually Isabella stretched, her arms aching from the unaccustomed exercise. She shook back her hair, enjoying the warmth of the sun on her unprotected face.

'Enough,' she said. 'I'm going to put on my bonnet and go and sketch! It is far less exhausting, and won't give me freckles!'

'A competition before you go?' Thomas urged. 'Go on, do! Just six shots each and see who does best. You're bound to win.'

She laughed, happy in their approval. 'But after that I go. Bess is bored with archery!'

It was a long time, she thought, since she had laughed, or had so enjoyed her brothers' company.

They took turn and turn about, removing the arrows after each three shots. Predictably, Isabella's shots came steadily nearest to the centre, but the boys were pleased with their efforts, at least they were reaching the straw each time.

'Last turn,' William said. 'No one has scored a bull's eye yet. Come on Izzie!'

'Don't worry,' she laughed, breathless after running to retrieve her favourite arrow before Thomas grabbed it. 'I'll finish off with something special.'

It was at that moment that she turned back towards the store, and saw Lord Alladay leaning against the wall in the sunshine, idly stroking Bess's ears and watching them. He raised one lazy hand in greeting, but she turned abruptly away, pretending she had not seen. Her light-hearted mood evaporated, and she swung into fuming resentment, hating to expose herself before this man's gaze.

'Your turn, Izzie,' William was saying. 'Look, I've shot my best yet. See if you can beat that!'

She debated simply walking away, but it would be impossible to escape with any dignity from her brothers' recriminations if she did not complete their tournament.

'Look, there's Anthony,' Thomas said. 'Show him, Izzie, show him what you can do!'

'Anthony?' she exclaimed in shocked surprise. 'You know you should call him . . .' She paused. She had been going to say Mr D'Estine. 'It is not at all proper, and Papa would be most affronted. You should call him Lord Alladay,' she finished reluctantly.

'No, we shouldn't!' Thomas retorted. 'He told us to call him Anthony. We wouldn't have done it otherwise. He said it is silly for us to call him Lord all the time, and as he is not to be our tutor any more he will adopt us as temporary younger brothers and we are to call him Anthony. And Papa ordered us to do everything our tutor told us. So we are. I dare say he'd let you call him Anthony too if you want. Have your turn, Izzie, do!'

Abandoning this fruitless discussion, she took the bow and arrow and walked forward, raised it, aimed and shot almost in one casual movement. With a resounding thud the arrow hit the centre of the target. Isabella tossed her head, and grinned.

The boys were loud in their applause, and ran off ahead of her to tell Lord Alladay of her skill, their own successes.

Isabella, her features composed, strolled coolly over to collect her things. Alladay's smile was unexpectedly appreciative.

'You keep secrets, Miss Larkham. I had no idea you were an expert at archery,' he said.

'There is no reason at all why you should have,' she replied, taking the things he had picked up for her, dangling her bonnet carelessly by its ribbon. 'Come on, Bess!'

With a further flick of her head that set her fair curls bouncing in the sunlight she walked swiftly away across the field, Bess, to her great satisfaction, obediently following. Behind her, Anthony, Lord Alladay, gave a reluctant grin as he watched her go.

The heat of the day after luncheon found Isabella up in her room, debating with Ruth which dress to wear to replace the morning's muslin, grubby from the long-stored archery equipment and from Bess's muddy paws. Ruth stroked the cloth of each gown with an envious awe, relishing the textures and colours, making Isabella look anew at dresses she had long treated with dissatisfaction or indifference.

'Wear the blue silk, miss, oh, do,' she was saying. 'I dare say you're right that it's a bit formal, but think how it will match you eyes——'

Suddenly the sound of horses' hoofs and the scrunch of wheels approaching at speed sent them both to the window to peer down. With a flourish, an elegant black curricle, with matched black horses, was swung to a halt on the weed-strewn drive outside the main door. The driver snapped his fingers at his tiger, who jumped nimbly down from behind to take the horses' heads, while the driver languidly flicked dust from his many-caped coat. It was not until he removed his beaver hat to brush the dust from its surface that Isabella realised who the visitor was.

'Oh, no!' she breathed.

Ruth looked at her anxiously, and she pulled herself together.

'It is my fiancé, Lord Carlton Crue,' she said briskly. 'I was not expecting him to call today. What a *wonderful* surprise. Quickly, that blue silk. You are quite right, it will be perfect.' She was in the dress and buttoned up in a quicker time than she had thought possible. 'Now my hair. That style I showed you yesterday, can you do that?'

'Ooh, yes, miss.'

Caught up in the romance of the occasion, Ruth laboured her best. She had never before seen such an elegant equipage as awaited her mistress, or such a languidly elegant man as had climbed out of it. Her mouth full of hairpins, she tried for a fairy-tale perfection, and the result was passable even to Isabella's critical eye.

'And you're truly going to marry him, miss?' she asked, wistfully, pushing back her own lank brown locks.

'Certainly I am.'

Ruth frowned. 'Well, maybe Nurse Pusey's not always right, her and her dogs——' she was beginning, when there was a knock on the door, and Nurse Pusey herself was standing there.

'Hopkins called up to say there's a visitor for you, dear,' she said, 'in the green room.'

Hopkins was waiting for her at the foot of the stairs. A rosy-cheeked, comfortable-looking man, with a fatherly smile, he was not what Isabella imagined the ideal butler should look like, but he led her along a length of marble floored corridor that led off the main hall, and flung open the door of a room Isabella had not previously entered, announcing, 'Miss Larkham,' with suitable solemnity.

The room was indeed green, though the colours were fading now. The woodwork was green, the paper striped in white and green, the carpet a green pattern, and the furniture and curtains all of a rich design of swirling leaves and birds, green upon green. It was a bit like discovering a room underwater, Isabella thought, as she stood uncertainly on the threshold. Then she walked in.

Lady Kintrove was there, talking with scrupulous politeness of the weather and the effect of the dry spell upon the roads, sitting opposite Lord Carlton Crue, who was obviously listening with the scantest of attention. Lord Alladay stood silent by the fireplace, glancing from his mother to Lord Carlton Crue to the toe of his boot. They all looked up as Isabella entered, and Lord Carlton rose smoothly to his feet.

'Isabella, my dearest,' he murmured, taking her hand and raising it to his lips, holding it there too long for mere courtesy while he gazed into her eyes. 'How very, *very* good it is to see you again.' He stood back and held her away, looking her over slowly, a smile playing across his lips. 'My dear, I am impressed. You look more beautiful than ever.'

Isabella could feel the heat of her flush run over her face. His look seemed to be running over her like the touch of fingertips. She pulled away a little, but he held her hand tightly, smiling more broadly. She knew that he had watched her blush, and had enjoyed it. He put her hand on his arm.

'I have told Lady Kintrove I am taking you out for a drive,' he said, bending over her a little, edging her close. Then, turning to face the others, he added, 'I shall return her to you, reluctantly...' he patted her arm and smiled '...later this afternoon.' His tones were suavely polite.

'Do you wish to go out for a drive with Lord Carlton Crue?' Lady Kintrove asked mildly. 'If you would prefer, for the roads are very dusty, you could remain here and show him the gardens.'

A trace of his irritation showed in the hint of a frown that crossed Lord Carlton's handsome face.

Isabella looked at Lady Kintrove, avoiding her kindly brown eyes and seeing her calico skirts and the mud under her fingernails, then at Lord Alladay, who was staring down at the grate as if his mind was far elsewhere. Her hesitation was brief, then she raised her eyebrows disdainfully.

'I would love to go out for a drive,' she said, and, feeling as if she were jumping into an icy lake, she flung Lord Carlton Crue a dazzling smile.

He helped her up into the curricle, not taking her arm as she expected, but with his hands tight about her waist, lifting her, leaving her breathless and blushing on the seat as he walked round and jumped up beside her. She expected the tiger to accompany them, but Crue waved him aside, and he stood back from the horses' heads with a leering grin.

'Oh, but...' Isabella began nervously.

'We are engaged, Isabella,' Crue said. 'We can dispense with the chaperon.'

She glanced anxiously back. Alladay was standing in the doorway watching the curricle move away. The horses sprang forward, turning sharply, and Isabella was thrown against Crue, forced to hold his arm to steady herself. When she looked back again Alladay had gone.

Crue kept up the pace, faster than Isabella enjoyed, and scaring her a little, so that she was continually forced to hold on to him, until they were well clear of Long Trovers. He had driven in silence, only glancing down at her occasionally, and smiling. She risked the occasional glance back.

He was handsome, in a dark, lazy, self-confident way. He was old, forty-five she had heard, and his skin was swarthy, faintly pocked, but his hair was very thick and black, his brows heavy, his dark eyes surprisingly bright and intense under the heavy lids, his nose long, his lips thin and mobile over very white teeth. She knew he had a reputation for his attractiveness to women, and for his treatment of them. She shivered a little, and swallowed nervously.

He allowed the horses to idle along a quiet lane that wound gently down beneath trees into a small valley.

'The horses are tired,' he said. 'I have driven up from Worthing.'

'Have you?' She felt very young and tongue-tied.

'I have taken a house there for the summer. It means I will be able to visit you, when I am free.' He gave a sudden bark of laughter. 'Poor Isabella. I should think you will need someone to visit you, or you will die of the tedium. What a morgue! Place is about to tumble down, struck to the quick by neglect and near bankruptcy, by the looks of it. And what a family! The Kintroves have been known for a streak of eccentricity, but that woman...what a fright!' He paused, and looked down at her. 'So how does my pretty little fiancée spend her days in such a place?'

Isabella shrugged. 'I become bored, I become lonely. I long for interesting company...' here she shot him a glance, and wondered if he knew about Harry '...and I sketch the views of scenic neglect. All of the views,' she added with bitter feeling, 'and all several times already.'

He laughed, surprised to find himself genuinely amused.

'Poor little Isabella. Tell me all about it. Has no one any conversation?'

Isabella, flattered and encouraged by his interest and laughter, welcoming anyone who understood her world, her expectations, her amused disdain for the occupants of Long Trovers, began to describe her life there so far.

She painted a cruelly funny picture of them all, Lord Kintrove in his corduroys tied with string endlessly pushing his wheelbarrow, Lady Kintrove with her calico and onions, Miss Pickering spattered with paint, trailing loose ends of cotton and scattering pins. Particularly she mimicked Alladay, the tedious tutor, always with her brothers, his conversation stuck at their level. Crue's unfeigned laughter and malicious appreciation spurred her on, and she spoke of the lack of servants, and imitated Nurse Pusey instructing her to wash in the scullery.

'I don't believe it,' he said, still chuckling. 'This you *must* be inventing.'

'No, I swear it is all true,' she said, her face bright with her success in amusing and entertaining this experienced and sophisticated man. 'All true.'

'What stories you give me to dine off, Isabella. You are worth your keep already. I shall have to visit Long Trovers frequently, shall I not?'

He had unobtrusively turned the ambling horses so that they wandered to a halt off the lane under some trees, and they were now standing lazily in the dappled shade, twitching their flanks against the flies.

'I begin to think we might deal very well together, Isabella,' he said.

She racked her brain for further stories to amuse him, starting to babble the tale of William shooting the chicken, while she watched with horrid fascination as his hands knotted the reins loosely on to the rail in front of him. He turned towards her and laid one gentle finger on her lips.

'Enough talk now,' he said. 'You have displayed your lively conversation for my delectation; now you must charm me in other ways.'

He ran his hand down her cheek and beneath her chin, feeling for the ribbon of her bonnet. She could not suppress a shiver of half-horrified excitement as he slowly pulled the ribbon, and he smiled again as he lifted the bonnet.

'No, please,' she protested weakly.

'A fiancé's privilege, my dear. I can assure you, there are many, and all of them are pleasant.'

He dropped the bonnet on the seat beside him, and took her face gently in both hands, pulling her close. Her eyes were wide with apprehension, and her lips parted.

'Very nice,' he murmured approvingly, and lowered his mouth on to hers.

She wanted to be horrified, to pull herself free, and she jerked beneath his hold, her hands pushing ineffectually at his chest, but he held her firm, and touching him brought a dreadful fascination as she moved her hands against his body. Her thoughts flew wildly to slapping his face and leaping down from the curricle, but then, most horrifying of all, she was finding his questing lips seductively persuasive. His kisses were so much more experienced and insistent than Harry's soft, tentative offerings, much more exciting. She felt herself reacting, responding to his touch, as if her newly awakened body was acting independently of her wishes, wanting to lead her on to further dark delights. Suddenly frightened, she pulled abruptly away.

Crue rested his hands on her shoulders, preventing her twisting away from him, and regarded her with interest.

'Well, well, little Isabella,' he drawled. 'Perhaps you are not so very little after all.'

He was watching her, his eyes narrowed.

'And where did you learn those pretty tricks, I wonder? Not when your Papa was watching, I'll be bound. From that absurd young Exton pup, perhaps?' he mused. The colour flooded her face. 'I see. Obviously I underrated the boy. Let us hope his journey to the Indies will be exceedingly stormy.'

He took her bottom lip between his finger and thumb and squeezed slowly. She was breathing fast, and tears sprang into her eyes, but his tones were light, almost teasing. 'You will keep all those pretty little tricks just for your fiancé now, won't you, my dearest? No running after the gardening boys or the poor crippled tutor.' His voice held menace beneath the banter. 'And your tricks will give me something to hurry back for, won't they?'

Her face glowed red with shame, rage and humiliation.

'You insult me, sir——' she began, but he interrupted.

'Oh, spare me the maidenly blushes now, dear girl,' he said, tossing her bonnet on to her lap and taking up the reins. 'I am not quite certain that they suit you.'

She was silent throughout the drive home, but Crue whistled to himself, quietly satisfied.

'I think, my dear Isabella,' he said as he handed her down at Long Trovers, 'that you and I will come to understand each other very well.' He gave her a knowing smile. 'This arrangement could offer more than I had dared hope. But I must depart. Make my apologies to your hosts, dear girl. I could not contain my mirth were I to meet the geriatric in string and corduroy, and my faultless social reputation would stand in ruins.' He flicked her cheek. *'Au revoir.'*

And he was gone, leaving Isabella forlorn, adrift on the gravel before the great wooden door of Long Trovers.

CHAPTER FIVE

ISABELLA'S dreams were filled with anxiety, twisting tortuous paths around Lord Carlton Crue, his smile, his touch, his lips, and calls for Harry, who never came.

She awoke suddenly, abruptly wide-eyed in the early light. Her thoughts ran relentlessly on in the coils of her dreams, worrying and brooding on the events of yesterday. She was frightened but fascinated, repulsed yet flattered. She hated the way Crue had spoken to her, she was angry and confused. She felt deeply shamed by her response to his kisses, and degraded by his reaction to that response. Yet still a whispering corner in her mind was excited and wanted more of his touch, winding dark hope among the reproofs with which she chided herself. She was guiltily aware that her caresses with Harry seemed but childish games in comparison.

And there was no escaping the fact that Crue *was* her fiancé. Her father had given her over into his care. He had a right to do these things. He would become her husband. Harry would have to be forgotten. She shivered, and pulled the blankets tighter about her. She tried to imagine herself married to this man, running his home, raising his children, lying in his bed . . . and her thoughts flew panicking away like startled sparrows.

Ruth found her new mistress to be withdrawn and irritable when she brought up her breakfast tray, and hopefully attributed this to a lovesick heart. She had thought Lord Carlton Crue both rich and handsome, and had been regaling the servants' hall with imagined stories of Isabella's romance and true love, ignoring Nurse Pusey's snorted disbelief.

'I expect it was wonderful,' she said wistfully, half to herself, as she brushed the blue silk and checked it carefully for mud splashes.

'What was wonderful?'

Isabella had finished her toast, and was sipping her chocolate, leaning back in her pillows.

'Ooh, driving out with such a man, so handsome, and in such a curricle, so . . . so dashing!'

She sighed at the wonder of it all.

'Oh, yes,' Isabella said expressionlessly. 'Wonderful.'

'I knew it! I told them downstairs as how it was all true love, and Nurse Pusey, she looked daggers, her and her story about the dogs!'

Ruth laughed. Nurse Pusey had been with the family for so long that she sometimes acted as if they were her own personal possession, and she the fount of all wisdom about them. This could be very annoying. It was fun to know more than she did.

'What story? What dogs?' Isabella asked crossly. She disliked the idea that she had been discussed in the servants' hall.

'Why, the old family legend, of course. Have you never heard it? Everyone who lives round Long Trovers knows of it, that and the treasure. Those are the two stories everyone tells.'

'Well, I don't live round Long Trovers, do I? I live in London, or so I used to believe. So I wouldn't know your precious story, would I? So tell it to me.'

'Yes, miss. Sorry, miss.' Ruth was only momentarily daunted. 'Well, it's like this, see. The dogs here, they are the only sort like them in all the country. They are Trovers spaniels, and have been bred by the family for I don't know how many generations. There's always some, here in the house, and out on the farms round the estate. And there's stories about them. If they all die out, see, the Kintrove family will die out too, everyone knows that.

'And as for the other story, though I don't know as how I believe it, it's said they always choose the new lady for the eldest son. That's how the tale goes. When the eldest son brings a lady home the dogs know if she will be the next lady of the house. If they accept her, then she belongs here. If they don't, well, nothing will come of it.'

Ruth shrugged.

'Nurse Pusey believes it all as gospel truth, so when Mr Anthony, or Lord Alladay as I should say now, when he brought you home and the dogs carried on so, well she reckoned she knew what to think. But don't worry, miss. I told them all how it was with you and Lord Carlton Crue.'

Isabella lowered her cup and stared at Ruth in unfeigned outrage.

'Do you mean to tell me . . . do you seriously mean to tell me that that nurse, that horrible old witch, has been gossiping in the servants' hall, implying I would . . . that I might . . . heaven forbid, *marry* Lord Alladay!'

Ruth nodded.

Isabella could hardly speak, she was so angry.

'Unspeakable! The impertinence! How dare she? As if I would even dream of such an impossible thing!'

Even Ruth looked surprised by the strength of this outburst.

'Don't fret, miss. It's only an old story. No sense in it. I told them how it is with you and Lord Carlton Crue, and there's lots of us don't mind seeing Nurse Pusey wrong for once.

'If truth be told, we all know Mr Anthony will have to marry an heiress if he's to save the estate. He can't be picking and choosing, whatever his heart might say. It'll have to be a fortune for him, and a big one I reckon, no matter what she looks like.' Ruth giggled. 'No, miss, you take no notice of what old Nurse Pusey says.'

'You can rest assured,' said Isabella, pushing her tray aside, and jumping out of bed, 'that I shall take no notice whatever!'

Later, as she made her way downstairs, Isabella was waylaid by Hopkins.

'Your young brothers were looking for you, Miss Larkham. I told them you were not down yet, and they asked me to ask you to join them outside, where you were shooting the arrows, yesterday.' He smiled. 'They sounded very keen!'

She smiled back, pleased they wanted her again.

'I expect they want some more target practice. Yes, I'll join them.' She was turning away, then she said, 'Thank you, Hopkins.'

Bess, who had, as usual, materialised with the breakfast tray, was joined now by several of the other dogs.

'All of them her sons and daughters,' Hopkins said, regarding Bess proudly.

'Is that so?' Isabella said, giving a quick frown. Hoping to escape their attentions, she went hastily outside.

She could, as usual, hear her brothers before she could see them. They were inside the store where the archery equipment was kept, so, expecting them to be lugging at the heavy target, she ducked into the doorway out of the bright sun and stood smiling and blinking in the gloom.

They were not collecting any of the archery things. They were busily unpacking boxes of bolts of cloth, cloth that appeared, to her bemused gaze, to be silk. And they were not, as she had expected, alone. Lord Alladay was with them, straightening up as he saw her, a length of red material in his hands. His terse greeting was drowned by the cries of the boys.

'Thank goodness you've come, Izzie. We really need you to help us sew this. Just look how big it will be!'

'Do you know what it will be? I bet you would never guess! It's going to be a balloon! A huge balloon that we can fly in!'

'Yes, truly, we are going to fly! Just like the Montgolfier brothers in France. Do you remember about them? Anthony taught us. And now he is going to help us to do the same, but we need you to do the sewing.

If we sewed it, it would be full of holes and all the hot air would come out!'

'Go on, Izzie, say you will!'

Isabella's first instinct was to refuse outright, to escape from the store at once. She was beginning to shake her head when Thomas added despondently, 'If you won't help we'll have to ask Nurse Pusey, and she's so old she'll probably die before it's finished.'

Isabella paused and frowned at the mention of the old woman's name. Awful to think of her down here, sewing and spreading her impossible gossip. She glanced at Alladay, but he seemed engrossed in studying a design printed on a sheet of paper. She shrugged as if indifferent.

'I might,' she said, ungraciously. 'I suppose there is nothing better to do in this God-forsaken place.'

'Thank you, Izzie.' The boys were overjoyed. 'Come and look at the plans. See the picture of it finished?'

They clustered around Alladay, pulling Isabella with them, and he spread the paper for them all to see. It was headed in dashing script, 'A Unique Opportunity to Defy Gravity!' and claimed to give detailed instructions, with scaled-down pattern pieces, for the construction of your own personal hot air balloon. 'Astound your family and friends as you float above their heads!' it concluded. 'Of inestimable convenience to the householder inspecting roofs and guttering, or for the easy discovery of distant game for the gun!' Then, in very small print, 'Silk, thread, ropes and basket not included!'

Alladay spoke.

'We ordered the plans and the silk while we were still in Town,' he said flatly to Isabella. 'They have only just arrived. It seemed an ideal thing to try over the summer.' Then he turned to the boys and his face lit with an infectious, boyish grin that seemed to Isabella to shut her out. 'Some of us just couldn't resist it, could they?'

Setting her shoulder towards the man, she looked in amazement at the picture. The balloon would be enormous! 'However could you afford all this silk?' she asked, accusingly.

Alladay made as if to reply, but Thomas was quicker.

'We used the money Papa gave us for staying down here,' he said cheerfully. 'After all, it was supposed to be used for us!'

Isabella turned to Alladay, aghast.

'The money our father paid out for our board and bed? You spent it all on silk! That is more than irresponsible; it is absurd!'

He regarded her coolly, his eyebrows faintly raised, and she registered surprise at this new, aloof assurance. It was a very far cry from the role of Mr D'Estine, the tutor, and once again she felt set at a disadvantage.

'Your father entrusted the money to me. He expected it to be spent on his children; that is what I have done.'

She glared at him.

'It was to have been paid to your parents,' she said. 'They are the ones who are lodging us. It was not yours to dispose of.'

'My parents welcomed you into their home because I requested it. They would never have dreamed of accepting money from you,' he said quietly, and his voice was chilly with disdain. 'They have accepted you as my friends. Their hospitality is not to be bought,' he regarded her bitterly, 'no matter how much gold is dangled before me.'

'Then,' she paused, staring at him with stormy eyes, before continuing tautly, 'then we are forced to become your guests.'

'Of course,' he said. 'What else? You have been my guests since you arrived.'

He returned her look levelly, and, flushing slightly at the memory of her arrogant behaviour, she dropped her eyes, unable to meet his gaze. Confused, she turned back to the paper, where her brothers were eagerly pointing to the designs for the sections of silk.

It took some time, and much eager discussion on the part of the boys, before a full-sized pattern of one of the silk balloon sections had been measured, drawn, and cut out from great lengths of faded, rotting, purple curtain that Alladay and Hopkins removed and brought back from windows in one of the many disused rooms.

To Isabella's great relief Alladay left them then, excusing himself to her brothers by pleading an appointment with the Long Trovers' agent. His farewell nod to Isabella was cool, and she spoke to William, ignoring his departure.

'We then use this as the full-size pattern to lay on to the silk, and cut around it. Look at the instructions, William. How many sections must we cut?'

Isabella found she was enjoying helping, once he had gone, despite having to crawl about on the dusty floor.

She drew outlines, and cut out shapes, joining with her brothers in a lively discussion of how to balance the colours. They had chosen silks in patriotic red, white and blue, and needed to ensure suitably alternating stripes.

The three had worked for some time, and were all growing tired, when an amicable argument over the arrangement of the stripes, degenerated rapidly into a parade of giggling Romans in swathes of silken toga. Isabella, who had a fondness for home dramatics, was dying agonisingly slowly to breathy groans of *'Et tu, Brute?'*, amid her brothers hilarity and enthusiastic stabbings, when she noticed that Alladay had reappeared in the doorway of the store.

Angrily embarrassed, the laughter wiped from her face, she dropped her length of silk to the floor, and began to spread the pattern on to it, resenting his help when, seeing her problem with keeping the material flat, he quietly knelt down to assist. Sensing her dislike, he shrugged and moved away.

She became aware that William was speaking to her, kneeling beside her as all four of them began carefully to cut out the vast shape in rich blue.

'Lord Carlton Crue called to see you yesterday, didn't he?' the boy asked, quietly. He sounded worried.

'Yes, he did,' she said.

'Are you truly going to marry him, Izzie? Truly? We would never have fun like this again if you did. He is so old! He is one of Papa's friends! As old as Papa. And, anyway, I don't like him! Nor does Thomas.'

She frowned reprovingly, acutely aware of Alladay, just across the store, holding the material taut for Thomas to cut.

'Papa arranged it, William. I have to do what he says,' she answered, a touch desperately, hoping he would drop the subject. 'I really have no choice in the matter, do I?'

She noticed a quietness across the room, and realised that Alladay was very still, his lips gripped tight as if in disapproval. Disapproval of her engagement? Or was he, too, thinking of Harry? She glared. 'Besides,' she continued, her eyes still on Alladay, 'I like Lord Carlton Crue!'

She watched with satisfaction as Alladay's face seemed to set a little sterner. How dared he set himself up to disapprove of her and her fiancé! What right had he to an opinion?

'You like him, Izzie? Are you sure?' William's voice was filled with doubt. 'I thought you and Harr——'

'Oh, yes,' she interrupted deliberately, raising her voice a little. 'Yes, I am quite sure. I like him very much.' She kept her eyes on Alladay's profile. 'You are really too young to understand, William,' she said kindly, 'but Carlton is a *very* attractive man!'

William only shrugged, but Alladay turned and gave Isabella a long look. He said nothing, but she thought his eyes seemed full of contempt. She stared defiantly back, though she felt her colour rise, and she gave a light laugh before turning back to smooth the silk and continue cutting. Shortly afterwards Alladay left them again, pleading necessary work to be completed in the estate office, for his afternoon was to be taken up with visitors.

'I hope you will come and meet them, Miss Larkham,' he said stiffly, as he was leaving. 'The Grice-Hewsons are old friends of my parents, and I had thought...' he paused, and she wondered if he was regretting his thought '...I had thought that their daughter Sarah might be congenial company for you.'

Isabella looked at him with a faint smile. Visitors! At least that would be a welcome novelty!

'I shall be delighted to meet her,' she said.

The Grice-Hewsons were to arrive at three o'clock that afternoon. Isabella had ordered Ruth to bring up extra hot water after luncheon, and had thoroughly cleaned away all traces of her morning's work in the old store, which, though swept by the boys, was far from clean.

After much thought, and many suggestions from Ruth, she eventually decided to wear a deceptively plain white muslin, with a simple flounce above the hem and a low scooped neck, which tied high under the bosom with a white satin sash. It looked, she knew, very demure, but also very becoming, setting off her silky skin and rich golden hair to perfection. She had Ruth brush her curls out loosely, and just catch them back with a single white ribbon, then she smiled at her reflection. It would do very well.

She ventured downstairs to the green room just before they arrived. Alladay and his parents were there. Lord and Lady Kintrove had both changed from their workaday clothing, and presented a picture of unassuming and somewhat old-fashioned elegance, Lord Kintrove in black with ruffles of rich Brussels lace at either wrist, his lady in a dress of rust-brown silk. Alladay, she noted with surprise, was immaculately clad in brown breeches and a jacket of dark green superfine, his cravat falling in perfect folds. His fair curls had been trimmed shorter, and were brushed back in attractive disorder. His eyes, looking oddly dark, regarded her thoughtfully.

After a brief word of greeting he ignored her, and she sat down beside Lady Kintrove, who was competently repairing some worn embroidery on a large tablecloth, and immediately begged assistance in matching colours.

Hopkins announced the visitors with a wide smile, and was almost overtaken by their enthusiastic entrance. The parents swept over, smiles beaming, hands outstretched, to greet everybody, but Isabella's eyes were caught by the daughter.

Sarah Grice-Hewson was a small, vivacious girl of perhaps seventeen, with sparkling green eyes and bouncing, glowing curls of rich copper red. If she was the smallest bit plump it was plain that it would always be forgiven her, for it suited her rosy cheeks, and, besides, it was immediately obvious that she would be everybody's darling. Isabella watched her dubiously.

'Anthony!' Sarah said, clasping her hands together. 'Oh, Anthony, it has been such ages since I saw you.' She ran lightly across the room to where he stood, and took his hands in hers, nodding appreciatively. 'Oh, very handsome, very nice,' she teased. 'Have you come to break all our hearts? I can see you have lost none of that Kintrove charm. Go on, give me a quick kiss for old times' sake.'

He laughed, and obliged with a kiss on each cheek, his face alight with amusement and pleasure.

'You don't change, do you, Sarah?' he said.

'I don't intend to,' she replied cheekily. 'Life is far too much fun! But wait now, I am forgetting my manners!'

She danced over to greet Lord and Lady Kintrove, kissing each one very prettily on the cheek and stopping to talk a moment, before settling down beside Isabella.

'I have heard so much about you,' she said. 'I have been longing to meet you. You must know that I am relying on you to tell me all kinds of outrageous stories of Anthony's doings in London so that I can tease him about them! I suffered so much from his teasing when we were young that it is high time, now I am home from school and a lady grown, that I am able to get my revenge.'

She chuckled, looking up at him from under her lashes.

'Do you remember that time you put me on your new pony, swearing it was the most docile thing alive, when really it was the most excitable beast?' She turned to Isabella. 'It immediately took exception to the flapping of my skirts and fled hysterically down the field.'

'Oh, I think it is a moot point who was the hysterical one!' Alladay put in, laughing.

'You may laugh,' she went on, in mock indignation. 'That was all you did then, you and your brothers!' She turned back to Isabella 'I may tell you that I was clinging on for my life through three fields while they did no more than roll on the ground curled up with laughter! I landed up in a bramble patch, and Jasper had to fish me out, all scratches, blood and tears! How I hated Anthony!' She looked at him and laughed.

'I am surprised you bothered to call on them again,' Isabella remarked.

'Not call again! My dear, you don't understand! *All* the little girls round about...' she chuckled '...and those not so little, would give their eye teeth for a visit to the Kintrove boys!'

'We still have that pony, you know,' Lady Kintrove put in. 'Older, wiser and more sedate now. He is out in the Long Meadow, I believe. Why don't you walk over with the girls, Anthony, and take him a carrot or two? You don't want to stay in here all afternoon. I'll order tea when you get back.'

Sarah took Isabella's arm as they went out, throwing a saucy smile over her shoulder at Alladay.

'I intend to pick Isabella's brain for every one of your darkest secrets, you know! Nothing will be safe from me!'

'Then my presence will be quite unnecessary. Shall I leave you two ladies alone?'

'Good heavens, you can't think to escape that easily! You may only leave us to fetch the carrots. We will be walking towards the meadow, deep in conversation!'

Sarah giggled as he left them.

'Dear Isabella, you don't know how often I have hated you! To think of you, living in London with the last of the Kintrove boys all to yourself! Oh, I wept for weeks when Bardolph died. It was bad enough when Jasper was killed, though of course he was so much older than me...but Bardolph! He was so handsome, and when he was in his uniform... Did you ever see him?'

Isabella shook her head.

'What a heartbreaker! We all swore we loved him distractedly, of course, and he was a terrible flirt!' She giggled again. 'But I always thought Anthony was the most handsome of the three. You must not mind when I tell you that you can have no idea how pleased I was when Mama told me your engagement had been announced to Lord Carlton Crue! Oh, I meant to congratulate you! I am afraid I don't know him, I hardly ever get up to Town, but he must be very special if you preferred him to Anthony! Oh, dear, I do rattle on, don't I? Don't tell him a word I have said, will you?' She leant nearer and whispered, 'I really think Mama and Papa hope we will make a match of it, but they say I must wait to make any attachment until I am older and have had my London season, next year.'

'But don't you object to his having worked as a tutor? Or to...well, to the way he walks, his limp?' Isabella found herself asking with a hint of disdain.

Sarah looked at her in surprise.

'His old job is not important now he has the title, is it? And his bad leg? From when he fell out of the walnut tree? I was here when that happened, you know. It was horrible, I thought he was dead. But no, do you know, it is not that I don't mind it, I don't even seem to ever notice it. Look.'

Alladay was coming up to join them, chewing on one of the carrots he had brought for the pony.

'It is hardly there at all, really. It's just...well, it's just Anthony!'

Sarah had paused, waiting for him to join them.

'You gluttonous beast,' she said. 'Fancy eating the carrots and depriving poor starving Pippin!'

'Wait till you see him,' Alladay rejoined. 'Poor starving nothing! He is like a barrel. I shall have to get William and Thomas to give him some exercise if I can ever drag them away from their balloon!'

They spent a lively half-hour feeding carrots to Pippin and the other plump pony, Bramble, and under the influence of Sarah's irrepressible cheerfulness even Isabella relaxed and laughed and chatted about the balloon they were making and the boys' plans for flying it. They were wandering back to take tea, and Isabella was feeling more at ease at Long Trovers than at any time since her arrival, when she found herself saying impulsively, and somewhat wistfully, 'Oh, I do hope we will soon see you again!'

'I only wish you could,' Sarah wailed. 'There is nothing I would like better, but my dear parents have taken a house on the coast, in Worthing, for the summer, and we are to leave at the end of the week. So unless you can persuade Anthony to bring you down on a visit...'

She raised her eyebrows hopefully at Anthony, and giggled, fluttering her lashes.

'Go on, Anthony, say you might. You could bring the boys down for a day by the sea,' she coaxed.

'Oh, I don't know,' he rejoined gloomily. 'I am going to be very busy with the management of the estate...' then he took pity on her disappointed face and finished with a grin '...but I might just consider it!'

'Dearest man,' she beamed at him. 'I knew I could rely on you.'

'You are a shocking flirt, Sarah Grice-Hewson! I wonder that your parents dare take you to Worthing,' he responded with mock severity. 'You will have the place by the ears in five minutes!'

'Do you really think so?' She seemed delighted. 'That will compensate me for life without you!'

'Minx!'

Isabella felt very much the outsider in this exchange. She was not sorry to rejoin the elders and take her tea and cakes. She felt thoroughly disconcerted to discover that a girl of obvious wealth and excellent family should consider her despised Mr D'Estine a most desirable catch, and, more, a most desirable man. She wondered if hers might be the fortune he needed for the estate. She looked across at where they were sitting together, Alladay laughing and shaking his head at something she had said.

Was Sarah right? Could he be thought attractive? She gave a mental shrug. He was certainly changed. Despite her dislike of him she could see that it was more than just the different garb. He seemed to be more mature, to have taken on an added assurance that made him quite independent of her and her father. She knew with a sudden certainty that no amount of her father's money could buy Alladay back to work for him now.

He looked up and caught her eye, holding her gaze across the room. Isabella frowned and let her eyes fall.

CHAPTER SIX

THE following morning Isabella went to the store, hoping to find Thomas and William alone there, maybe to set up the archery target.

She had been invited to accompany Lady Kintrove and Miss Pickering to pay a few calls in the village. They had been welcoming and friendly, and she had almost accepted, but her awareness of her own inadequacy in their spirited conversations, and her embarrassment at the curious figures they seemed to cut in their unfashionable clothes, made her self-consciously refuse, and she knew her refusal had sounded churlish.

As a result, she felt oddly discontented with herself when she reached the store. She found her brothers had not yet arrived. She paced irritably up and down the worn red-brick floor, running her hand against the coarse flint of the wall, thinking of Harry, not wistfully now but with some anger, for still no letter had arrived. And she brooded on her unsettling fiancé, Lord Carlton Crue, whose presence filled her with such an uncomfortable turmoil of emotions.

So abstracted was she that she caught her knuckle on a protruding edge of glassy grey flint and drew blood. She sucked at it crossly, then with a sigh she settled down to cutting out the last of the pieces of silk, kneeling on a remnant of the old purple curtain in a hopeful attempt to keep her skirts clean. Bess, naturally, was with her, and, as Bess liked to doze in the sun, and Isabella liked to spread the silk in the sun to gain the best light, the appropriation of the patch of sunlight near the door was in permanent dispute.

'You are too fat, too hairy, and always in the wrong place!' Isabella remarked to her severely, as the old dog rolled yet again on to the white silk. Bess heaved a soulful sigh.

'You are not even anything of a conversationalist, which is a great pity, seeing as you seem to be the best I have got.'

Bess's tail twitched sympathetically.

Isabella heaved a sudden despairing sigh.

'Wretched dog. I don't now why I bother to talk to you. Here am I, so horribly miserable, and lonely and... and confused, and what do you do? Do you answer me? Do you advise me? Do you help? Never! You just lie there and thump that hairy tail of yours. And what use is that to anybody?'

Bess, basking in so much attention, lolled on to her back, rolled her eyes at Isabella, and thumped her tail on to the floor hopefully.

'No, I don't want to spend my morning scratching your belly! Believe it or not, I have better things to do!'

'Oh, she won't believe you,' came a voice from the doorway. Alladay was standing silhouetted against the brightness. 'In her view there *is* nothing better to do! Is there, old girl?'

He came in and squatted down by Bess, stroking her belly while she lay, ecstatic, against his boot. Isabella, perturbed and angered at the thought of him listening to her one-sided conversation, bent her head over her cutting and scowled at Bess, who was responding to Alladay's touch with traitorous adoration.

'I have sent your brothers off to exercise Pippin and Bramble,' the man continued mildly, concentrating all his attention upon Bess, running his long fingers up and down her throat while she lay sprawled on her back, all four legs lolling in the air. 'Old Bill has taken them. He taught my brothers and me to ride, so they are in good hands. They will return when he has had enough of them! I thought you might be here, and might be wondering what had become of us all.'

'Oh, no,' she said, irritably removing her gaze from his fingers' rhythmic stroking. She smoothed a rumple in the silk. 'Nothing of the sort. I was enjoying the peace and quiet.'

'Ah.'

He stood up, walked across the store, picked up the instruction sheet and began to read, studying the shapes already cut, and frowning slightly. Isabella finished the piece she was cutting.

'I believe that is the last piece,' she said, thinking to escape.

He nodded. 'Yes, you're right. We have to start stitching now, and that is going to be a very long and tedious job. Whatever the boys may think, we are all going to have to do our bit. You could not possibly stitch it all alone and Nurse Pusey has enough sewing in the house to keep her fully occupied. But first is the question of what joins to what.'

Isabella straightened up and looked at the pile of pieces. It had not occurred to her that the tutor might contemplate taking his turn with a needle and thread. The thought amused her. An absurd vision of Lord Carlton Crue daintily stitching a sampler swam into her mind, and she stifled a giggle.

She had always been good with her needle, and had enjoyed on occasion making additions to her wardrobe. But this was a secret pride. On the completion of the first gown she had attempted she had proudly displayed it to her father. Her weeks of work were greeted with the irritable remarks that had he wanted a seamstress for a daughter he wouldn't have worked to get himself where he was today, and why couldn't she go to a French dressmaker like any other lady of quality? It pleased her now occasionally to pass off her own creations as those of Madame Defayne.

She studied the pieces of silk with an increasingly professional interest, then glanced at Lord Alladay. His attention was entirely taken up by the instruction sheet from which he appeared to derive little enlightenment. He did not seem to be teasing her. The sarcastic remark that had risen in her mind died unsaid before a desire to do something that she thought she could do well.

'It might be easiest,' she suggested diffidently, 'if I were to roughly tack the first pieces before we begin sewing. So they are held into the correct place.'

'Thank heavens!' he said, looking relieved. 'Someone who knows how to do this! I don't want the boys to be disappointed now we have got this far.' He delved into one of the boxes. 'Here are the needles and cards of thread that we ordered. Show me what you mean.'

Uncertainly at first, then growing in confidence, for the pattern really did seem very straightforward to her, she arranged the first vast pieces.

'Look. If you could hold these together for me, I could tack them quickly, then we could sew them at our leisure.'

She deftly matched corners and edges, and gave him pieces to hold.

'Did you not order pins?' she asked, and she heard her voice sound critical.

'No.' He frowned, and she thought he would make some sharp rejoinder, but his face suddenly broke into a rueful grin. 'I didn't know we needed them.'

She shook her head, but, 'Men!' she ventured, and he chuckled.

She made him stand holding several pieces while she tacked the long side seams together. She thought he seemed a little friendlier, less disapproving than on the previous morning, and she was surprised to find herself relieved, even pleased.

'I enjoyed meeting Miss Grice-Hewson,' she volunteered.

His face lit in a spontaneous smile.

'I hoped you would. We all find Sarah irresistible, and we have known her so long she seems quite one of the family. It is a pity she and her family are going to be away. I had hoped we would be seeing her regularly.'

'Yes.'

He seemed very enthusiastic. Perhaps Miss Grice-Hewson *was* the necessary heiress. Ruth will probably know by now, Isabella reflected with an inward smile; I shall have to ask her.

'But you will see her again if you take the boys to Worthing,' she said.

He looked up at her, a frown in his eyes.

'It is *you* she wished to see,' he said, his tones touched by renewed irritation, 'not your brothers. Her invitation was to you. Couldn't you bring yourself to enjoy a trip to Worthing? Certainly we would have to wait until her family are settled in, and, yes, it would be a long day, but the weather seems set fair. Surely the trip *could* be pleasurable?'

Surprised at his spurt of irritation, Isabella paused before answering, pulling firm the thread at the end of the seam and nipping neatly through the cotton with her teeth. Struck by an uncomfortable thought, she did not make her instinctive, angry response. Was she really always as ill-tempered about any suggestion as his tone implied? Did she always find such fault that he automatically expected it? Ashamed, her thoughts flicked to her refusal to go to the village with Lady Kintrove. Her son must know of that.

She contemplated a trip to Worthing. In her mind Worthing was full of visions of Lord Carlton Crue. Where was he staying? she wondered, and how did he fill his days when he was not driving to Long Trovers? Would he be angry if he saw her out with her brothers and 'the poor crippled tutor'? Would he complain to her Papa? Abruptly she was defiant. She hoped that he would complain. Papa had buried her here in the countryside, depriving her of all the outings and picnics they had planned. They could all be angry. She did not care.

'Yes,' she said firmly, allowing herself a small, satisfied smile at his surprise, 'I should love a trip to Worthing. It sounds most enjoyable. Let us go as soon as may be convenient.'

She turned away and settled down to finely stitch the seams, but almost immediately the boys arrived, very noisy and full of their riding experiences, smelling strongly of stables. There was a moment's peace while they went, reluctantly, to wash their hands, then they were back, and learning to handle needle and thread with vociferous complaints. Alladay excused himself at this point—he had a meeting with a tenant—and Isabella was left alone to organise the boys' efforts.

It was a more arduous task than teaching them archery, but by the time he returned they were both managing competent seams. He duly admired their handiwork, and, catching her eye across the spread silks, he smiled his admiration and approval at the improvement she had brought about. But she found the warmth of his smile and his friendly words more difficult to react to than when she could be angry and sharp-tongued, or resentful of his disapproval. After sitting for a while feeling awkward and tongue-tied, she pleaded a headache, and made good her escape from the store.

As Bess seemed to feel that the reason for leaving the store could only be to walk in the sunshine, Isabella ambled idly after where the old dog led. She was unaware of Alladay's gaze watching her through the cobweb-straddled window of the store.

Over the last four years Alladay had frequently had the opportunity to watch Isabella, usually unnoticed, accustomed as he had been to her utter disregard for his existence.

He had seen her first as a gangly, uncertain schoolgirl, her thick blonde hair tied demurely back from her face. He had watched her frown uncertainly as she was pushed by her father to bring home schoolfriends who were rich, well-connected, or, preferably, both. He had pretended not to see her hide her tears behind the nursery curtains when she was forbidden the friendship of a girl her father deemed unsuitable. He had seen her artfully coax and cajole her father to his face, but regard his back with wide-eyed anxiety. And throughout, she had regarded the tutor with contemptuous disdain.

The atmosphere in the Larkham household had not been a happy one for a lonely, motherless girl, and Alladay's opinion of the shallow, simpering Aunt Caroline, who occasionally took a mother's place, was low. She had offered none of the advice and affection Isabella needed, only shown her own selfish, silly ways. Alladay's tentatively sympathetic approaches to the young girl had been suspiciously rebuffed, however. It was clear that Isabella resented his friendship with her brothers. She clung hopefully to the brittle friendships made at her seminary.

Isabella had grown beautiful. It would have needed far more than the spectacles he affected to blind Alladay, or all the multitude of admirers she had acquired during her London season, to those huge, long-lashed blue eyes, pert little nose, pouting red lips and tumble of blonde curls.

She had been, of course, an instant social success. For a little time then, in her heady excitement, it had amused her to flaunt herself before her brothers' tutor, swirling her wonderful, rustling new skirts and fluttering her long lashes, innocently confident that her teasing was safe. As indeed it had had to be. Whatever feelings might have been aroused, the tutor had known that as an impoverished younger son, and an employee of her father, no response was possible, and he had watched her with a cynical raised eyebrow, squinting horribly through his spectacles, and hunching his back.

Affronted by his immovability, and the suspicion that he was teasing her in return, she had been briefly spiteful in her jibes and taunts, then had coldly ignored him. Later, hurt by the fickleness and unkind betrayals of jealous schoolfriends, she had seemed to grow hard and uncaring. She had flirted shockingly, had grown more wilful, petulant and irritable, and had spurned all suitors with impatient contempt. Many a time Alladay had itched to give her the set-down she deserved, or to pick her up and shake her out of her silly, affected mannerisms. Only her constant fondness for her brothers had redeemed her in his eyes.

Until the day she had met Harry Exton. After she had met Harry, with his soft, languid airs, his delicately boned white hand flicking back the Byronic lock of dark hair from his forehead as he had gazed into her eyes and murmured poetic couplets, and his willowy, tall figure draped elegantly beside her wherever they had gone, Isabella had seemed to forget her brothers altogether, and Alladay had lost patience with her entirely.

He had managed to be civil to Mr Larkham when that man had announced that it was necessary for his daughter to accompany her brothers to Long Trovers. But only just. What he would do with that irritable, wilful, petulant, contemptuous, lovelorn daughter at his eccentric parents' home had given Lord Alladay much unresolved thought, from the hilarious to the despairing.

He frowned after her retreating figure. And now Lord Carlton Crue had appeared on the scene, to further complicate matters. He shrugged. No doubt things would resolve themselves one way or another. His duty was to her brothers, and he turned away from the window to give his attention to their noise.

Isabella was similarly deep in thought, thoughts triggered by Alladay. He had considered her family 'ignorant, uncultured Cits'.

She kicked angrily at a clod of earth, then glared more angrily at the mud stain it left on her jean half-boot.

She hated him for what he had said. But, the idea wormed in her mind, was he right? Was that what they were? It was a deeply humiliating thought.

Isabella had never previously questioned her father's ban upon visiting, or even mentioning in company, his family, and his brother in the north of England who still ran the family woollen mills. She had been taught to pretend they did not exist, and to laugh with her acquaintances at the pretensions of upstart Cits with neither culture nor breeding.

Was she really so different from those Cits? What right had she to an assumption of superiority? Was she one of them? It was a disturbing thought, questioning everything her father, and she herself, believed about her position in society.

Her father's diplomatic career was funded by those same despised mills, as was their entire way of life. This money had paid for her to attend the very select seminary where she had learnt, at her father's insistence, to share the prejudices of the daughters of the greatest in the land—to admire wealth first, then breeding—learned to hide her own origins, to live a partial pretence.

She thought then of something else Lord Alladay had said. That taking the post he had done with her family had helped him to mitigate his prejudices. What had he meant? Had he meant that he was no longer so ready to despise those underbred Cits, those self-made men?

She thought of her own, or her father's ideas about the importance of wealth. The Kintroves had none. But it had gradually become plain to Isabella that not everybody would despise them for that as her father obviously did. Other people could find things to value in such a family. She thought of kindness, courtesy, generosity, and honesty, qualities of little value in her father's world, and she was suddenly ashamed of him.

Her reflections, so questioning of her father, left her with a vague feeling of panic, as if she was cutting herself adrift from the structure of her past, but had yet to build a raft to carry her into the future.

Isabella's thoughts had drifted randomly, and her feet had rambled as far as her thoughts. Bess had led her across the fields in front of the house, following a pathway that led through a series of wooden gates, towards a rounded mound topped by a copse of trees. As they neared the trees Bess ran ahead and vanished among them, towards muffled, irregular thudding sounds.

Isabella followed the path and emerged in a circular clearing at the centre of the copse, on the very top of the mound. Before her was the base of a large, stone, circular hollow structure, without door or windows, now standing about five feet high. Beside it was a wheelbarrow, piled high with old stones, many patterned by moss, lichen or old ivy roots, and beside the barrow was Lord Kintrove, a large square stone in his hands. He was lifting it up to place it on the wall. He smiled at her, but spent some little time settling the stone to his satisfaction before standing back to survey it with approval, then turning to speak.

'You must forgive me, dear girl. I see you have come with Bonny...' here he bent and caressed Bess's ears affectionately '...so I know I should know your name. But, I have to confess, it escapes me. I do forget so much nowadays, if I don't have dear Clara to set me right.'

He beamed at her hopefully.

His wispy white hair floated up in the hint of breeze. He was wearing the corduroy breeches, and they were indeed both patched and tied at the knees with string. His hands were earthy from the stones. His face was warm and kindly, his smile innocently unselfconscious, his eyes growing just a little anxious as she did not immediately speak.

'Oh, dear, oh, dear! Have I offended you, my dear, by forgetting? I can assure you it is nothing personal. It happens all the time. So foolish.'

He seemed quite distressed.

'No, of course not.' Isabella was quick with reassurance. Perhaps the old man is quite mad, she thought, with a mixture of amusement and alarm, and a corner of her mind pictured the story she could tell Lord Carlton Crue. 'It is not at all important.' She held out her hand. 'I am Isabella Larkham. I came down to stay for the summer, with my young brothers.'

'Ah, yes, good. It is always good for the boys to have company. They love to have friends to stay...' His voice tailed off, and he frowned, reaching out his hand to hold the stone he had just placed in to this strange edifice. He looked back at her sadly, and sighed. 'They used to,' he said. 'When they were young and all still with us. Such times they had. Jasper always leading them into any sort of scrapes.'

He smiled gently, apologetically, his face as open as a child's.

'Well, you'll know the story of the parson's old saddleback sow, and Bardolph as the highwayman, holding up old Lady Greening... Such times...' He rubbed his forehead. 'I find it hard to understand that it is all gone. Jasper gone. Bardolph gone. Only young Anthony left, and he away at some tomfool job in London. But there. I do what I can to remember them. Something to remind me that once they were here.'

He patted the stone wall proudly, and his face, which had been creased in painful memories, assumed an air of hopeful pride.

'This will be their memorial,' he said. 'Not down in the church, but here, on their land, where they should be remembered, and built from the stones of their tower, their inheritance. I can't afford a professional job, you know...' he leant forward, his tones earnest and confidential '...for I won't burden my tenants to pay for such a thing, and in a way I am glad. Money is not everything. I like to do the work, and I believe my boys would prefer their memorial built with time and love.' His voice was strong and certain now. He was gazing beyond her, speaking to perhaps something only he could see, away in the trees. His living audience was forgotten. 'One should remember one's family with honour and with pride. When it is built this tower will stand high above these trees, a permanent monument to my sons.'

Head thrown back, hand on the stone, he had a strange, compelling dignity that left Isabella filled with awed hilarity, but also compassion, and reluctant respect. He might be old and confused, but as she watched him the desire to mock drained from her. She remembered again her descriptions to Lord Carlton Crue, and his scornful laughter, and she was ashamed. She hardly knew how to reply, and was relieved when he continued, in everyday tones.

'There now, dear girl, I have kept you long enough. Look.' He pointed to a bundle wrapped in a red spotted handkerchief. 'I have brought my luncheon, and I believe I will stop to eat before I do any more. Would you care to share a bite? No? Then could you be so good as to tell Clara that I will be eating here? She worries, you know, if she thinks I am not eating properly. Fusses when I don't come to meals. Tell her, would you, that I will eat here? She is back from the village. She'll be in her garden, I dare say.'

'Yes, of course, Lord Kintrove,' Isabella said.

They shook hands again solemnly, and he waved to her as she left the clearing. He was seating himself on the stones in the wheelbarrow, opening his handkerchief.

It was not until Isabella was almost at the house that she noticed that Bess must have remained behind, hopeful of a share of Lord Kintrove's luncheon. Feeling oddly bereft, she walked along the front of the house to the doorway in the brick wall that she knew led into the vegetable gardens.

There were a succession of large, enclosed gardens, their walls of high red brick, linked by doorways down the central gravelled path. Smaller grass or earth paths divided the rows of plants and bushes. Isabella walked down the centre, looking about her, but there was no sign of Lady Kintrove. She ventured through the doorway at the far end of the garden. Here there were glasshouses along one wall, and Isabella could hear voices coming from near them. She took one of the grass paths that led between fruit trees in what she hoped was the direction of the sounds.

Turning a corner at the end of the path, Isabella was brought to an abrupt halt by the sound of her own name. It was obvious that the soft grass had muffled the sound of her approach, and the speakers were continuing a conversation just out of sight around the corner of the glass house. Despite herself, Isabella hesitated, and listened.

'But it is so *sad*, Clara. She reminds me of a painted doll. She doesn't have two thoughts to rub together inside that pretty head, and whatever *is* in there seems constantly ill-tempered. Such a shame. Such a waste.'

'Mary—pass me some more peas, would you? Thank you. I will surprise you by telling you that Isabella reminds me very much of myself at that age. Truly. I too had a sheltered, cosseted childhood, thoroughly spoiled by whatever money could buy, and not ever expected to have a thought in my head beyond the next ball. Which I didn't, of course.

'It took marriage to Wilfred to make me realise I had a mind of my own, and could use it. He is that rare jewel among men who treats a woman as an equal human being, not just as the source of his comforts and heirs, but as a friend. He taught me to read widely, he listened intelligently to my ideas and, more, he valued them. I was *so* lucky that this was the man my parents chose, and it was pure chance, you know. Their other possible choice was Locksey, and, well... you know how he treated his wife!

'No, I believe there is an intelligent woman waiting to develop inside Isabella's pretty head. What really bothers me is whether she will ever have the chance to find that woman if she is married off to Crue. Poor child, what a fate!'

Lady Kintrove paused, and Isabella was about to creep shame-faced away when the voice began again.

'Now, the other thing that perplexes me is why Crue is keen on the marriage at all. He is not the man to be trapped by a pretty face. He has always had any number of those for the asking... Have you finished the peas? Good. Let's just rake that over... No, there must be a clever deal in it for a man such as him somewhere, but I have no idea what. She has no reputation as a great heiress that I ever heard, though I am sure there will be a respectable settlement. What else could he be after?

Ah, well! Nearly time for luncheon. Pass me the rest of those marker sticks, would you, Mary?'

Isabella, her cheeks burning, crept away silently up the grass path. She almost ran away altogether, but her assurance to Lord Kintrove held her back. She waited a moment to compose herself, then walked noisily down the gravel to deliver her message.

'Thank you, Isabella. It was kind of you to let me know. I do worry about him. Now his memory is so shaky he will often forget to eat altogether, and it does him no good.'

Lady Kintrove and Miss Pickering were dusting themselves off at the end of a long row of smoothed earth.

'Two rows of peas done.' Lady Kintrove waved a hand at the row. 'I love to know they are in, waiting to shoot.'

Isabella forced a smile.

'Congratulations,' she said, stiffly. 'It must have been a great deal of work.'

Miss Pickering looked surprised, but Lady Kintrove laughed.

'It was indeed, my dear. Come along, let's all go and find something to eat. I am sorry you missed our trip to the village. Mr Rose, at our "Great Little Trovers Emporium"—christened by the boys, I should tell you, with small regard to veracity—has in some very pretty new lengths of ribbon. You might like to see them...'

CHAPTER SEVEN

THE days continued to pass with what seemed to Isabella a yawning tedium. No letter arrived from Harry, and the deepening hurt and disappointment coloured everything she did, from the moment she snapped at Ruth when she woke up, to the moment she dropped blurring tears into her diary as she huddled over it under the fluttering candlelight at bed-time.

Most days she put in some time on stitching the huge balloon, as did her brothers, and, occasionally, Alladay. Isabella attacked the work with an irrational, discontented determination. She enjoyed the time with her brothers when Alladay was not there, but when he was she felt ever driven to puncture the peaceful atmosphere with sharp comments, needling him into an angry response, for his cool courtesy was a source of constant irritation to her. She seemed to be taking an unhappy pleasure in fulfilling Miss Pickering's hurtful accusations of ill-temper. If he gave way to anger she would smile, then loftily ignore him in a way that led her brothers to regard her with perplexity, indignantly accusing her of deafness.

To escape, she sometimes walked up to the copse on the mound, and admired the progress of Lord Kintrove's monument. He was always pleased to see her, although he never remembered her name, but she found an unlikely comfort in his rambling, undemanding conversations about his sons.

Isabella's thoughts fretted over the conversation she had overheard. Her initial reaction of raw hurt and outrage, that had left her continuing to avoid Miss Pickering with haughty aloofness, had led to some furious words directed at a bemused but fascinated Ruth.

'How do I look, then?' she had asked, angrily, on the evening of that day, as she had dressed for dinner, and flounced with irritation before the mirror.

'Ooh, lovely, miss. Pretty as a picture,' Ruth enthused. She still found Isabella's wardrobe a source of wonder and delight.

'Oh, a picture! Just a painted picture! Not a painted doll, I suppose? An ignorant, uncultured, empty-headed, painted doll?'

How bitterly the words still rankled. Ruth, instantly wary at her mistress's tone, shook her head earnestly.

'No one could say such things about you, miss.'

'Oh, but they could, Ruth.' Isabella pulled irritably at her hair. 'They have! Do something with this mess, for heavens sake!'

'Yes, miss. Whoever could have said such a thing?'

Ruth, ever sharp-eared for a snippet of gossip, was keen to encourage details.

Her mistress shrugged irritably.

'Just some irrelevant, out-moded, opinionated, ill-dressed old trout, for one! I suppose my conversation bores you, does it, Ruth? Lacking that sparkle of witty literary criticism, that intellectual discussion of current political events, or the way to electoral reform, or the education of the masses, or the legal rights of women?'

She shook her head crossly as she thought back over the various conversations that had enlivened the Kintrove dinner table or visits from friends. Ruth, understanding none of this, shrugged slightly.

'I like it when you talk, miss. You tell me about fashion, and handsome men and life in London. That's what *I* think is interesting. Please hold your head still, miss, or I'll never get done.'

'I suppose I should be wonderfully reassured to know that my interests are on a par with those of my maid.' Her voice was sarcastic. She paused, then said, 'Lord Carlton Crue seemed to like my conversation well enough.'

Ruth's face lit up, as it always did when Crue was mentioned.

'Of course he does, miss. He loves you! *He* won't mind *what* you say, he'll always think it perfect!'

Isabella shifted irritably. Lady Kintrove's words about her fiancé had sown unwelcome seeds of doubt in her mind. Or had they only confirmed the unacknowledged doubts that had always been there? Why *had* Lord Carlton Crue agreed to the marriage?

She thought of his smooth talking, and practised address. She knew, of course, that he did not love her. She was fooling herself when she felt a pride in her conquest. It was depressing, but she had to accept that there had been no conquest. A part of her shame at her reaction to his kisses was because she knew this. How could he love her? They barely knew each other. He held her in no affection. That was not uncommon in arranged weddings, but, as Lady Kintrove had so bluntly pointed out, he would not be trapped by her face, no matter how pretty. Her conversation, she thought bitterly, was obviously fit only to amuse her maid. So, why *had* he agreed to the engagement? It was a question to which she had no answer, but she reflected back on his visit with an increasing resentment, aware she was just a pawn in some game played by Crue and her father.

'Don't chatter, Ruth. Just finish my hair.'

Ruth worked silently, pondering with fascination over the identity of the old trout, before she steered the conversation back to the gratifying topic of Miss Grice-Hewson, who had, so the servants' hall gossip averred, a considerable fortune, and whose exuberant return from school into Lord Alladay's life was causing Nurse Pusey some wary teasing by lesser members of the staff.

Isabella ignored her, engrossed in her own thoughts. Until now Isabella's interests, and those of her friends, could fairly be summed up as fashion, eligible men, and entertainment. Nothing more. Now a part of her felt reluctantly ashamed of her ignorance, and one result of that thinking led to her requesting privately of Lord

Kintrove that she might occasionally visit his library and borrow something to read.

She had no very clear idea what she would read in order to expand her mind, and was too uncertain and too proud to ask for advice, but she spent some time browsing amongst the crowded shelves. Some were stocked with volumes of obvious value and antiquity and had glass-panelled doors closed across them. Others were filled with tomes that daunted her by their sobriety and learning, many volumes of collected sermons, or treatises on matters scientific or philosophical.

She was beginning to conclude that she would have to remain a mere empty-headed painted doll, when she found the shelves of well-thumbed books, books of poetry, novels, letters and diaries. Far more hopeful now, she took several back to the large leather armchair that stood near the window.

After much dipping and sampling she selected Mrs Radcliffe's *The Mysteries of Udolpho*. She knew this to be a 'must', on the reading list of any person pretending to culture. To it she added Volume One of a novel called *Clarissa* by a man named Richardson, all three volumes of a novel entitled *Sense and Sensibility*, by A Lady, and some poetry for good measure; *Lyrical Ballads* by somebody called William Wordsworth. She had not heard of any of these last three, but they seemed as good a way as any to begin improving her mind. She secreted them up to her room with a quiet satisfaction.

The comments she had overheard from Lady Kintrove gave her more of a kindness for that lady. She began, rather diffidently, to seek out something of Lady Kintrove's company, learning to enjoy her straightforward, kindly manner.

In an effort to appear helpful, Isabella offered to take responsibility for arranging the flowers when further visitors were expected.

Several people called, and Isabella was always introduced as a welcomed guest of the family. There were friends of Lord and Lady Kintrove, a ruddy-faced general and his wife, a baronet from a neighbouring village, and an outspoken Lady Brockton with a tongue-tied daughter in tow, who made great point of welcoming Alladay home and drawing attention to the fact that her daughter Gertrude was now officially 'out'.

Isabella began to make the reluctant effort to travel with Alladay and his parents to return some of the calls, creaking through the dusty summer lanes in the ancient family carriage. She could not deny to herself that she derived enjoyment from these breaks in the daily pattern, and a certain satisfaction from the belated realisation that, as the guest of the Earl and Countess of Kintrove, she was treated with respect by those they called upon.

She gained no satisfaction from the behaviour of Lord Alladay upon these outings, however. She would watch with a smouldering eye the amusement that blatantly lurked in his eyes as he went out of his way to engage her in lively, friendly conversation, at times when the presence of company forced her to politely respond in kind. Resentful glares, or attempts to aloofly ignore him seemed, infuriatingly, only to increase his misguided sense of humour.

Younger, more congenial visitors to Long Trovers were friends of Alladay's, handsome young men, some languidly foppish, like Algie Carstairs, who reminded Isabella just a little of Harry, others energetically sporting, like the Beaumoyne brothers, Arthur and Edmund, but all congratulating him on abandoning his foolish attempts at earning a living, and returning to the world of polite society. They made great play of envying him his proximity to Isabella, with many extravagant compliments to her, bemoaning the fact of her betrothal.

She thought she would be amused and flattered by their company, and tried flirting with them to irritate Alladay, while her relations with him remained icy cool. But she was for the first time made aware of how her betrothal had changed her status. These pleasant young men knew she was engaged, and officially out of bounds. Naturally, they politely respected that position. Just as her father had hoped, she thought, very bitterly, as she felt Alladay's sardonic eye upon her.

She felt isolated, unable to join in their banter, and she would soon excuse herself from the easy camaraderie. Alladay spent much time out with them, riding or fishing, when he was not working on the estate, or entertaining William and Thomas. Isabella was lonely, and her sketch pad grew fuller.

She was bringing a basket of young carrots from the gardens up to Mrs Stoke in the kitchen one afternoon, when Hopkins came hurrying out to find her and tell her that Lord Carlton Crue had once again come to call. There had been heavy rain that morning, and, although the sky had now cleared to a rich blue and the leaves were steaming in the sun, it was still very wet underfoot, and Isabella was keeping to the gravelled paths. She quickened her pace, regarding Hopkins anxiously.

'Where is he now?' she asked.

'I put him in the green room, Miss Larkham, but there is no one to entertain him, for my lord and lady are outside and Lord Alladay is visiting a tenant at Long Common.'

If only I too had been out, Isabella thought.

She was frightened by the prospect of seeing him again. Resentful of the restricting engagement, uncertain of his true motives, unsure what he would expect of her, she was horribly unsure what her reaction to him might be. A flush of shame tinged her face as she pushed away thoughts of his kisses. Hateful man. She debated asking Hopkins to say he had been unable to find her, but pride prevented her stooping to the lie.

'Please make my apologies to Lord Carlton. I will be down when I have changed. Perhaps it would be possible to offer some suitable refreshment? Oh, and could you please give these to Mrs Stoke?'

Hopkins bowed and went on his way. He had seen the look on Miss Larkham's face, and quite wished that he *had* been unable to find her.

It was some little while before Isabella reluctantly escaped the eager ministrations of Ruth and, leaving the maid full of eager plans to run down and attempt conversation with Stoat, Crue's tiger, while he partook of liquid refreshment in the kitchen, descended to the green room.

Clad in an elegant creation of fine French cambric in a soft golden shade that echoed the sunlight in her hair, she still paused uncertainly at the door, reluctant to impress him, yet reluctant to incur his scorn. Then she put back her shoulders, tilted up her chin, and pushed the door open.

'I am sorry to have kept you waiting, Lord Carlton,' she said. 'I trust you have enjoyed some refreshment?'

Carlton Crue had been waiting for an hour, and he was not famed for his patience. He had found it an intolerable bore to have to talk with the eccentric Kintroves on his last visit, but at least he had gained many a laugh among his friends and acquaintances when later describing them. It was a great deal worse to be ignored, and to be kept waiting by this chit of a girl. He swallowed his irritation, however.

'No wait can seem too long if it is rewarded by such a vision. My dearest Isabella, you look quite enchanting.' He took both her hands in his and raised them to his mouth, deliberately kissing each finger. It amused him to see her disconcerted. She pulled her hands away.

'I thought you might like to walk about the grounds,' Isabella began, hoping to avoid another trip in her fiancé's curricle, but he interrupted her with an incredulous laugh.

'Paddle about in the mud in the Kintrove farmyards? No, thank you very much my dearest girl. I have a drive planned that I think you will enjoy, and I do not wish to keep the horses waiting any longer. Come.'

He took her arm. She was led irresistibly out to the vehicle before she could think of any excuse, and lifted firmly up to take her seat. Then with a sway of the springs he was beside her, and Stoat, grinning knowingly, was waved free to hurry away to the kitchen door.

'In what rustic delight were you disporting yourself that the beating of your heart did not instantly apprise you of my arrival?' he asked her, springing the horses over the rutted lane. 'Put your arm around me, my dear. That way you will feel quite safe.'

Isabella resisted this offer, and clung to the side of the curricle. She could hear the sneer behind his light words.

'I wish you would drive at a safer pace, my lord,' she said, endeavouring to remain cool and aloof.

'But I find a safer pace so tedious, don't you? A little danger holds an excitement that I suspect you enjoy as much as I do. But you have not told me. What *were* you doing?'

'I was bringing in carrots to the kitchen, my lord.'

He gave a hoot of laughter.

'A veritable rustic wench! I can only hope your father is not away too long. We will find you milking the cows and feeding the pigs! I trust the tutor takes care of the turnips, and the old lady digs the potatoes! But tell me, have you braved the scullery yet, and succeeded in obtaining a wash?'

Crue was still feeling irritable, and it showed in his tones. He had not wished to take the drive up from Worthing, where his time had been very happily occupied, but he considered his long-term interests to be best served by regular visits to Long Trovers. He was finding it hard to remember, however, looking at her poker stiffness, what he had found amusing in the girl's conversation. He glanced sharply down at her, surprised she had not answered.

Isabella was confused. Not only did his tone lack the amused, bantering flattery she had previously enjoyed but, however much she was prepared to complain about it herself, she found herself unexpectedly resentful of the way *he* was speaking of her life at Long Trovers.

'I am sure I told you, my lord, that I am now privileged to have hot water brought to my room,' she managed, 'and I undertake to give you due warning when I intend to begin feeding pigs. Perhaps the threat will bring my father back all the sooner and I will be able to return to a civilised life in Town.'

She searched her mind for witty things to tell him, and attempted comical descriptions of the visits that had been made to and from Long Trovers. The curricle lurched and rocked through the lanes, constantly jolting her against him. Isabella shifted further away on the seat. She found herself oddly reluctant to ridicule all the Kintroves' friends, although she managed a maliciously cutting portrait of Lady Brockton, and her stories tailed off.

He, glancing at his heavy gold watch, found it hard to hide his lack of interest.

In desperation, eventually, she asked him about his life in Worthing, but he merely laughed and remarked that he doubted she would find it rewarding listening.

She saw him stifle a yawn behind his York tan glove.

'Perhaps, sir,' she burst out angrily, 'you would find less to yawn about if instead of expecting me to entertain *you* like some performing circus dog, you put a little more effort into amusing *me*. You have hardly been the most enlivening companion today!'

They had entered a small village by this time, and Crue pulled up outside a long, low inn, timbered and thatched, that stood back from the road. A couple of other vehicles stood in the yard.

He sat regarding her for some moments, eyes narrowed, an unpleasant smile hovering on his lips.

'Is that so, Miss Larkham? I apologise. I must certainly make amends, must I not?' His tone seemed affable, but held that undercurrent of menace she had sensed in him before. 'I know this place well. There is an excellent private parlour, and the landlord is commendably discreet. In addition, the ales are surprisingly potable. We will stop for some refreshment.'

Isabella frowned. She was accustomed to at least a show of consulting her wishes, and she found his tone not pleasingly masterful, but insultingly dismissive.

Her annoyance grew when the innkeeper hurried forward down the stone-flagged passage, rubbing his hands together in hopeful welcome, and, after a quick glance at Isabella, offered the 'usual private parlour' in lowered tones. She was filled with an overwhelming desire *not* to retire to the private parlour with Lord Carlton Crue. She had no wish to discover how he intended to entertain her.

It was with relief that she just then spotted the general and his wife who had visited at Long Trovers a few days previously. She was taking coffee in the main parlour, a long, heavily beamed room with a huge open fireplace at the far end, while he leant against the bar with a large, pewter tankard of ale.

With a cry of delight that was only a little feigned, Isabella hurried over to greet them, to introduce Lord Carlton Crue, and to sit firmly down beside the general's wife at the polished oak table, and, breathing in with relief the welcome tang of coffee, request a jug for herself.

Crue, who had planned this drive with the express hope that the privacy offered by his usual parlour would enable him to get to know his fiancée a little more intimately, could hardly drag her away. His inescapable conversation with the general was terse.

Isabella watched him over her coffee-cup.

She was relieved that she had managed to escape that time alone with him. She resented him, and even feared him, but the memory of his kisses still had an unwanted power to disturb her. Her breath quickened nervously as she surreptitiously studied the hard lines of his mouth, the hooded lids over the disdainful eyes, but she was proud of herself when she managed to look away with what she hoped was haughty composure when he turned a brooding look towards her and caught her eye. It was the laugh he gave, having watched her, that made her blush, then he laughed again, and, having paid his shot, escorted her back to the curricle.

He drove in silence until they were some way from the inn.

'So,' he remarked, letting the reins slacken and turning to face her, 'my little haughty miss was afraid to share a private parlour with me. Why might that be, I wonder?'

'The results of a proper upbringing, perhaps?' she replied sharply.

'Now, what could it have been about our last meeting, dearest Isabella, that ensured that was the last explanation that might have occurred to me?'

Perhaps he expected some flirtatious sally in return, and for a split second Isabella could clearly see her choice of roles with this man. An arch look or a knowing giggle would place her squarely in his world, as one who played the sexual games he recognised. She could visualise the role, and for an instant the picture of herself acting the cynical sophisticate was tempting, but, for reasons she did not clearly understand, she could not adopt it. Almost without her conscious volition she raised her hand to slap his face.

It was an ineffectual gesture. He caught her hand before it was half raised, and twisted her arm roughly behind her back, forcing her against him. She thought he was going to kiss her then, and turned her face aside, but he spoke scornfully.

'Don't panic, proper little Miss Larkham. I do find your attractions resistible, you know. But I do not tolerate chits of girls brandishing their little kid-gloved fingers at me, nor is that the sort of behaviour I will look for in my wife. Is that understood, Isabella?'

He took her chin and turned her face towards him.

'Is it?'

'Yes, Lord Carlton.'

Her voice was small, and hid a fury of resentment. She turned away to hide the tears that welled up in her eyes.

They were silent for most of the return drive, until the sight of Alladay, walking across the fields with the dogs at his heels and a spade over his shoulder, provoked a series of speculations from Crue.

'Tell me, do, has our heroic crippled tutor turned his attentions from labouring in the brains of your brothers to labouring in the fields like a peasant? A romantic return to the realities of nature, perhaps? What could he have been doing? Indeed, what *does* one do with a spade? Clear pigstyes? Empty cow byres? The mind can hardly encompass such barbarisms. Thank heavens I have never had the delights of finding out. But you, Isabella, with your acquaintance with carrots—doubtless you know all there is to be known about spades?'

'No, my lord. But in view of your consuming interest, naturally I shall endeavour to oblige you by discovering.'

She was all the angrier when he merely laughed.

As before, he pulled up outside the main door, but he paused before setting her down. He regarded her thoughtfully, and she glared back, her colour high.

'It has been an interesting visit. We learn a little more of each other each time we meet, do we not? Always an enlightening process.' He caught sight of Alladay, who had just breasted the hill and was walking down the slope of the fields towards them. 'Time to enjoy a fiancé's privilege, my dear.'

He had an arm about her waist before she could wriggle away, and his other hand at her chin. His kisses were more proprietorial than passionate, and to her relief her only responses were shame and anger. She was horridly aware of Alladay's approach, and the rows of eye-like windows behind her. As soon as he released her she jumped down unaided from the curricle, and hurried into the house.

Crue drove off at a leisurely pace, but the greeting between the two men, as he passed Alladay, could not have been cooler.

Isabella hid in her room and immersed herself in a book, finding escape in following the fortunes of Marianne Dashwood, rather than dwelling on her own. She hugged Bess forlornly as they curled up together on the bed.

'How could you understand?' she muttered reproachfully to the dog. 'You were never trapped in an engagement you hate. I don't want to marry him, Bess. But I am afraid of making him angry, for I don't think I can escape. My father would never allow me to break the engagement. Oh, Bess, what shall I do?'

Later she excused herself from dinner by pleading a migraine, and Ruth brought her a light meal on a tray. She felt she even preferred Ruth's interminably rapturous descriptions of Stoat to facing conversation with the Kintroves. Particularly she did not wish to face Lord Alladay. She was certain she would see his contemptuous disapproval of her writ clear in his face.

CHAPTER EIGHT

'Go on, Izzie! Do come. You're bound to like it. And it might even cheer you up!'

Certainly Isabella was stiff and tired from sitting on a straw bale stitching silk. But Alladay had been so silent that she had several times contemplated refusing to be further involved with the making of the balloon, and withdrawing once again to her sketching. Nothing she said seemed capable of provoking him to anger; he had no infuriating laughter in his eyes. He remained morosely silent. Would he want her to go riding when he took the boys, or was he eager to escape her company? Which would annoy him more, for her to go, or to toss her head in refusal? She frowned at his back, unsure.

'I have not previously ridden outside the parks,' she said, stalling.

'Don't worry, Izzie. Anthony will look after you, won't you, sir?'

Thus appealed to, Alladay looked up.

'What are you committing me to now, Thomas?' he enquired.

'If we go riding, you can look after Izzie if she thinks she's going to fall off, can't you sir?'

He looked across at Isabella.

'Oh, *please* don't trouble yourself,' she said hastily. 'I have no wish at all to come. I shall walk with Bess——'

'Nonsense!' he said, suddenly decisive, standing up. 'Of course you shall ride. My mother's mare has perfect manners, and is in need of exercise. You will be doing Mama a favour by taking her out.'

He strode out of the store before she had time to muster arguements.

'I need to change my dress,' she countered crossly, glaring after him.

He did not look back, however, and William replied.

'Lord, Izzie, don't fuss so. You look fine, and, anyway, that dress is already dirty—it can't make any difference. Do come on.'

'No. I must run and change. Tell Lord Alladay he will just have to wait,' she pronounced, and with a show of nonchalant indifference she sauntered off towards the house.

When she returned, in her elegant dark brown riding habit and pert beaver hat, the boys were already setting off across the fields on the round, shaggy ponies. Alladay was waiting in the yard, chatting idly to old Bill. Captain was saddled up, and a pretty bay mare with liquid brown eyes stood ready beside him, resting her nose on his neck.

'I trust I have not kept you waiting too long, sir?' she said, with a bright, provocative smile.

'Not at all,' he said calmly, and made not the least mention of her outfit, which was new, and became her rather well. 'This is my mother's mare, Marina. She has perfect manners, and should give you no trouble.'

He did not offer to help her up, but quietly led the horse to the mounting block and waited for Isabella to arrange herself comfortably in the saddle. Then he swung himself up on to Captain's high back, and led the way out under the archway, across the gravel and into the fields beyond. A breeze was stirring the summer air, ruffling Isabella's hair on her shoulders and snatching curls across her cheeks. She drew a deep breath, and impulsively gave a soft laugh. It was good to be on horseback with open fields ahead. Alladay glanced at her in surprise.

'I thought we might go up on to the downs.' He nodded his head towards the long sweep of hill that stretched its flanks down into the fields, but he seemed unenthusiastic. 'There are good, clear gallops along the heights.'

Intolerant today of this dullness of tone, suddenly eager to stir up some excitement, to forget her confused emotions, to simply enjoy herself, Isabella urged Marina up alongside Captain.

'Come on, then,' she said impatiently. 'If you will only stop looking so gloomy! I thought bad temper was supposed to be *my* role! Do you know? I do not think I have ever galloped! I have only ridden in the park, and I was forbidden to be indecorous. Naturally,' she risked an arch look at him, 'I obeyed. But surely it is not so very hard?'

They were trotting side by side up the hill slope. Alladay frowned at her, shrugged, then half laughed.

'Only a question of sitting right! Do you want to try? It is a long flat ride along the hilltop.'

She nodded, excited, wanting to be reckless.

'Hold on, then, and just follow me.'

The horses were lengthening their stride as they topped the rise. Marina seemed to sense Isabella's exhilaration, for with a toss of her head she took off after Captain with surging burst of speed.

Isabella thought that that gallop was probably the most wonderful, terrifying, exhilarating event in her life so far. It occurred to her briefly that perhaps Crue was right, that she did find it good to live a little dangerously. She had simply never been allowed to try. But, she thought fiercely, she would choose her own dangers! She would not have them inflicted upon her for someone else's amusement. She laughed aloud, revelling in the rush of the wind on her face, and the thudding thunder of hoofs beneath her, willing the wildness to carry on for ever.

But Captain smoothly slowed his pace as they neared a copse far along the ridge of hill, and Marina obediently followed his lead, until they came to a panting halt at the edge of the trees.

Alladay was laughing, slapping Captain's neck, when he turned to speak to Isabella.

'Well?' he asked.

She was half laughing, breathless, filled with excitement, her hair blown into a wild halo of gold about her head, her eyes as bright and blue as the sky above and around them. He stared at her, then turned abruptly to scan the ridge for her brothers.

'I thought I was a timid rider,' she was saying. 'Cooped up in the park, that poker-faced groom of Papa's always there watching, and nothing to do but gossip with friends and notice what everyone was wearing. You know what it was like. The riding seemed dull, just a social necessity... But this!' She spread her arms wide and her face was filled with delight. 'This is entirely different.' Her joy was so unaffected he thought she must have forgotten she was speaking to him. Then she paused and laughed wryly at herself. 'Not that there was any skill on my part. I was not once in control of the entire proceeding, and had Marina not got such perfect manners I would doubtless have vanished way over the horizon by now!' She felt tipsy with excitement. She stroked the mare's neck, and straightened her mane.

'Oh, Marina wouldn't have gone any further,' Alladay said neutrally. 'She adores Captain. She would never go on without him.'

'They must come out together again.'

The wind whipped a tangle of blonde over her eyes and mouth, and she laughed as she pushed it aside, turning her face into the wind so her hair streamed behind her from under the beaver hat.

'Lord Alladay?' She spoke without any premeditation, on a whim as impulsive as the wind which whipped the words from her lips before she could regret and withdraw them. 'Shall we declare a truce?'

She was almost as startled as he by the words she had spoken and for a few moments they stared at each other in speculative silence. Thinking her happiness had merely made her vulnerable to his contempt, she began to shrug and turn away, but his voice stopped her.

'I am sorry, I am sorry! I have to confess a small element of surprise! But yes. We will declare a truce.

An honourable truce, with safe conduct for all participants, and much waving of white flags!'

She regarded him suspiciously, thinking he was mocking her again, but his smile was unexpectedly bright and friendly, and he solemnly pulled out a large white linen handkerchief, and waved it above his head. He grinned.

She pulled a dainty scrap of lace-edged white muslin from her bosom, and, mock solemn, she waved that above her head. Marina and Captain sidled restlessly in the wind. She regarded his grin thoughtfully.

Alladay stuffed his handkerchief back in his coat-tail pocket.

'So, now we are no longer declared enemies, are we possibly friends?'

'Possibly,' said Isabella cautiously. She wondered if she would regret this impulse.

He gave her a speculative look.

'Well, this could be more interesting than arguing, couldn't it?' he remarked.

'Perhaps!' she dubiously replied again.

They began to amble back to where Thomas was still trying to remount after tumbling off halfway along the hilltop. He was hopping angrily, one foot in the stirrup, while his pony moved gently across the fine turf seeking the choicer morsels to graze upon, and William sat secure in his saddle, laughing.

'Useless whelps!' Alladay commented mildly, as he leant over to take Bramble's reins and hold him still. 'Stand, you gluttonous brute,' he commanded the pony, and Thomas, shame-faced, scrambled back into the saddle. 'Now, give them some exercise. Gallop down to the trees.'

With many encouraging shouts, and a flurry of barks from the dogs, the boys set off, and Isabella and Alladay made their way back through the fields.

This tentative truce resulted in several rides together. Their arguments became, to the relief of William and Thomas, a little more guarded, even light-hearted. There was an exhilaration about this carefree riding that made bad temper difficult to sustain. Sometimes the boys would accompany them, and sometimes Algie Carstairs or the Beaumoyne brothers, but other times Isabella and Alladay would set out alone. Always Isabella wanted to gallop, to experience yet again that thrill of rushing along the sun-drenched hilltops as if skimming the roof of the world. She grew bolder, throwing taunts at Alladay and Captain, and urging Marina on to race faster and faster, and Alladay would laugh, narrow his eyes, and take up the challenge, keeping Captain always one maddening stride ahead.

They went on occasionally to explore the estates, for Alladay was keen to see for himself what was being done with every part of their acres. Isabella would affect a yawn and listen with only half an ear when he expounded his plans for improving the farming methods, then jeer at him for a turnip-head when she considered he was becoming tediously enthusiastic upon the subject. When desperate, she would wave a white handkerchief flag, or turn and gallop for home, her taunts left hanging in the summer air. But she met and spoke with numerous of the family's tenants, beginning to recognise them, remember their names and ask after their children. She was surprised and pleased when she saw their obvious pleasure at her attention, and her interest in them and their lives began to grow.

'Dear Lord, I wish I had never given in to your persuasion to buy this wretched balloon,' Alladay remarked one morning, pushing away the yards of silk, and grimacing at the boys. 'Thank heavens I was not born a seamstress. Never shall I think lightly of their efforts again. They have my every sympathy, and I regard each shirt I pull over my head as little short of a miracle. Can't that maid of yours finish it off for us? Nurse Pusey complains she does nothing but chatter idly. The work would do her good.'

Isabella chuckled as her needle flew neatly on up the seam.

'You cannot possibly be so faint-hearted as to give up now. We are so nearly done, and you have done so *very* little of the work! And only think of the excitement of actually flying! Better than the longest gallop. It is worth any amount of effort.'

He looked across at her in sudden consternation.

'Miss Larkham, you do not seriously hope to fly in this maniacal contraption, do you? I have been beginning to have nightmare doubts about the sanity of subjecting your brothers to the dangers of a trip...' here he paused to quell the outcry from Thomas and William '...but with them I seem to have no option, and they are agile enough to scramble to safety if need be I suppose. But you?'

'Don't underrate me, sir. I am quite as agile as they are, and more than twice as sensible!' She grinned at their predictable retorts. 'Don't be such a pessimist! Don't think of the dangers! Think of the excitement! Think of actually flying! Think of the wonder of it! And please don't start an argument, for I would have to fight you to the death! Not even a washing line full of white handkerchiefs would deter me after all this interminable sewing!'

He shook his head dubiously. He had a sinking feeling that she would insist on having her way, and he knew he should endeavour to prevent her. He did not give a lot for his chances of success. He had many a time before seen Isabella with her mind set upon something.

'The Montgolfier brothers,' he remarked darkly, to no one in particular, 'have a great deal to answer for!'

Isabella chuckled, and made a face at him.

'I have to visit Nunn's Farm this afternoon,' he remarked neutrally, after a short while, changing the subject and postponing any argument. 'I don't know if you would like to come, or if you would find it tedious waiting while I talk with Farmer Nunn.'

She paused to consider. She had a letter to write to Jane, who had written describing her stay with her aunt in Bath as a non-stop whirl of social excitement brimming with the attentions of deliciously eligible men. Jane was delightfully exhausted. She begged to know whatever dearest Isabella could be doing to fill her time at Long Trovers. Isabella frowned and jabbed her needle into the cloth. Jane could wait!

'I'll come,' she said. 'Marina would hate you to take Captain without her.'

The Nunns' farm was some miles away from Long Trovers, over the hills, then beyond the course of a long, narrow, tree-lined valley. It made a cool and pleasant ride. They allowed the horses to amble.

'Tell me about when you were a nasty little boy,' Isabella asked, watching the sunlight spatter through the leaves overhead. His face was patterned as he turned to her. 'That nasty little boy who tormented poor Sarah!'

She noticed the way his face lit up when he smiled. Harry's smile had been warm and slow, and had set her heart pounding and jumping. Lord Carlton Crue's smile discomposed her; it was so knowing, or sneering, that she always felt stupid and very young, shut outside his private humour. But Alladay's smile lit his face up with infectious mischief. He looked younger, happy, his dark-lashed eyes very bright. His face seemed to have grown leaner since they had been in the country, his hair had bleached to a paler gold in the constant sunshine, and the fine lines of his nose and cheeks had acquired a golden tan and showed a smattering of golden freckles. All golden, she thought. Not like her darling Harry. Harry had seemed wonderfully dark and mysterious.

'What about when I was a boy?' he was asking. 'You must remember, it was such a very long time ago. I may not be able to recall.'

'Fool!' she countered. 'Why, compared to Lord Carlton Crue you still *are* a boy!'

She saw the smile fade from his face, his mouth pinch closed, and he frowned, staring forward between

Captain's ears. The horse, sensing his sudden change in mood, sidled and danced a little. Alladay quietened him. After a moment he turned back to Isabella.

'I am sorry. It is not like Captain to be fidgety. Had you any particular incident in mind?'

The light had gone from his expression, and it seemed he was merely making polite conversation, but when Isabella, irritated at his change of mood, crossly asked about the story of the parson's saddleback sow, and Bardolph as the highwayman, he laughed.

'Who mentioned that to you? My father? I noticed you have been walking up to talk with him. I did not realise he had been betraying family secrets! It was he, poor man, who was left with the problem of pacifying the parson and Lady Greening.'

He told a good story, bringing each character leaping to life. Isabella watched him, her head a little on one side, moving gently with the rhythm of Marina's ambling walk.

He described the day he and his brothers had slunk in to Lady Greening's acres with Jasper's terrier, intent on raiding a rabbit-warren famed for the plumpness of its coneys. How the foolish dog had instead given chase to one of Lady Greening's pampered cats, and the three boys had watched aghast from the shelter of the trees while the terrier caught the cat's tail and grimly hung on, ignoring all the whistles and bellows of his owner. Of how Lady Greening had appeared like a fury from the house, clutching an enormous butterfly net, and, before their horrified eyes, scooped up the terrier and marched off with it struggling in the net, while her butler retrieved the terrified cat, now, unfortunately, minus half its tail.

Isabella chuckled.

He described Jasper's fruitless attempts to regain his dog by charm, apology and reason. Then, when there had no longer seemed to the boys to be any hope of retrieving the dog by conventional means, he told how they had concocted The Grand Plan. A plan to hold up her coach one dark night, steal her jewellery, and offer to trade its return for that of the dog.

'It seems incredible, looking back, but we truly thought it would work! Of course, Jasper thought of it, and Bardolph and I were long trained to consider everything Jasper planned to be indisputably the best.'

He was grinning, totally absorbed in his reminiscences.

'Go on? What happened?' Isabella was impatient.

'Well, we knew she was visiting the parson that evening, so we decided to waylay her in the dip just beyond the parsonage. Jasper and Bardolph had their ponies, Jasper brandished a pistol they had secreted out from the gun-room, and they both tied handkerchiefs about their faces. To my great chagrin they deemed me too young to take a part in the hold-up. I was to be the lookout, and let them know when she was on her way.

'Out she came from the parsonage, an awesome sailing galleon of bombazine as black as the night, and climbed into her closed carriage. I waved my handkerchief down the road to warn my brothers to be ready. Then I determined that I *would* not be left out of the excitement. I crept round to the parsonage yard, and opened the half-door to what I thought was the parson's grey cob. Out ran the largest saddleback sow you ever saw. In desperation I flung myself at her, and, grabbing an ear, got a leg astride her back.

'I still can't say precisely how it happened, but at the moment that Jasper fired his pistol into the air and scared his pony into a witless bolt that took him almost to the next parish I appeared rocketing down the road astride the parson's pig, howling like a banshee! Bardolph, totally bemused, was still chanting, "Stand and Deliver", when Lady Greening marched down from the carriage, grabbed him by the arm and the seat of his breeches and swung him neatly off his pony and into her carriage before he could squeak. She turned the carriage and drove straight to Long Trovers, and the rest of the story doesn't bear recalling!'

Isabella was laughing.

'But the dog? Did Jasper get his dog back?'

Alladay chuckled. 'Oh, yes, eventually. And the parson his pig. And we retrieved Jasper. But it seems we still haven't lived down the tale.'

Isabella heaved a wistful sigh.

'It sounds a good childhood. Extraordinarily, I could even wish I had known you then!'

'You?' Alladay spurred Captain on, and spoke back over his shoulder. 'You would have been *far* too young to be considered in our games. A mere babe in arms! And a *girl*! What could be worse?'

Isabella, incensed, kicked up Marina and gave chase, so they were both travelling with unseemly haste when they swung into Nunn's farmyard, startling the chickens into a rout of squawks and flying feathers, and setting all the farm dogs barking.

The shadows were beginning to lengthen when they started back from the farm.

Isabella had been regally entertained. She had wanted to sit in the comfortable kitchen, where worn beech-wood chairs stood round a spotless deal table, rag rugs scattered the stone flags, and a vast dresser stretched the length of one wall, laden with pewter-ware plates and tankards, and bright blue and white patterned crockery. It had been warm and redolent of recent baking. But Mrs Nunn had been outraged at the thought, and had escorted her firmly through to the best parlour, where despite the summer weather a faint aroma of mildew had tinged the air. She had ushered her into an armchair bristling with horsehair, set before a polished brass grate. Above the fireplace a portrait of Mr Nunn had stared, ferociously glassy-eyed, and in garish colours, from an improbable landscape.

Here she had sipped a glass of elderflower wine and eaten a scone, while Mrs Nunn stood determinedly watching, two small children peering out from behind her patterned calico skirts and crisp white apron at this unusual visitor. Isabella had been embarrassed, but touched, and had made an extra effort to admire the wine, the scones, the portrait and, above all, the children. She was thinking of Mrs Nunn and those children as they travelled back up the valley.

'You care a great deal about your tenants, don't you?'

She watched Alladay's face. She was curious, remembering her father's attitude to servants and dependants.

'Of course. I believe we have an obligation to them. But also, as landowners it is in our interest to attend constructively to our tenants' grievances. In return, contented tenants work well, keep the land in good heart, make the estate productive. It is an arrangement that should suit us both. But there is so much more I could do. I only wish my hands were not so tied by lack of capital.'

'Is there really so little money?'

'Really! My grandfather was a bad lot. Extravagant, gambled, bled the estate for all he could. Left no end of debts. Those have been settled by my father, but everything that could be sold off went then. The town house in Grosvenor Square, the estates in Gloucestershire, and all the land in Lancashire. We only have Long Trovers left and the land around here. The trick is to get it to pay its way and support that museum of a house, when father will not even contemplate raising the rents.' He grinned ruefully. 'But that is my problem, and I should not burden you with it.'

'My maid, Ruth,' Isabella said thoughtfully, 'told me that it is common knowledge that to save the estate you will have to marry a fortune. I suppose she must be right?'

Alladay's brows snapped together in a frown.

'It appears to me that Ruth's tongue is far too busy. You should not waste your time listening to idle servants' gossip.'

'No, sir, of course I should not.' She grinned at him. 'But that having been agreed, it doesn't alter the fact that what she said was true, does it?'

Alladay glared.

'My personal life is not a matter for any servant's speculation, or for yours, Miss Larkham. I will thank you not to encourage such talk.'

'Whatever you wish, sir!' Isabella was amused by this abruptly pompous Alladay, and quite unrepentant. 'Miss Grice-Hewson is a charming girl, is she not? When are we to visit her in Worthing? I have been told that she is exceedingly wealthy in addition to being beautiful! Would that be true, do you know?'

This last she flung over her shoulder as she cantered ahead, laughing.

Whether it was the regular exercise she was taking now, or some general improvement in her spirits, was not clear, but Isabella seemed to have found, to the relief of her hosts and her brothers, some contentment.

Although still no word had come from Harry, the sharp edge of embittering despair had, except for a nightly self-inflicted revival while she studied his letters in her diary, faded. She was noticably more ready to smile. The boys found her good company, willing to ride, or practise archery. She occasionally helped Lady Kintrove with jobs in the garden, to the surprise of them both. Even Miss Pickering cautiously revised her opinion of the 'painted doll', and admitted to Lady Kintrove that perhaps she had been right; there could be more to Miss Larkham than had been evident at first.

Only Lord Carlton Crue was unaware of any change. On his next visit, when Isabella came down to the green room where he was making heavy work of conversation with Lady Kintrove, who sat imperturbably stitching at her embroidery, Isabella pleaded a headache. She declined his invitation to drive, insisting that the cool green light of the room where they now sat was most soothing, and asked him to forgive her if she remained to talk with him there. Lady Kintrove sat immovably over her tablecloth, occasionally asking Isabella if she would not prefer to go and lie down. It was not long before Crue, bored and irritable, made his excuses and left.

When Hopkins had ushered him out Lady Kintrove laid aside her needlework and regarded Isabella shrewdly.

'I dare say your headache is a little better now?' she enquired wryly.

Isabella smiled. 'Just a little, thank you, ma'am!'

'Isabella... I want you to remember that if ever there is anything about your situation that you wish to discuss, anything at all, then I am always here to listen, and I have only your happiness at heart.'

The girl looked across at her. It was the kindly expression she saw now, not the weather-beaten face. 'I do know it now, ma'am, and I am grateful.'

She almost looked as if she might say more, but she did not. She smiled, though, at Lady Kintrove, and for the first time her hostess recognised in that smile a genuine fondness and warmth.

CHAPTER NINE

WHEN an invitation arrived from the Grice-Hewsons, asking Viscount Alladay and his guests to spend a day with them in Worthing, immediate excitement gripped the boys. They hurried to shake the duckweed from their bathing suits, and to set aside balls and hoops to use on the beach.

Isabella did not intend to disrupt the Grice-Hewsons' day by insisting upon immersing herself in the waves, however beneficial salt water was deemed to be, but she put some thought into what she would wear. If there was even the slightest risk of suffering an unexpected meeting with Lord Carlton Crue and his friends she intended to avoid his jibes about her rusticity.

Alladay's suggestion that they take the closed carriage was vociferously opposed by William and Thomas, and, when appealed to, Isabella insisted that she too would prefer to run the risk of rain and take the open chaise. Then, perversely throwing caution to the winds, she selected a dress of lemon-striped jaconet, with lemon kid gloves and half-boots, and a pelisse of green shot sarcenet with a high collar and three capes. To this she added a pagoda-shaped quilted parasol in lemon and white, a fine moss bonnet with a lemon and white trim, and a lemon silk scarf at her neck. Ruth's comments, as Isabella twirled before the discoloured bedroom mirror, well pleased, were entirely satisfactory.

'And you want to look your best, miss, as you are certain to meet Lord Carlton Crue,' she finished, her tone faintly querying.

Ruth regarded her mistress hopefully. Nurse Pusey had been looking increasingly smug recently, and Ruth was anxious for confirmation of Isabella's affection for the dark, shiveringly handsome man with the sleek curricle and pair. She would have like to know when he and his swift-talking tiger, so full of brash Town charm, would call again at Long Trovers. Stoat had not proved averse to Ruth's trusting, flattering gaze, and Ruth's heart was smitten. But Isabella's response was disappointing.

'Possibly,' was all she remarked in offhand tones, and turned to brush some fluff from her half-boots.

Ruth sighed.

'And you're certain you'll not be needing me, miss? It'd be no trouble to come.'

She had had great hopes of this trip to Worthing.

'No, Ruth, thank you. But don't worry. I doubt you would have seen Stoat, anyway.'

Ruth sighed again.

The morning chosen for the trip could not have been better, its hopeful beauty quashing to almost nothing the effort needed by Isabella to achieve the unthinkably early start that Lord Alladay deemed necessary. A shower of rain overnight had damped down the worst of the dust, but now the sun was rising high and clear into the heavens. The journey would take at least three hours, but Isabella felt that no amount of jolting over the rutted clay roads could subdue her spirits. As they pulled away from Long Trovers she felt an unusual sympathy with the ramblings of Old Bill.

He was sitting proudly at the back of the chaise, his face as wizened as a walnut, grinning like a monkey and exclaiming happily and repetitively, 'This is more like it! Just like the old days, eh, Master Anthony? Ah, but it's good to have you back home! Brings a bit of life to the place. You push 'em along, my boy. Do 'em good. Push 'em along!'

Alladay, catching back his whip with a flourish, was content to indulge Bill and let him ramble on. The day was too good to waste in repressing old retainers! It held a heady sense of freedom.

For four years he had stubbornly persisted in keeping a job with an employer who could be both antagonising and humiliating. What had started as something of a jest between himself and Bardolph had come to seem a necessity to a younger son with no prospects. Not only had the job enabled him to support himself, but he had been able to occasionally contribute to his family.

He had enjoyed teaching Thomas and William, but it had none the less been galling to have emphasised that their irritating, arrogant chit of a sister, Isabella, was to be considered utterly unapproachable. It had been drearily clear that the best qualifications a man could have if he wished to continue in employment in the Larkham household were a total lack of prospects, an unprepossessing exterior, and a silent tongue in his head. He had needed to retain the job.

Thus had developed the public persona of the downtrodden tutor, a very different character from the lively man the boys had learned to appreciate when they were alone with him. They, with the uncanny astuteness of childhood, had supported these changing roles.

Those years had taken their toll. They had been years of hard work, swallowed pride, drab clothes, suspended or lost friendships, and grief. Grief at the seemingly impossible deaths of his two older brothers.

It was partly an inability to accept those deaths that had made coming to terms with his inheritance so difficult. For months he had continued to work in London, ignoring the unwelcome title and responsibilities that had become his with so much unhappiness.

It was only now, now that he had at last come home, that he was accepting and beginning to enjoy his new position. He had had to learn to shake off the character of penniless younger son and fulfil the role of heir to a long and once great tradition. He still occasionally viewed himself with a wry amusement and disbelief, but the land called him as it had called generations of his forebears, and he was coming to accept that he would pour effort, thought and time into restoring the estates.

The acceptance of his new status had benefits. For the first time in four years, a long time in a man of only twenty-six summers, he was dressing to please himself. He was remembering that long-hidden Kintrove charm, and how to employ it. He was also being brought to appreciate, through the changed attitudes of the mamas and daughters of his acquaintance, that his status on the marriage mart, though not the best, on account of the family poverty, was, by virtue of his title and expectations, more than acceptable. It was not surprising that he viewed the more determined mothers, whom he had watched chasing Jasper and Bardolph in their turn, with a degree of cynicism, but many girls, like Sarah, had long been friends, and there was no denying that their admiration was pleasant.

All this was an exhilarating mixture, and his cheerful assurance brought an infectious gaiety to the party. Isabella had eyed him with covert approval, liking the coat of rust-coloured broadcloth that fitted so immaculately across the shoulders, the pale cream pantaloons, the Hessians with tassels in rust, the cravat in deceptively simple folds, and the jauntily angled beaver hat. She determined to give him no inkling of her approval. He was looking far too pleased with himself already. Anyway, she was certain that the talkative Sarah would be loud in her appreciation.

The journey was uneventful apart from one stop at a small wayside inn to quell the thirst of the travellers with lemonade, or a sample of the landlord's best brew. They did not take the new road into Worthing through Ashington and Findon, but reached the coast down a track beside the Adur river, already looking low after the hot dry spell, and emerged by New Shoreham. Everyone was exclaiming excitedly at the views of the sea. The tide was high and the sea reflected all the blue of the skies above. They drove slowly on past Lancing, breathing deeply of the beneficial ozone, and pointing and remarking at the merchantmen and men-of-war to be seen in the distance.

It was gone eleven o'clock before they arrived at the small town house Mr Grice-Hewson had taken for the summer season. Set back from the water, in Ann Street, it lacked any sea views, the rooms were small and the furnishings only adequate, as Mrs Grice-Hewson pointed out at length, but much had been done to improve it. The family had brought luxuries with them from home, many small details that could add an elegance to the apartments, and the principal first-floor drawing-room had a pleasant balcony on which to take the air, and which was only a little disturbed by the noise from the market at the far end of the street.

The travellers were immediately offered refreshment after their long drive: cold meats, cheese, fresh bread, assorted fruits, biscuits and cakes. It was an offer enthusiastically appreciated, and the family joined them to eat and talk, so it was some time before they considered venturing out to explore the town.

Sarah's parents asked Isabella, when the sightseeing walk was discussed, if she intended calling on her fiancé during her visit. She was puzzled to notice their reserved tones, and their efforts to conceal their surprised relief when she was embarrassed to confess that he had not even furnished her with a direction for his lodging. Alladay regarded them with a frown of concern, but nothing more was said.

As they made their way down to the street Sarah admitted that she had looked out for Lord Carlton Crue with keen interest, and had thought to introduce herself as a friend of Isabella's, but had found no one who seemed able to point him out to her, let alone make an introduction. Alladay considered this to be strange in the small, close-knit community that was polite society at a seaside resort, but he kept his thoughts to himself.

The boys ran ahead to find the beach, each clutching their costume, a shilling for the bathing machine attendant, and strict instructions as to which machines were for the use of gentlemen, and which for ladies! As Mr and Mrs Grice-Hewson had professed themselves content to remain indoors and peruse the *Morning Post* and the

Lady's Magazine respectively, Alladay, Sarah and Isabella walked out together.

'So you persuaded this idle man to make the arduous journey to Worthing?'

Sarah, looking charming in a peach silk pelisse over a dress of white muslin, was resting her hand on one of Alladay's arms, and talking across him to Isabella, who had been offered the other. She fluttered engagingly cheeky looks up at him as she spoke.

'Did you have to be *very* persuasive to engage his co-operation? I confess, I was all anxiety for you when I remembered how *gloomy* he had been when I mooted the visit. You wouldn't think that a man who can appear looking so elegant and distinguished could be so ungracious, would you?'

She chuckled.

Alladay was about to protest in defence of his good name, but he was forestalled. Isabella shot him a challenging look and joined forces with Sarah.

'My dear, you are right. You would not believe the hours of persuasion it has taken! And the sacrifices I had to make, enduring his company! Can you imagine the tedium of suffering all those hours of supposed conversation, listening endlessly to why wheat would do better on Ten Acre field, which strain of turnip to introduce, how many extra sheep could be run on the downland, and whether or not to fell Niddy's Copse? Niddy's Copse! Can you conjure up a more riveting subject for conversation? And all this suffered in order to have the pleasure of seeing you again!'

Isabella was affecting a doleful face, shaking her head, but Sarah was openly giggling.

'Not Niddy's Copse!' she exclaimed. 'Niddy's Copse indeed! It is too much!'

'I would have you know,' Alladay remarked severely, with looks of quelling solemnity, 'that the fate of Niddy's Copse is the subject of much heated debate in Long Trovers. It has great bearing upon the energies of our gamekeeper, and upon the livelihood of at least four local poachers that I can call to mind on the instant, not to mention, which naturally I shall not in the presence of ladies, the necessary and convenient privacy requisite upon the courtship rituals of the local enamoured. I am—can it be doubted?—all consideration for their comfort. Never let it be said,' his voice took on tones of exaggerated self-righteousness, 'never let it be said that I ignore the views and welfare of my tenants!'

'Pooh, what stuff!' commented Sarah rudely. 'Such vulgar excuses! None of that is any reason for boring a young lady with tales of Niddy's Copse! For penance you must listen with every appearance of fascination and delight while I take you on a tour of the sights of Worthing! I trust you are all attention?'

'What a termagant you have become, Sarah! You will have me terrified!'

'And insolence to add to his faults! It will be an even longer tour of the sights of Worthing! We have just passed the theatre, there, with the four pillars and the balcony, now we shall continue into the market!'

On the corner of Ann Street and the High Street, the market was impressive. A pump stood in the centre of a handsome paved quadrangle which was bordered on all sides by covered stalls, each separated by a pillar. Wrought-iron gates gave access at either end.

They wandered in and looked at the goods displayed. Sarah was pointing out the locally caught fish: mackerel, sole and plaice, and the rustling baskets of live shellfish, when Isabella, with a malicious little smile at Alladay, and a murmured comment about thinking of the good of his estates, professed an overwhelming interest in the poultry on the far side of the square.

'I just want to go and look,' she said. 'Don't hurry! Lord Alladay, you *must* stay and listen to Sarah! I know she has been looking forward to your company.'

With a whisk of skirts she left them alone together and stood feigning an intent interest in the hanging chickens, duck, geese and turkeys, and the piles of tiny wheatears, or English ortolans, until the pressure of the fat farmer's wife in charge of the stall drove her on to contemplate the venison on the stall beyond. Here Sarah and Alladay caught her up, Sarah still chattering happily, but Alladay gave Isabella a repressive look and a frowning shake of his head. She smiled at him, all airy innocence, as they walked back into the High Street and headed towards the sea.

'Do you know Worthing, Isabella?' Sarah asked.

'Not at all, though I visited Brighton when I was very young. The last time I was by the sea was when Papa took rooms in Ramsgate for the summer. He left us children there with Miss Huckstable, our much-detested governess. She disapproved of the seaside, having an abhorrence of sand in the house, and made herself so disagreeable that I believe she drove him back to town. We were left to her tender attentions, and spent the days in view of all that splendour, but forbidden ever to walk on the sand!'

'No wonder the boys have rushed to the beach,' Alladay remarked, but Sarah, happy to have an uninformed visitor to show around, was already speaking, her serious tones belied by the amusement evident in her face.

'You must both promise to be impressed by all you see! Impressed without thought of comparison. You must understand first of all that we in Worthing do not believe in the superiority of Brighton! We never, ever admit that there might be anything in That Other Town along the coast that we do not have here! *All* the resort facilities are here. Our beach is as fine, our sea as tempting, our ozone as invigorating, our company as refined and our assemblies as elegant as at any Other Place that you might not wish to mention! You see Warwick House here? It is one of the best houses anywhere on the south coast, always taken by one of the first families. This year the Duke and Duchess of Glendoon are staying here with their young children. Why, we even have our royal patronage. Did you know Princess Amelia visited here in 1798? And Princess

Charlotte has spent a season here? You didn't? Such ignorance!'

'But,' asked Alladay solemnly, 'the question is, do you have a Pavilion?'

Isabella joined in, regarding Sarah sadly.

'The poor man,' she said, shaking her head. 'He has undoubtedly suffered from an excess of the sun on our drive down. He must be hallucinating! Pavilion? What Pavilion? I have heard nothing of any Pavilion, have you?'

They regarded him pityingly.

'He'll be hallucinating about some Prince Regent next!' Sarah added, and they both broke into giggles.

'About this guided tour of Worthing...' Alladay remarked, darkly on his dignity against the combined attack.

'Ah, yes! Well, there is the Colonnade Library. It is kept by Mrs Spooner. One can usually find something worth reading there, oh, and the Post Office is there too, very convenient for us in Ann Street. And this delightful area before you is the Steyne which, as you may know, is a promenade for you to take the air and display yourself to the other visitors. And if you should have a faint suspicion that you might have promenaded along another, longer Steyne, Somewhere Else, then do not remark upon the fact!'

They paused to look about them. The area had been laid out at right angles to the sea, designed before sea views became popular, which Isabella felt was a shame, but it was a pleasant place, with laid-out gardens surrounded by a neat dwarf wall coped with Portland stone surmounted by iron railings. They entered the gardens. People were walking about enjoying the sunshine, their appearance in the most part genteel but not in the height of fashion. Sarah greeted several of them before pausing to point out the buildings of the surrounding square.

The west side of the area was taken up by the Steyne Hotel, with its adjoining Marine Library and assembly rooms, and various respectable lodging houses. All were built in the attractive local cream-coloured brick. To the east stood another hotel, and gardens.

'It may not have the view of the fabled unmentionable edifice to recommend it,' Alladay remarked, 'but it is a very pleasant spot none the less.'

Sarah chuckled.

'Of course, it is not so bad, any of it. But *how* I wish we were in Brighton. Mama prefers Worthing because it is quieter. She considers Brighton to be a rackety place, full of characters who are quite unsuitable to make my acquaintance.' She sighed wistfully. 'And naturally Papa obliges her, and is well pleased because prices here are so much cheaper! But, oh, how I wish . . . But there, I am letting my tongue rattle away again. Come, let us walk down towards the sea.'

It quickly became obvious that the walks along the foreshore were the favoured meeting places of the younger visitors to the resort, and that Sarah had not spent too much time in pining for the more exotic attractions of Brighton. Several young men and girls hurried over to greet her, and it was clear she was a favourite with them all. She eagerly introduced her visitors, and Isabella endeavoured to engage the attention of some of the other young ladies, leaving Alladay free to monopolise Sarah should he so wish. It would not be through any fault of hers, she determined with an inward smile, if he failed to attach the necessary fortune! Talk, however, became full of plans of which assemblies to attend, which tedious musical evenings to avoid, knowledgeable talk of card parties, and assignations to meet at the Marine Library if the weather became wet.

Alladay raised his eyebrows at Isabella with a slight, irritated gesture of his head.

'Shall we walk on slowly and view a little more of the beach, while Sarah talks with her friends?'

Sarah regarded Alladay with an arch look, and called cheerfully that they could desert her if they must; her heart would not be *entirely* broken, they needn't think it; and she was not so short of admirers that she could not dispense with Alladay for ten minutes! She defiantly returned to flirting with two gangly and blushing young men tricked out in the first stare of fashion.

Isabella frowned reprovingly at Alladay as they moved away.

'You will never catch a fortune if you abandon it so casually, you know! You cannot be certain that a heart captured in a childhood bramble patch will remain unswervingly true! You must bestir yourself to make more effort. Look at the competition you have back there!'

She chuckled.

Her companion did not look amused; quite the reverse. He spoke staring stiffly ahead.

'I will thank you, Miss Larkham, to abandon this busy contriving of my path to matrimony. I suspect your interest to be no more than mischievous. It is as unwarranted as it is unnecessary!'

He sounded impossibly pompous.

She coloured up, and glared at him.

'Tell that to your tenants, sir! See if *they* think my concern is mischievous! Tell it to the Burden family with that leaking roof, or those in Longcroft Bottom whose one shared plough finally broke this summer. Or Mrs Bollings who has buried three children this year from that dilapidated hovel they call a home. Or Widow Samson whose only cow died, or——'

He flushed angrily, and interrupted.

'Colwick and I do our best. Heaven knows, the rents are low enough. If only my father would consent to raise the rents of those who *could* afford to pay perhaps I could do more for the less fortunate. But . . .' he paused, suspicious, and regarded her through narrowed eyes '. . . since when have *you* concerned yourself with the fate of those less fortunate than yourself? Never! No, this is a mere excuse for your meddling!'

He glared at her and, undaunted, she glared back.

'I have *learnt* to care, sir, since I have, on *your* estates, had the opportunity of meeting such unfortunate people.

There were precious few I was likely to meet in my father's world. But here, I have ridden the estate with you. I have talked to those wives while you are so busy with their husbands. You do not hold the monopoly on caring!' She drew breath, then re-attacked on a different front. 'And why should I not encourage you towards Miss Grice-Hewson? She is charming, pretty, fond and wealthy! Could you ask for more?'

'She is no more than a child, and she talks too much!'

He sounded so truculent that she giggled, and reluctantly Alladay also gave a rueful smile.

'I cannot help the truth,' he said.

'No, no, of course not! Let us talk of something else or we shall be in grave danger of breaking our truce.'

They wandered on. The beach comprised some shingle on its higher reaches, but the tide had been receding ever since their arrival, and sand was now exposed, gleaming smooth, wet and level in the bright light, as far as the eye could see, a sparkling contrast to the wooded slopes behind. Long wooden groynes divided the beach, and Isabella politely asked their purpose.

Alladay, equally punctilious, explained the problems of the landowners whose properties abutted the foreshore, and who had arrived each summer to discover that they owned a little less land than they had the previous year, the winter storms having taken their toll. The groynes had been constructed at the end of the previous century to preserve the beach, and thus the properties adjoining it, and enhance the prospects of the town.

Beyond the groynes the bathing machines stood, pulled well out into the waves, and beyond again, leaping in the swell while watched by a grey-clad attendant, could be seen the matching scarlet-suited bodies of Thomas and William.

'Thank heavens you have worked to improve their swimming skills,' Isabella remarked, watching their antics.

'Thank heavens, indeed. I have no wish to repeat my heroic dash into the water to rescue the little beasts! My memories of the fate of my boots and waistcoat are horribly fresh in my mind, and think of my embarrassment at the Grice-Hewsons should the same fate overtake them again!'

She raised an eyebrow.

'I was exceedingly displeased with you, Lord Alladay,' she said reprovingly. 'I still believe I was used abominably! Your boots and waistcoat deserved no less.'

'I would not dare to contradict you! Hence my relief that your brothers have proved so able in their aquatic studies!'

Several other people were taking to the water, the men in brightly coloured suits, some of the women in the bathing coverings provided for the purpose by the guides who worked the machines, others in their own voluminous bathing preservers. The screams and laughter of the women entering the cold water mingled with the cries of the seagulls overhead. Beyond them all the Dieppe packet lay at anchor, a lone rowing boat just pulling away from its side.

Fishing boats had been pulled up along the shingle and upturned. Various weather-beaten men and boys were at work inspecting nets, and the smell of hot tar drifted from a bucket over a small fire of driftwood. Near it a burly old man puffing on a clay pipe was repairing the hull of his boat. Women with flat woven baskets full of freshly caught fish were offering them for sale. Isabella was just wondering whether it was feasible to transport a gift of fresh fish back to Long Trovers and the attentions of Mrs Stoke, both as regards the journeying of the fish and of themselves, when she felt Alladay start.

He endeavoured to turn her discreetly back along the foreshore. Surprised, she looked up to see what had disturbed him.

Emerging from the broken-down gate of a dilapidated property overlooking the beach, and turning to walk down the foreshore towards them, was Lord Carlton Crue.

He was so engrossed as to be quite unaware of their presence. His attire gave him an air of rakish disreputability that Isabella had not seen in him before. His coat hung casually upon him, unbuttoned, his cravat was tied in a loose knot, and he lounged along, scraping the pebbles with his boots. But it was what slowed his progress that transfixed Isabella to the spot.

Draped upon his arm was a woman whom even Isabella, with her almost total ignorance of the *demimonde*, could have no hesitation in placing accurately. Her tiny turban with its plume of ostrich feathers was placed provocatively amid an undisciplined mass of chestnut curls. Her dress was so diaphanous that it clung to every accomodating curve with the movement of the breeze, yet despite its revealing nature it was still cut so low across the bosom that the lady's more than ample charms were dangerously displayed. The generous rouging of her cheeks was unmistakable, but it was her wide eyes with the darkened lids, and her pouting mouth as she pressed against him to cajole and tease, that spoke most clearly of the intimacy of their relationship. Isabella watched, frozen.

'Miss Larkham, come away, now.'

Alladay was insistent.

'It can only hurt you to remain here.'

She looked up at him. It was clear that, for the moment, the fury that was revealed in his face was overridden by his concern for her feelings. Crue was closer now. She heard his guffaw of laughter at something the woman said. Abruptly her frozen shock was wiped away by a feeling of undiluted rage.

'No!' she said, controlling her fury with an effort. 'If you have no objection, my lord, we are going to walk on. I see no reason to interrupt our plans. No reason at all!'

Her head was held high, although there was a bright spot of colour on either cheek. She put her hand out imperiously.

'Are you sure this is what you want?'

'Oh, yes, Lord Alladay. Quite, quite, sure!'

He could see no way to stop her. In her present mood he was certain she would not hesitate to go on alone.

She took his arm and they walked towards the oncoming couple, who remained absorbed in their own conversation. As they drew near Isabella startled Alladay by giving a quiet, bitter laugh. Then, as if suddenly coming to a decision, she murmured, 'Just act the part for me, do!' She clung close on his arm, and gazed provocatively up at him with a flutter of eyelashes from under her bonnet. With her free hand she pointed down at the beach. When she spoke her voice was strained, a little too high and loud.

'Oh, look, Anthony! A pony and trap giving rides down the beach. Such fun! Do take me, dearest Anthony!'

Alladay's utter astonishment was immediately superseded by a burst of inward amusement when he looked at Lord Carlton Crue, now immediately before them, and saw that mirrored reaction in his face. Astonishment, shock, dismay, and anger chased each other across the swarthy lordly visage.

'Good heavens!' Isabella was continuing in exaggerated amazement, her voice ever a little too high. 'Just look, Anthony. It is Lord Carlton Crue! How *do* you *do*, my lord? What a *delightful* surprise. Naturally I would have given you notice of our arrival had you not unfortunately omitted to leave me your direction.' She allowed her haughty gaze to touch upon the woman on Crue's arm. 'It really *was* an unfortunate omission, was it not? When we reached our friends' house our *first* thought was to secure your address from them, but they assured us they knew of *no one* who had been introduced to you! *At the time*, I was amazed . . .' she allowed herself another supercilious glance at his companion '. . . now, of course . . . However, we must not keep you.'

She favoured Alladay with a breathtaking smile.

'Dearest Anthony! The pony and trap?'

Alladay took a measured look at the outrage on Crue's face, and smiled. He deliberately raised the hand of Crue's fiancée to his lips, paused, and regarded Crue across it. 'Whenever you wish, Isabella. You have only to say.' He lowered her hand, but retained it in his clasp, before nodding briefly at Crue. 'Servant, sir.' And turned to move on.

'Miss Larkham!'

Crue's tones were icy with fury.

They half turned, Isabella's eyebrows faintly raised.

'You wish to introduce me to your companion?' she asked quietly.

Crue's colour rose as he glared at her impotently, and his temper was not improved when the girl on his arm favoured him with a faintly malicious smile.

'Go on, Carlie! Be a gent. Introduce me to your lady friend!'

'I will thank you to keep your mouth shut, Clorette.' Crue's tones would have curdled milk.

She made an exaggerated moue of distaste, and shrugged. Then she caught Isabella's eyes, grimaced towards Crue, gave a brief smirk, and dropped a slow, conspiratorial wink.

Against all her expectations, Isabella laughed.

Crue ignored them both, and turned his rage towards Alladay.

'And you! You shall answer for this!'

'For what, sir?'

Alladay's tone held no more than polite enquiry, but he allowed his gaze to linger on the diaphanous lady and the hint of a sneer raised his lip.

Crue glared at him for a moment longer, swung abruptly on his heel, and strode away, the lady half running to keep up.

Isabella and Alladay walked on in silence. When they had covered some distance she stopped. The fury had abruptly drained from her and she began to shake. She looked up at him. Her lips were quivering, and tears filled her eyes.

'I am sorry,' she said in a small voice that strove pathetically for dignity and maturity, 'to have embroiled you in that tasteless scene. I am afraid I exploited your presence shamelessly. I should not have done that.' Tears spilled over on to her cheeks. She sniffed crossly. 'I do not usually cry.'

'It is the shock,' he said gently, putting an arm lightly around her shoulders and leading her over to a small upturned dinghy. 'Sit down for a moment.'

She collapsed on to the worn timbers and thankfully accepted a large linen handkerchief.

'You have nothing for which to apologise,' he said, standing looking down at the top of her jauntily trimmed bonnet.

She was staring disconsolately at the pebbles. A seagull flew screeching overhead, and the tumble of waves made a constant background murmur.

'In fact,' he continued, 'your intervention was probably the only thing that prevented me from making my feelings about that man known in ways that would have been much cruder, more physical, and likely to cause you extreme embarrassment. What I am really saying is...' he paused, then continued '...now we have our truce, you know, you need never have any qualms about enlisting my help and support in any way you wish.'

She blew her nose angrily, barely hearing what he said.

'I was just so furious! I had heard...' she flushed '...I knew he had a reputation for the women he... well, the people he associated with.'

She paused, then, 'Clorette, indeed!'

She scowled at her clenched fingers.

'In a strange way I was proud...proud that despite his past he had eventually chosen me. But to see him...after all the things he had said to me... I hate him!' she said passionately. She stamped on the crunching shingle.

The futility of the gesture seemed to deflate her anger. She paused, and it was obvious she felt she had been shaken into speaking too openly.

'I am sorry. I should not burden you with things that are none of your concern. Please, do me the favour of forgetting all that has passed here, everything that was said. It is a problem I have to solve for myself.'

She blew her nose again, defiantly, squared her shoulders, and stood up.

'I should like to ride down the beach in the pony and trap, if you have no objection. It will give me time to compose myself before we rejoin Sarah.'

'Of course,' Alladay said.

After the ride they collected the boys, who were warming up after their swim, beating their hoops wildly along the sands. Crue and his companion had vanished. They walked back to where Sarah and the other girls were holding court, dividing their attentions generously between the hopeful young sprigs of fashion who preened themselves like jealous peacocks.

Alladay regarded her cheeky wave to them with mixed feelings.

'If she enjoys herself so much in Worthing there will be no holding her when she has her London season next year!'

'Why, yes,' Isabella said, dully, 'and I am sure you will be there with her.'

The realisation that by that time she might well have become Lady Carlton Crue she found overwhelmingly depressing.

She was subdued throughout the rest of the visit, and quiet during the drive home, despite having to share the chaise with assorted fish, three live crabs and an enormous lobster that Thomas and William had insisted on purchasing as souvenirs.

Alladay, thinking back over the events of the day, ruefully considered the challenge that he had silently but recklessly thrown down over Isabella's hand. He had not intended to be pushed into making such a gesture, and was uncertain where that rash, irresistible impulse would lead him.

One relief, he reflected, was that, although there was no doubt at all that Crue had been aware of the apparent challenge, and would doubtless respond, Isabella herself seemed to have been so engrossed in her own anger as to have been quite oblivious.

CHAPTER TEN

ISABELLA spent much of the following morning fretting over the composition of a letter to her father. She found it difficult to know how to compress her emotions into the cool reason she felt might best sway Mr Larkham to her point of view, and on occasion despaired of her ability to do so.

Long empty minutes dragged past while she gazed blankly from her window at the distance hillside, stirring her quill idly round and round in the little cut-glass ink-well. She watched Alladay vanish over the horizon with a pickaxe over his shoulder and was roused to curiosity, then his father struggle up to the copse with a wheel-barrow full of stones, and was moved to pity. She grew irritated with her hair falling about her face, and dragged it angrily back with a tortoiseshell comb. She sighed, and scratched at the paper again.

Bess, as devoted as ever, sighed as if in commiseration from her position sprawled heavily across Isabella's feet, and groaned each time Isabella, her toes becoming numb in their soft silk slippers, endeavoured vainly to heave her to one side.

As time passed, many pieces of paper were aban-doned, sadly blotched with ink or tears. She evolved flowery phrases and ladylike euphemisms, then angrily scored them out and wrote pages giving full rein to her outrage. Ashamed, she tore these up. She reverted to what she hoped was a restrained simplicity. At last she managed a draft of which she felt at least that she could make a neat copy.

Dear Papa,

I am writing to tell you how unhappy I am with the engagement you arranged between myself and

Lord Carlton Crue.

I have made every endeavour to oblige you and be content, but I have been made most painfully aware of the incompatibility of our life styles. Lord Carlton Crue does not appear to live by the gentlemanly standards that I am sure you would wish for in my husband, and his behaviour has been a source of grave embarrassment to me.

I do not believe, Papa, that you would wish your daughter married to a man whose lewd behaviour can make her a laughing-stock before her friends. I trust therefore that you will oblige my most earnest wish, and release me from an engagement that can cause me nothing but unhappiness and disgust.

With every best wish for your good health and your speedy return,

I remain your most obedient daughter,

Isabella.

She regarded the round looped handwriting on the stiff paper for some time, then resolutely folded it and sealed it down. As she had no idea of where her father was, it would be necessary to post the letter to her father's secretary, who dealt with all Mr Larkham's business in London during his absence. Mr Dawson was reliable, and would certainly forward it as soon as he was able, but still, it could be many weeks before Isabella received a reply. Even when it came, it might not be one she would wish to read.

She sighed disconsolately. She thought of the days when life had been nothing but a thoughtless round of social pleasures, when her love for Harry had filled all her dreams with happy anticipations that barely looked beyond the next ball or soirée, and Aunt Caroline had been too empty-headed to ever concern herself over her niece except to accept invitations, and promise treats and outings. How simple life had seemed then. Now Harry was just a memory. How long must she dream, and wait for him to return? If only he would write!

She curled up on the bed in a patch of sunshine, and reached for her book. She had finished *Sense and Sensibility*, all three volumes of it, and was secretly inordinately proud of herself, although she had been a little disappointed with the ending. She was not convinced that her favourite heroine should have ended the book marrying a man who wore a flannel waistcoat!

Now she was deep into *The Mysteries of Udolpho*, and it held her enthralled, full of villainy, suspense and thwarted love. Isabella lived and breathed with Emily while she read, she gasped her way through awesome mountain passes, shuddered at the evils of Montoni in his castle stronghold, and shed bitter tears over the missing Valancourt.

Some pages of accompanying Emily in following a trail of bloodstains through dark castle corridors surrounded by enemies reconciled Isabella amazingly to her own lot. In fact, she mulled earnestly, a frown of introspection on her forehead, in many ways her life at Long Trovers *could* be deemed an improvement upon her London days. She *had* been an empty-headed doll, thinking of nothing but her own pleasure. Now, like Emily, she had to think for herself and decide what was right or wrong in her life, and act upon it. She had taken the first step in writing that letter this morning. The thought gave her great satisfaction.

She was so absorbed by her book and her thoughts that she missed the knock on her door. It was Bess who ran over wagging her tail.

'Come in!' Isabella called.

It was Alladay. He frowned round the edge of the door at her.

'Are you ill?' he asked, abruptly.

'Such tender solicitude! I will take care not to go in to a decline when you are about! If you suspect I am ailing you should be sending up calf's foot jelly, thin gruels, hot bricks and smelling salts, not gruff enquiries! Come in, if you have anything to say.'

The rest of him appeared around the door, and he made his way to the chair at the table by the window where she had sat writing her letter. He swung the chair around, and sat astride it, resting his arms along the back, and his chin on his arms.

'You were quiet on the journey home yesterday. I feared perhaps the day had proved too tiring. Six hours of journeying in the sun can be exhausting. You have not been downstairs at all yet today.'

'I was unaware that my movements were constantly monitored!' she exclaimed. 'What is it to you if I spend a morning in my room?'

Then she shrugged, laying Mrs Radcliffe's epic aside on the counterpane.

'It was not the journey that exhausted me,' she muttered to herself, her head bent, avoiding Alladay's scrutiny.

Bess leaped back on to the bed beside her and stretched herself out comfortably.

'I did wonder if you would wish to discuss any aspect of your connection with Lord Carlton Crue,' Alladay ventured, tentatively.

Isabella frowned.

'I can see nothing to be gained by discussion,' she began, picking irritably at the pattern of the cotton counterpane. 'My father has arranged the engagement. It has his complete approval. What choice has a mere daughter?' She scowled harder. 'Oh, don't look so understanding and concerned. What could you do? Nothing! There is nothing to be done! If you were a true gentleman you would not have raised the matter again. I specifically requested yesterday that you would not do so. I am content in my engagement, do you understand? I have no choice but to be content.' She was glaring at him, although her bottom lip quivered. 'Your interference in my path to matrimony is as welcome as mine is in yours. There is nothing to be done, nothing to be said. My relationship with my fiancé is my concern alone. I would be grateful if you could learn to remember that.'

She reached for her book, pointedly turned it over and began to read. Alladay remained where he was. She looked up to see him regarding, with raised eyebrows, her letter to her father, which lay sealed upon the table. He met her glance with a look of query, but she made no explanation, and her look dared him to ask. For some moments they remained, their eyes locked.

'Oh, go away!' she said.

'Shall I take this down to be franked?' he asked mildly.

'If you wish.'

He moved slowly to the door.

'You might like to know,' he said, pausing halfway into the corridor, 'that I arranged this morning for Colwick to have another cow delivered to Widow Samson. He tells me that a bit of cheese-making was her only source of income.'

'Well, one good thing came of my "meddling", then, did it not?' Isabella replied, sounding cross, not wanting him to see that she was pleased. 'You probably have an old plough on the estate somewhere in all those out-buildings, if you did but look.'

He laughed. 'Possibly. You make an improbable champion of the common people, Miss Larkham. I rather like you in the role!'

He had gone and shut the door before she could respond.

It was some days after this that Isabella was invited down to the green room to make the acquaintance of a family, new to the area, who had arrived to take up residence in a large property in the next village.

News of them had, of course, preceded their arrival. Algie had called, assuring Isabella that there were two daughters, both attractive, lively girls with generous portions, and a brother. Edmund Beaumoyne was certain the girls were heiresses; the parents were vastly wealthy, for the crates of goods arriving from Town had stunned Witchbourne. Their brother had some cracking cattle, and it was felt he was certain to be a dashed good sort. Isabella had listened with amusement to the various tales, and decided she must immediately assess these reputed heiresses as possible saviours of the Long Trovers estate!

The Whyle family looked quite at home by the time Isabella arrived at the green room. Mrs Whyle, a large lady in a yellow silk dress that would have better suited a woman of half her age and half her proportions, was keenly admiring Lady Kintrove's embroidery, while her eyes flicked to different items of furniture, assessing their age and worth.

Mr Whyle, dressed with a sober good taste that spoke of wealth, was discussing the local beauty spots with the Earl of Kintrove, while his son, Julian Whyle, struck a pose, one arm resting along the mantelpiece, the other with the thumb hooked into his waistcoat pocket. His head was thrown back, partly to display his profile to hopeful advantage, partly because the height of his cravat made any other stance impossible. His thin brown curls sprang in artful disarray. He looked Isabella over swiftly, then accorded her a surprised and over-appreciative greeting. She took him in immediate dislike.

Alladay was seated on the couch, a girl on either side of him. Chloe and Clytia Whyle were in earnest discussion of the entertainment to be found in the neighbourhood, or rather, the lack of it!

'I cannot believe,' Chloe was exclaiming, 'that none of the better families regularly entertains the young people. Why, when we were in Hertfordshire the Bigginses had dances every month, and so did we. The Hoyles gave regular musical evenings, and there were always card parties, everybody gave them!'

'You must help us, Lord Alladay,' Clytia chimed in, fluttering her thin brown eyelashes at him. 'As soon as the house is straight we will start to hold regular dances, won't we, Papa?' she called across the room. He beamed and nodded in response, and she chattered gaily on. 'We shall expect you to give us the names of all the people in the area whom we should invite. What fun it will be, getting to know everybody.'

'Of course,' it was Chloe who chimed in again, 'we shall have you and Miss Larkham on the top of our list!'

They were not *bad*-looking girls, Isabella decided. Their hair was certainly thin and inclined to lankness, but they had done everything to improve this that money could pay for. It was a shame that Clytia had the very slightest of squints, but that was nothing to deter a man's affections. It was a shame too that their mother had dressed them in matching over-frilled muslins, be-looped and bowed in pink ribbon, which did little for their sallow complexions. But one should not, she reprimanded herself virtuously, judge their clothes on the one meeting.

Isabella smiled to herself, and determined to discover how generous a portion each girl could expect! Alladay could not complain that he lacked a choice of heiresses! When they rose to leave after the required half-hour, planning and promising all sorts of entertainment, she was well satisfied.

Another visit of interest was that made by Lord and Lady Alnstrop, accompanied by a nurse and their small son Henry. Although quite a young couple, they were treated very much as long-standing friends. It emerged that the Alnstrop estates bounded with those of Lord Kintrove for some considerable distance, so, although the houses were not close, they considered themselves neighbours.

Isabella liked them at once, and was enchanted by Henry, who sat and gurgled plumply on her lap, solemnly handing her his silver and coral rattle to shake, then equally solemnly taking it back to shake himself. Lady Alnstrop, obviously delighted to find another person as charmed by her baby as she was herself, begged Isabella to call her Louisa, confessed that she was expecting another addition to the family in the autumn so her travelling might be limited soon, but invited Isabella to come to Alnstrop House whenever she wished. Isabella, both flattered and genuinely pleased, hoped it could be arranged.

Before they left, Lord Alnstrop insisted on visiting and admiring both the vegetable gardens, and Lord Kintrove's growing monument up in the copse. Isabella, appreciative of his thoughtfulness, wished her father could have seen him.

It was while they were out riding one cloudy day in early July, with a damp breeze that hinted at drizzle tugging Isabella's skirts, and lifting his hair back from his forehead, that Alladay unexpectedly turned to Isabella, who had been engrossed in her own thoughts, and said something that persuaded her to pay a visit herself.

'I am surprised you don't see more of Miss Pickering,' he remarked. 'She is an unusual woman, quite an eccentric in her way, but it is extraordinary what she has done in the east wing. You have an artistic eye. I think you would be interested, and I am sure she would appreciate hearing your comments.'

'Why, whatever does she do?'

'You don't know? Then I shall not spoil the effect by telling you. You will have to go and look for yourself.'

Intrigued, Isabella persisted.

'What effect? What will I see? Don't be so infuriating, sir, creating mysteries out of nothing! Why should I bother going to the east wing if I don't even know what is there?'

Alladay chuckled.

'You will go because you will not be able to resist! Curiosity will tug at your mind, unanswered questions will torment your brain, and your footsteps will wend their involuntary way towards the hidden mysteries of the east wing!'

'Infuriating beast!' she retorted rudely. 'It would serve you right if I took no notice whatever!'

'And you should know,' he went on as if she had not spoken, though his eyes were full of amusement, 'that you will need to visit soon. Miss Pickering goes regularly to live with families in Brighton and teach young ladies French and Italian. She is an excellent linguist, you know; a very intelligent woman in her own way. One of her regular families has written to say they wi. be in Brighton from next week, and requested she joir them, so she will be gone for some time.' He paused and smiled, teasing her. 'The east wing will be locked up once she has gone, and all its mysteries hidden! Think of the torture of never finding out!'

'Oh, yes? But do I care?'

She swung Marina ahead and cantered away from him, up on to the hilltop. There she urged the mare into a gallop and set to race Alladay home, but Captain's long stride brought him steadily closer until he thundered by her side, and traitorous Marina, content to have him there, would make no effort to outstrip him. Alladay laughed across at her vain efforts to spur on the horse, until she laughed herself, and slowed, breathless, to a trot.

'Wretched horse!' she exclaimed ruefully. 'How am I ever expected to put you in your place when she will only nuzzle up to Captain as if he is the light of her life? It is too bad!'

'It is indeed,' he laughed. 'Perhaps I should ride out on Pippin or Bramble to give you two a sporting chance!'

She gave him an indignant glare, but addressed herself to her horse. 'If you had any sense at all, Marina, you would turn round right now and bite him!'

Marina trotted blandly on.

'I always suspected that horses were a great deal more stupid than most people believe,' Isabella remarked darkly, to no one in particular.

She heard him chuckle.

'Captain begs leave to differ,' he said. 'We are of the considered opinion that Marina shows remarkable good sense, good taste and discretion!'

'There speaks the male of the species,' Isabella observed, and her voice held a bitterness that surprised her. She pushed the mare into a canter and did not speak again until they reached the stableyard.

'Go and visit Miss Pickering, though,' Alladay mentioned again as they unsaddled the horses and left them to the attentions of Old Bill, who was whistling tunelessly round his one tooth.

She regarded him with her head on one side.

'I might!' she said, 'I might.' She snapped her fingers to the waiting dog. 'Come on, Bess.'

With a toss of her head she left him there, still holding Captain's saddle.

The truth was that Isabella had to some extent avoided Miss Pickering. They talked politely when they met at meals or in the gardens, but Isabella had not forgotten Miss Pickering's opinion of her, and found the conversations daunting. Far from despising her as she had at first, after weeks of listening to her artistic comments and critical discussions Isabella now would have liked to feel she could gain the older woman's approval, but doubted her reading had yet extended far enough for her to do so.

That afternoon Isabella decided to forestall further teasing by Lord Alladay, gather up her courage, and visit the east wing.

She was walking round the outside of the rambling house to the garden door of the wing, rather than endeavouring to make her way through the maze of corridors, when she saw a smart closed carriage, newly painted in a glossy dark green and cream, with matched bay horses, sweeping down the drive to the front of the house. Intrigued, she stopped to watch, and maybe greet the visitors. It was not a carriage she recognised.

It was with indignation and some alarm that she watched Lord Carlton Crue jump down from inside the carriage, stretch himself, and wave a contemptuous hand towards the house, speaking to someone still inside the vehicle. A man who must have alighted from the door the other side walked round to join him. Isabella glanced frantically to and fro. They had not yet acknowledged her presence, but she was too far from any door to reach it undetected.

She looked down in despair at the old faded dimity she was wearing, and thought angrily of the comments it would draw. It was only later that she decided she would have preferred to greet him in mud-stained calico complete with a spade.

'By God, I do believe that's her!'

Crue was staring across at Isabella.

'Come here, Isabella.' His voice was peremptory, amused and confident. 'I have a friend who wants to have a look at you. Here we have your rustic impersonation of a kitchen wench, do we? But you lack the basket of carrots! I had promised him carrots.' He was openly laughing at her. 'There is no doubt, the sooner we take you back to the civilising ways of London, the better.'

He turned to his companion.

'Well, Barney, what do you think? A fine little filly once she's put to the curry comb.'

The man approached Isabella and held out his hand.

'How d'you do, Miss Larkham? Sir Barnaby Croft, at your most humble service. Yes, indeed...' he glanced at Crue appreciatively '...you are everythin' Carlton promised. More than happy to wish you joy, old boy. Quite green with envy!'

He gave a throaty chuckle, and opened his plump fingers, letting drop Isabella's unwilling hand. He was a stout man, with a florid complexion and full, pouting lips. His protruding eyes looked her over with a lingering attention to detail that left her quivering with outrage.

It was plain that Crue was amused at her fury and discomfiture. Her eye caught movement in the carriage, and she could distinguish flounced skirts through the open door. His grin broadened.

'I have no wish for this meeting, Lord Carlton——' she began stiffly, but he broke in.

'Not wish to meet old Barney? Come now, my dear. You will cast him into despair. He always thinks himself such a favourite with the ladies!' He turned aside to Sir Barnaby. 'Marvellous what anger does for the complexion; quite irresistible!'

He stepped closer and took her hand, raising it swiftly to his lips. She snatched it back, but he tightened his grip, and bent his face close to hers. His voice was very quiet.

'You and I are sophisticated people, Isabella. We know the way of the world. I expect to enjoy my life, a fact you would have to accept sooner or later. As for you, my dear, *after* you present me with a son and heir, I dare say I could turn a blind eye to games with the tutor. But *after*, you understand. Not before.'

'How dare you?' she spat, white with fury and indignation. 'How dare you imply——'

'That is how a civilised marriage works, and we are civilised people,' he interrupted coldly, ignoring her outburst.

He pressed her hand firmly to his lips, but his eyes, regarding her over it, were not amorous. He let the hand go, and she hastily stepped back.

It seemed like a ludicrous nightmare to Isabella, to be standing out on the gravel, with the coachman, Sir Barnaby and the beskirted occupants of the carriage all pretending not to listen, discussing in such bizarre terms how she would spend the rest of her life.

'I have written to my father——' she began defiantly, but again he stepped in smoothly.

'Good, good. Horatio and I understand each other perfectly.' He glanced back at the carriage. 'We have so many interests in common. He will appreciate the situation. Let me know when you hear from him.'

He turned back to where Sir Barnaby was surveying the house and shaking his head sadly.

'Terrible state, terrible state. I swear that wing is quite fallen down. Depressin', y'know. Most depressin'.'

'Then we won't allow you to suffer any longer, Barney. Goodbye, Isabella. Glad we don't have to disturb the family. We only dropped by to see how you were. If there's anything you require?'

He raised his eyebrows queryingly, and she shook her head, furious.

'We are on our way back from a couple of days in Town. Well, no doubt I shall see you again shortly. Remember your manners; bid Barney farewell.'

Swallowing her fury, Isabella managed a choked courtesy of some sort. Crue, obviously struck by some thought, gave a grin and reached into the carriage. There was a feminine cry of protest, hastily pacified, then he turned back to Isabella, a collection of fashion plates in his hand.

'Allow me to leave you with these, my dear,' he said, pressing them into her hand. He looked her critically up and down. 'I am sure you will find them of interest. *Au revoir!*'

He jumped easily into the carriage and slammed the door. The coachman bestirred himself beneath his many capes, and the immaculate carriage moved away.

Rigid with outrage, it was some moments before Isabella flung the fashion plates passionately on to the gravel, swung on her heel and strode towards the house, her eyes almost blinded by tears.

She did not notice Miss Pickering until that lady rested a hand lightly on her arm.

'Isabella?'

She drew a long shuddering breath.

'I was on my way to visit you,' she managed to say.

'Then you shall do so.'

Without further comment Miss Pickering, her strange multicoloured attire fluttering in the breeze, led the way to the garden door of the east wing and inside.

'My parlour is upstairs,' she said.

The wing, near the stable blocks, jutted out into the gardens. A central stairwell rose before them, but while Miss Pickering bustled ahead, Isabella stopped in an amazement that even penetrated her present turmoil. Blowing her nose crossly, she paused to stare.

The entire wall surface, from floor to ceiling, right around the hallway and up the stairs as far as she could see, was intricately patterned with shells. Hundreds upon hundreds, in greys and yellows, pinks, mauves and whites, browns and blacks, striped, blotched or plain, they surrounded her in patterns that flowed along the walls like the waters of the sea themselves. Waves, swirls and curves blended into flower and fish designs of exquisite detail.

'Of course, you have not seen it before.' Miss Pickering paused at the top of the stairway. 'My interest, my hobby, my passion, my life. It totally absorbs me. But we will not look at it now. First things first. Come in and sit down, child.'

In something of a daze Isabella followed this eccentric woman up the stairs and into her parlour, a pleasant room with windows on three sides, overlooking the gardens, the lake, and the back of the stableyards.

She could see Alladay in the gardens, talking with Lady Kintrove. He was carrying a pickaxe again.

'Where on earth does Lord Alladay *go* with his pickaxe and his spade?' she asked irritably, watching him.

Miss Pickering spoke from where she was bending down, fetching something from a cupboard.

'I am sure he will tell you himself if he wants to,' was all she said, and Isabella frowned, turning away from the window to study the room.

It was chaotic, but comfortable. Isabella had never been in a room like it before. The walls, without a covering of shells, nevertheless were entirely decorated with paintings; sketches, watercolours and oils. Bright yellow curtains hung at the windows, exotically patterned rugs covered the floor, and more were draped over the furniture, in reds, greens, yellows and black, so that a chaos of colour leapt to warm you. Isabella stood blinking.

'Sit down, child.'

Miss Pickering was pouring wine into two delicate fluted glasses. She handed one to Isabella, and sat down herself.

'I saw him arrive,' she said shortly. 'That fiancé of yours. Not impressed. Not impressed at all. Met a lot of men of his stamp...' She broke off, leaving her words hanging darkly in the air. 'Talk about it if you want to,' she finished.

Isabella regarded the round homely face of the woman sitting opposite her, and was swung wildly between tears and hysterical laughter. She took large gulp of the wine.

'Were you ever engaged?' she heard herself ask.

Miss Pickering shook her head.

'My parents arranged a marriage. Many, many years ago. Nothing had been formally announced. I wanted none of it, but they were adamant. I ran away with the man I loved. He was an artist. No money, no prospects. Family disowned me. Name never to be mentioned again. We lived in Italy. Had five marvellous years before he died of fever. I worked there alone until I met Clara and Wilfred and they suggested I make a home with them here. Works very well. Never regretted what I did. Never.'

She stopped, and drained her glass, before fetching the bottle and refilling for them both. Isabella was staring at her in mute astonishment, her image of this dumpy woman utterly transformed. She had dismissed her as a drab spinster who had turned to books when life had passed her by. Those few brief sentences revealed a life more *risqué* than those found between the covers of a novel. She felt suddenly very young.

'Yes,' she said abruptly, 'I do want to talk about it.' She took a long gulp at her wine, and, finding she had drained it, boldly held out her glass for another refill in response to Miss Pickering's generous wave of the bottle.

'If you don't mind,' she said firmly, 'I would like to tell you right from the beginning.'

She began her tale with her love for Harry, and her father's reaction upon his discovery of that love. She spoke hopefully of Harry's return, but she could feel herself searching for excuses to cover the absence of letters from a man who had promised everlasting devotion. It was Crue, however, who filled her with indignant fury, Crue and her father. She told everything, her tongue loosened by the wine, and by the difficult weeks without any confidante except Ruth, or the dog.

She even muttered, shame-faced, her confused reaction to Crue's kisses, flushing and twisting the glass between her fingers. She anxiously argued her attempts to dutifully accept her situation, but how she still smarted under his sneers. She shook while she recounted the meeting in Worthing, the wine slopping so she paused to drink more, and tears of rage and frustration ran down her face as she described his words that afternoon.

Miss Pickering regarded her sombrely when at last she had finished. There was a pause before she spoke.

'Well,' that lady said with brisk determination, as Isabella scrubbed at her cheeks with her handkerchief, 'you are *certainly* not going to marry *him*!'

Isabella, staring dully out of the window, blinked, turned, and looked at Miss Pickering with new assurance. She drained her glass defiantly.

'No,' she said. 'You are absolutely right. I am *not* going to marry Lord Carlton Crue.'

She began, a touch hysterically, to laugh.

'Shall we empty the bottle to that?'

CHAPTER ELEVEN

THE balloon was finished. To everyone's astonishment the hours of stitching were at last over. The result was huge. Like the Montgolfier balloon used by Monsieur Pilâtre de Rozier and the Marquis d'Arlandes it would be forty-five feet in diameter and seventy feet high. Thomas and William had spread the vast empty bag out on the grass and were moving about inside it, draped shapes, checking the seams for holes. Alladay was measuring lengths of the fine silken rope, very light and strong, that was to mesh the balloon and attach it to the basket.

This basket, which looked like the base of a giant wicker picnic hamper, was fitted with buckled leather thongs that would attach the ropes from the balloon. Isabella fingered them, then tugged hard. Her life might depend on the strength of those buckles. They had tried the basket for size. The wicker had creaked alarmingly, and it was crowded for four people, but not impossible.

'It is the weight, though, not the space, that is crucial,' Alladay frowned. 'There is no guarantee that this contraption would lift Bess, let alone all of us! It may not be feasible for us all to travel.'

Aware of the drift of this conversation, Isabella regarded him firmly.

'Then the *heaviest* among us should offer to stand down,' she said. 'That, or the person who put least work into the stitching!'

He let the matter drop.

'I wish we had hydrogen,' she heard William remark from inside the balloon. 'Like Professor Charles. Six hundred thousand people watched his first ascension in

Paris in 1783. Six hundred thousand! Imagine if they came to watch us!'

Thomas grunted.

'We haven't any hydrogen, and, anyway, I don't expect there are six hundred thousand *cows* in the whole *county*, let alone people. I'm too hot in here. I'm going out.'

His lumped shape wriggled in the folds of fine silk.

'It'll be even hotter in here this afternoon,' said William, with satisfaction.

Alladay and Old Bill had built two raised platforms of piled bricks, between which the fire would be lit and from which the basket could be entered. Rearing above them on either side were two great tripods built from fruit-picking ladders roped together. A line slung between them would hold up the top of the limp balloon while it filled with hot air from the fire below. Isabella studied the construction critically. It looked makeshift, but sturdy. It looked as if it might work. With a little luck!

The printed instructions were unclear over the problem of how to get the hot air into the balloon without incinerating the basket, and they had all argued at length over the neatest solution. Thomas had argued for a large circular basket with a central hole through which the heat and smoke could rise into the balloon above, as he had seen in the prints of Rozier's ascent in the first manned flight. This had been vetoed on practical grounds. No one wanted to wait long enough while such a basket was especially constructed, or find the money to pay for it.

It had been William's wish for a movable fire that could fill the balloon, then be taken away while the basket was fixed in its stead, that had brought Isabella to tentatively suggest making the fire in an old iron horse trough. To her amazement her suggestion had been adopted enthusiastically, and the trough, on wooden runners, was now between the two platforms, filled with wood and straw, with planking above it to support the open mouth of the balloon. They were almost ready.

They trooped in for luncheon leaving Old Bill hammering stakes into the ground around the ascension platform, for anchoring the balloon once she was filled and tugging to be free.

'I am still not convinced...' Alladay began, pausing before making further inroads upon a generous helping of lettuce, bread and ham '...I am not at all convinced that you should undertake this trip, Miss Larkham. Perhaps later, once we have experimented——'

'I do not wish to begin this discussion again, Lord Alladay.' Isabella smiled sweetly at him, and neatly peeled an apple with a tiny silver fruit knife. 'I intend to fly!'

Lady Kintrove looked up at them from further down the table.

'And why should you not, my dear? It sounds most exciting!'

'Your son is of the belief that it will prove too dangerous for a mere female!'

'Mama——' Alladay began, but she was regarding him in saddened surprise.

'After all I have taught you, Anthony! Why must you persist in the erroneous belief that women are constructed of porcelain? Isabella is young, strong and intelligent. Better suited, without a doubt, to balloon travelling, than those two rapscallions down there!'

The boys looked up from their plates, deeply indignant, and she laughed.

'Mr Larkham might expect, or at least excuse, his sons taking part in such a venture, but certainly not his daughter. Think of the danger! And a woman is hampered by skirts. She cannot easily scramble to safety should the need occur,' Anthony argued.

'These are prevarications, not arguments, Anthony. If Mr Larkham is typical of the British gentleman then he will value his sons to a far greater extent than he does his daughters. Why, daughters are generally considered to be a financial liability! How much better then to risk the demise of a man's daughter than of his treasured sons and heirs!'

'Really, Mama!'

'Very true, ma'am,' Isabella interjected.

'As for the inconvenience of skirts . . . if you truly consider that to be a problem, why, lend the girl some breeches!'

'Mama!'

Isabella, after the initial shock of the idea left her, chuckled, ready for any recklessness.

'Do you think I should, ma'am?'

'Why not? It is a practical solution to a practical problem. I have not heard of any formal society guidelines laid down for lady balloonists, have you? And you will hardly be coming to land at Almack's, only in one of our fields! Wear whatever you will be most comfortable in, my dear. Anthony will have some old breeches from when he was a boy. There is sure to be something that will fit!

'I recollect one journey I made with my husband,' she continued, reminiscing. 'Do you recall, Wilfred? We were travelling in the wilder areas of central Italy, far from anything remotely resembling civilisation. I travelled dressed as a man for several weeks, for both safety and convenience, you know. Wilfred was forever complaining that I dirtied all his shirts and cravats; so difficult to wash in mountain streams!'

She resumed her meal, leaving Isabella as astounded as she had been by Miss Pickering's revelations of the previous week. Her son regarded her with irritation.

'You do not help me, Mama!'

She smiled at him fondly.

'Of course I do, Anthony. I help you along the road to a liberal understanding. Nothing could be more important. Your outgrown breeches will be in the oak chest in the old nursery!'

The breeches were buckskin, faded and patched. The shirt was linen and far too large, but Isabella tied her hair back with a red ribbon, tied a jaunty red silk scarf at her neck and felt ready to take on anything, even Italian bandits. She finished her ensemble with a pair of William's boots, far sturdier than her own, and, having quashed Ruth's comments, cheerfully departed, ignoring her stony silence.

Ruth was not enthusiastic. She was shocked, very shocked, at such extraordinary behaviour. Now she considered herself to be a proper lady's maid, she was beginning to have inflated opinions about the sort of lady she would like to work for! She could not wait to tell Stoat about these goings on. The sort of ladies his master knew in London would not do such things, of that she was very sure.

The boys had the fire well alight in the old trough when their sister joined them. Too well, for the flames leapt high and would burn the balloon. Alladay helped them heap damp straw on to the flames until they had a thick column of yellow-grey smoke rising.

'Now for the balloon.'

He stepped back, coughing and blinking.

They laid the mouth of the balloon on to the raised planking above the smoke, and William shinned up the ladders with the line threaded through the ropes on the top of the balloon, and secured it to the highest point of the tripod. After billowing in all directions until the boys were sore-eyed and choking, holding their breath while they endeavoured to hold open the base of the balloon, the hot smoke at last drifted steadily up into the huge silken bag.

The weather was cool and grey, the cloud cover persisting because there was no wind to shift it on. They had waited for a cooler day, wanting the contrast so that their hot air would rise more quickly. Isabella shivered. It was excitement, but Alladay held an old brown jacket towards her.

'Wear this. All aeronautical accounts tell of how cold it is in the higher atmosphere.'

He returned to feeding the fire. She stood back from the smoke, looked at the jacket with amusement, then pulled it on. Like the shirt it was much too large. The woollen cloth had a faint, masculine smell. It felt coarse and heavy after her fine, feminine fabrics. She watched him.

Isabella could tell that Alladay was anxious about the flight now it was imminent, worrying, she knew, not for himself, but for her and the boys. His face was tight with concentration, calling abrupt commands to her brothers as they hung from the tripods, holding open the silk. He was angry with her for insisting she would come, but she could not care. Nothing could make her stand back from the chance of flying through the sky like a bird.

The great stripes of red, white and blue began to heave and billow, humping and bumping between the tripods as the smoke coiled and rose, trapped in the silken folds, forcing them to spread. The fire was glowing red now, the heat more intense. Alladay hovered over it, watching for sparks, glancing from fire to balloon, his face reddened by the heat, beads of sweat standing across his forehead, his hands black-smudged. They watched and waited as the vast bag above them bellied and swelled. Isabella could feel the heat on her face, where she stood behind him, huddled into his jacket, head thrown back, gazing upward, her heart thudding in keen excitement.

'Check the guy ropes are secure, then be ready to pull the basket over,' he said, speaking abruptly over his shoulder without looking round.

'Me?'

'Yes, you, Miss Larkham. You are one of the crew. You are being treated like one.'

'Yes, sir!' she said with mockery of a salute, and walked over to the basket, conscious of the unaccustomed stride of her legs, usually so demurely draped. She tugged at the basket, and managed to pull it nearer to the fire. She waited, resting against the wicker rim, staring up at the huge balloon. Not even those interminable hours of stitching had prepared her for the great size of the multicoloured monster, bobbing and tugging now at its restraining ties.

'Release the top line, William, then come down here ready to move the trough.'

As the boys pulled away the line that had held up the top of the limp balloon, and shinned down their ladders, the balloon jerked and tugged more strongly, towering above them, dwarfing them all. Alladay continued to wait, watching the taut silk. Surely, Isabella thought, surely it can get no fuller? Surely now it is ready? She realised she was gripping the side of the basket so hard that her hands were sore, ridged and lined by the wicker-work. She drew a gulping, smoky breath. This is the most exciting thing, she thought, the most exciting thing I have ever done in my life. I am going to fly!

'Pull the trough away, boys! Miss Larkham, be ready with the basket. We must not let it all cool.'

She was laughing as she braced herself. The boys dug in their heels and pulled on the ropes attaching the horse trough. Nothing moved. They heaved again, then, re-gardless of the heat of the iron, Alladay impatiently tugged at it. The whole burning mass jerked forward on its runners and he leapt aside as the boys pulled it away, hurrying back to help Isabella lug the basket beneath the balloon. As she threaded the supporting ropes through the leather thongs he hastily made them secure.

'Jump in to weight it down,' he said to her, and to the boys, 'Get that fire well clear.'

Isabella scrambled up on to the platform, and slipped down into the waiting basket, taking secret pleasure now in the freedom of moving without skirts. She stood in the wickerwork, and with a gesture of finality pulled the string that closed the bottom of the silken bag, trapping the smoke and heat within. She could feel the basket shift and jolt as the balloon heaved above her. They were ready to fly.

Alladay had just given a last decisive tug to each knot when there was a shout from William, and a scream from Thomas. Heaving the trough backwards, Thomas had tripped heavily over one of the guy ropes and, falling, had unbalanced the wobbling trough on its uneven runners. It teetered, and rolled, tipping glowing embers, ash and straw all over the grass, and the frantically wriggling Thomas.

With a curse Alladay leapt to drag the boy clear, brushing the red hot coals from his boots and breeches with his bare hands, shaking him down. None of them noticed that William, in jumping back from the accident, had trodden on, and snapped, one of the stakes that held another guy rope, breaking it loose, causing the balloon to sway ominously.

However, it was not until the spilled, flaming wood, greedy for the tinder-dry fuel, had burned clean through the rope that had tripped Thomas, that the balloon rose up with a stomach-churning lurch. It hung, for a matter of seconds, a reluctant captive of the last two ropes. Isabella grabbed at one, thinking to haul herself down, down to the ground, but her pulling only loosened the stake, and it came away in her hand. The last stake, defeated, pulled gracefully out of the grass, and swung up lazily into the air. The balloon was free.

As if frozen, Isabella saw them all below her, transfixed, open-mouthed around the smoking embers. She saw Alladay leave Thomas and rush vainly for the dangling ropes, but she was being carried rapidly higher, and his expression was lost to her. Which was probably just as well, she thought, with a slightly hysterical laugh, as she clung to the side of the swaying, creaking basket and gazed down at the astounding vision of Long Trovers spread like a pictorial map below her. By the main entrance Lord and Lady Kintrove, tiny as ants, and the entire, microscopic household staff, were waving. Their joyous shouts floated clearly up, thin as the mewing of the seagulls.

The air on the ground had seemed still, but here, high above the sprawling house, a breeze was moving, cradling this unlikely companion of the startled pigeons, and moving its patriotic stripes over the rooftops, over the gardens, over the lake and the meadows. The cream-coloured cows raised their tails and ran in panic from the drifting shape, while its dull shadow slid silently over their field.

Isabella realised that she had been holding her breath. Her lungs felt tight and painful. Her stance was so rigid she was quivering, knees and elbows shaking. With a conscious effort she breathed, breathed deeply of this high, clear air. She loosened the grip of her fingers on the basket, and carefully turned around, terrified that an incautious movement would sent the basket tipping and her flailing body tumbling down.

But the basket swayed smoothly onwards, even as she moved to look behind her. A great bubble of delirious excitement filled her chest, and her face was rapt with delight. Behind her, everyone was out of sight, hidden by the bulk of the buildings. Then, even as she gazed, the balloon glided on, and trees rose up across her vision of Long Trovers, leaving her floating alone, drifting above an unfamiliar landscape.

Her thoughts flickered back to the others, so bitterly disappointed, though not, she thought with relief, seriously burned. She could not miss them. To be alone in the sky, light as air, flying free as the wind, exceeded all her dreams. She quivered with delight, gazing wide-eyed at the world far below.

The only nearby sounds were the movements of air over the balloon and ropes, the creak of the ropes or the basket.

Sounds from the distant ground reached Isabella with a startling clarity. A tiny puppet of a man behind a cottage was chopping wood, and the chock, chock, chock of his axe rang up through the skies. A heron flew along a stream beneath the basket, and its bitter complaining cronk, cronk, was loud and clear. High calls of children playing floated up from a lane, and the gruff calls of labourers in the fields, staring up and pointing. Plaintive sheep bleated, and crows circled warily towards her, cawing aggressively. A pony and trap pulled to a halt on a small road, and Isabella could make out the white face of its driver, gazing up in astonishment. She laughed aloud, and waved.

The air was moving rapidly over Isabella's face. She realised that she was both laughing and shivering. Alladay had been right. It was cold. She pulled his coat tighter about her, and fumbled to do up the silver buttons, fumbled because her fingers were stiff with cold where she had been gripping the basket rim. She turned up the collar, and tucked her silk scarf hopefully in at the neck.

The balloon was moving more slowly now, hanging sluggishly in the still air, almost as if uncertain which way to go. Below were trees, a deep wood of rounded hummocks of varying greens, soft and humped as an eiderdown. There was no doubt that these trees seemed closer than those she had flown over earlier. The balloon was losing height.

While half her mind hung suspended in delight over this roof of the world, gazing down in wonderment at the earth spread beneath her, the other practical half was reflecting that those rounded hummocks of tree would be twiggy and spiky to land in, and a very long way from the ground! She began to will the balloon to keep on a little longer, to wrest a fraction more life from the skies before it gasped out its smoky last upon the hard ground. Slowly, slowly it drifted, spiralling gently, over the tree-tops. Details of the trees became clearer, and songbirds flew out shrilling in alarm as the great shadow passed over.

Then, abruptly, ahead of her, the wood was gone. A dusty road bordered it, and fled beneath her anxious gaze. Beyond were meadows, and cows. The great bulk of the balloon slid gracefully over the edge of the trees, its trailing ropes snagging in the topmost branches.

The slow drift of the balloon seemed much faster now that she was near the ground. The last of the trees seemed to rush from beneath the basket, the road and a hedge to flash by in a blink, and the basket was touching, bouncing, juddering along the ground, bumping up and jolting down, tipping as the dragging weight was pulled behind the silken bag's dying bid for liberty. Isabella was tumbled and rolled. Tossed into the base of the basket, she huddled down to protect herself, arms over her head. At last, tipped on to its side, the basket came to a halt, and the earthy, secure smell of crushed and broken grass filled Isabella's sky-drenched lungs. She was down. She was safe. It was over.

She crawled unsteadily out of her wicker cage, fighting off the entangling ropes. Freed of her weight the balloon began to shift on over the meadow, bumping its basket behind. With a last burst of energy Isabella stumbled after the escaping, collapsing silk, and flung herself on to its colourful folds. She and the balloon fell to the ground together in a final, smoky gasp.

Alladay gazed in an agony of frustration at the rapidly receding balloon. Fury, anxiety and disbelief rendered him temporarily speechless, and it was some moments before he could think coherently. He turned abruptly to William and Thomas, brushing aside their cries of astonishment and indignation.

'William, run round to the gardens and watch the exact direction of the balloon's flight. Come and tell me in the stableyard. Thomas, see Nurse Pusey about that burn on your hand, and make sure someone comes at once to extinguish this fire. I will go after your sister on Captain. Now run!'

Alladay ran for the stables, cursing the slight uneveness of his stride that would fractionally slow his progress. Old Bill, who had watched the balloon ascend, came panting in after him.

'Saddle up Captain, quickly!'

Alladay ran through to the gardens, shading his eyes as he squinted into the sky. William, seeing him, flung up an arm to point.

'There she goes, sir!'

'She has gone so high, so quickly! She is well over Gibbet Hill and Long Common. If she keeps in that direction she will miss Witchbourne, but . . .' He paused, visualising the countryside beyond the hill. 'She will be drifting up the valley of the Ibben, I think, and then over Ibbenwood.' He frowned. Ibbenwood was big. If she came down in a tree-top in the middle of the forest... He did not like to think of her possible fate, or how long it could take to find her.

'Captain's ready, sir.'

'Thank you, Bill. We will need the trap later to bring back the balloon.'

And he was gone, down through the shrubs that edged the gardens, round the end of the lake, and up through the cattle meadows towards Gibbet Hill, pushing Captain on to gallop headlong, scattering once again the cream-coloured cows.

From the top of Gibbet Hill he caught sight of his quarry, floating jauntily ahead with its high, bright stripes. He almost thought he could make out the tiny speck that would be Isabella in the basket. Gripped by an irrational fury, he spurred on Captain, who surged down the hillside in a thunder of pulsing muscle.

How dared she have done this! How *could* she be so stupid? Floating there before them all, pulling out that stake. With her obstinate, arrogant insistence that she *would* come, that *she* knew best. When he had *told* her she should wait. But would she listen? Not Miss Larkham! Oh, no! Everyone must do what *she* thinks right. And now look what has come of it! She might be hurt. Dear God forbid, she might be killed. And she would deserve it. Any of it. He scowled furiously.

He breasted another rise and scanned the horizon, glimpsed the multicoloured shape far ahead, and thundered on without pause, down a long slope of field that led to a lane that would eventually take him up the Ibben Valley and into Ibbenwood. The furious turmoil of Alladay's thoughts goaded Captain onwards.

Once in the Ibben valley he was too low to gain any further glimpses of the balloon. He knew it to be several miles on, and to be heading, as far as he could judge, over the wood.

Once or twice he checked his course, calling out over the hedge to some fieldworkers, who nodded excitedly at his query and pointed on up the valley, and later asked a fat farmer in a trap, one of his own tenants, who confirmed the direction and was left staring bemused, shaking his head at Alladay's thunderous progress.

There were two ways past Ibbenwood. A longer, wider road, preferred by the local inhabitants, kept to bright daylight and skirted the edges of the wood, safe from whatever might lurk in its gloomy fastness. A narrow track, no more than a path, crossed it directly, and into this leaf-darkened tunnel Captain and Alladay plunged. It was more difficult to keep up speed here. Twigs whipped across their faces, knotted roots stumbled the path, and seeping springs reduced the track to stinking brown leaf-strewn bogs, but for the most part a steady canter took them onwards, Alladay looking about him all the time for signs of a wrecked balloon on the tree-tops, a small crumpled form lying at the foot of some steepling trunk.

He saw nothing. He would emerge with no idea whether to hurry onwards in panicking pursuit, or to turn back, searching back and forth in the gloom. Frantic anxiety swung in wild alternations with shaking fury as he burst out from the border of trees on to the dusty road. He stopped, fraught with indecision, reining in the tired horse. Captain's great flanks heaved as he breathed deep.

Alladay urged him into a trot along the road, looking for anyone who might have seen the balloon come over. It was as he scanned the fields for labourers that his eye was caught by a flash of red just beyond a second hedge. Taut with worry, he pushed Captain through a gap in the roadside hedge, cantered over the field, and slid hastily down to the ground, running as if with the dragging feet of nightmare towards the balloon. His eyes registered the spilled basket, and the scored ground where it had dragged along the grass. The great brave balloon was flat, and sprawled on it, motionless, was a small, breeched figure. With the hideous inevitability of nightmare, he was certain she was dead.

Isabella had been more shaken than she had thought. Collapsed upon the fabric of the balloon, clutching a rope and a handful of blue silk, she felt she could not move again to save her life. She was drained. Exhausted. She lay quite still, aware of the smoky reek of the cloth, too tired to care. No one had come running up, so she could only conclude that after her long drift over the lonely forest her descent had been unobserved. For the moment she was relieved.

It seemed later that she must have fainted, or maybe dozed. She drifted back to full consciousness knowing that she must bestir herself, find help, pack up the balloon, find her way back to Long Trovers. She knew that Alladay would be searching for her. It seemed inevitable, therefore, that when she heard footsteps running towards her she would turn over to find it was him.

'Isabella!'

Even as she sat up she registered that he had used her name. Also, that his voice was husky with anxiety. She pushed herself unsteadily to her feet, and smiled at him.

'I flew!' she said shakily, as he arrived breathless before her.

A spasm of disbelieving fury twisted his face and he gripped her shoulders, shaking her to and fro in his rage.

'How could you do this? Of all the stupid, irresponsible, selfish tricks to play... Pulling out that stake! You couldn't leave well alone, could you? Oh, no, Miss Larkham! You always have to meddle. Have to do what you think is best with your obstinate, arrogant, foolish, irritating, assumption of some absurd superiority!' At each word he jerked her to and fro, himself shaking in his rage. 'You could have been killed, you little idiot! Don't you realise? You could have been killed!'

Already drained and bruised, astounded at the unexpectedness and ferocity of his outburst, Isabella lacked the will to fight back. She stood, jolted, aching and sore under his punishing grip, her eyes wide in bewilderment. Tears began to swim into her eyes and roll uninterrupted down her cheeks.

'Dear Lord! Don't cry!' His voice was harsh, abrupt, painful. 'For God's sake, Isabella, don't cry.'

But she could only hang her head, and shake it dumbly, while the tears dripped down and splashed on to William's old leather boots like black stars.

With a groan he pulled her against him, cradling the slender form that shivered, dwarfed in his jacket. He pressed her head against his chest, and stood gently stroking her hair, soothing her softly, fighting to control his own ragged breathing.

'I'm sorry, I spoke like a fool.'

His fingers tangled in the brave red ribbon, already slipping out, and he pushed it down and away, loosing her hair to tumble on to her shoulders, stroking it gently, over and over, allowing his thumb to run lightly down her forehead and cheek, her neck, and on to the coarse wool of his jacket. His other arm held her hard against him, carrying her every quivering breath to his body, a reproof.

She gave a small sniff. Her head was still bowed against his chest.

'I have no handkerchief,' she said.

He reached into his pocket, and put one into her hand. She blew her nose, wiped her eyes, and blew her nose again.

'It was an accident,' she said in a small voice. 'I was trying to pull myself down——'

'I know,' he broke in. 'I suppose I knew all along. I was just so angry. So worried.'

He put a hand under her chin and raised her face up until he could look into her eyes.

'I thought you were dead,' he said, and his voice shook. 'Don't you understand? I thought you were dead!'

Tears were welling in her eyes again, and Isabella bit her lip, trying to stop its foolish quivering. Through the mist of tears she saw his gaze drop to her lips, and he raised a finger to touch them very gently. She felt the soft touch like a caress. Her lips parted and she drew a shuddering breath.

He lowered his face to hers. Briefly, her glance flew up with a wide-eyed query, and for a moment he paused, as she blinked and gazed into his bright hazel eyes, her breath quick and fast, but it was too late to turn back. This embrace held a strange, long inevitability.

His kiss was rough, demanding, bruising her lips with a hunger of long pent passion. She was breathless, reeling in his arms, quivering and dazed and uncertain. His mouth left hers, and she gasped, bereft, as his questing lips ranged over her face and pressed on to her eyelids, tasting the salt of her tears. She was crushed hard against him, unsure whether the thudding heartbeats she felt were his or her own, feeling the long lithe warmth of his body cleaving to hers.

Then his lips were again upon hers, gently, softly, filled with an overwhelming tenderness, lifting her swaying and dizzy, as his insistence grew, back into those heady moments of ecstasy, free as air, whirling in the heavens, until he lowered her gently down, down, until her feet were once again upon the ground.

She stepped a little back from his arms and looked up at him. Her lips were red, bruised, her eyes wide and dark.

'Isabella,' he whispered.

'Halloo! Halloo! Yoiks, tally-ho!'

They both started round towards the sound. William was forcing Bramble through a gap in the hedge, pushing aside a strand of thorn and waving his hat in the air.

'You found her! Are you all right, Izzie? I couldn't believe it when you floated off. I am so jealous! Was it wonderful? You came so far! I never imagined we would go more than a field or two. It was easy to follow you both. Everyone remembered the passage of a red, white and blue balloon followed by a maniac on horseback who fled by as if pursued by the devil! That is what one of them said to me! Old Bill is following in the trap but it will take him longer because he must keep to the roads.

Here William's bubbling stream of excitement halted abruptly; he slid down from Bramble's back, and stood before them, grinning.

'I'm sorry I stole the first trip, William,' Isabella said, shakily. 'I did not mean to.'

'I know that, silly. It is not important. We will go next time. It is not broken, is it?' His face was creased by sudden anxiety.

She shook her head.

'I don't think so. It was a bumpy landing, but only on grass.'

'Good!' he said. 'Let's pack it up, then. There were some children from down the road running after me. We don't want them touching it! Hold Bramble for me, Izzie.'

Indeed, several small faces were appearing through the hedge. Alladay sighed, and turned with William to the balloon, to spread it flat and fold it carefully. They packed it neatly into the basket, then, with the eager help of the staring children, carried it back to the roadside.

'I'll wait here for Old Bill, if you like,' William offered nobly, leaning against the basket and gazing with nonchalant superiority at the lesser mortals who lingered close. 'You two can get back. Izzie can ride back on Bramble. I can easily manage.'

They took up his offer. As they left they could hear his confident tones.

'Well, you *can* look in the basket, but only one at a time!'

'I would prefer not to ride through the villages, dressed like this,' Isabella said, her voice wan and tired.

'I will take you across country. We should not meet another soul.'

'I would like to get home quickly.'

He looked back at her and saw the exhaustion draining her face.

'It won't be too long,' he said, and, swallowing all the other things he wished to say, he swung Captain away through the woods at a steady trot.

CHAPTER TWELVE

ISABELLA wandered up and down the library shelves, picking down a book here, another there, flicking half-heartedly through the pages, while she listened to the dog snoring under the table at the far end of the room. She had already chosen a couple of volumes she wished to read, and knew she was stalling for time. She knew she ought to go boldly to the estate office, and request an interview with Lord Alladay. As soon as might be convenient. All the heady ecstasy of the balloon flight had evaporated, overwhelmed in her mind by what had followed. Something had to be said about the extraordinary events of yesterday. After a night much given to anxious thought, soul-searching, guilt, remorse, surprise, and startling memories, Isabella believed she knew what to say. She paced on, turning the pages of the book in her hands with little sign of enthusiasm.

It was with a mixture of relief and irritation that she turned at the sound of the opening door, and saw Lord Alladay entering, looking very brisk and cheerful in an elegant dark green jacket over a primrose-striped waistcoat.

'Hopkins told me you were here,' he said, closing the door and leaning back against it briefly. His gaze met hers, and his smile was warm.

He came towards her.

'Leave your books,' he said, holding out a hand. 'Come and talk.'

Dragging her eyes from his face, and the odd, unsettling thoughts it conjured, Isabella hastily sought to gain the initiative in this conversation.

'Indeed, we must talk, Lord Alladay,' she cut in abruptly, turning her back on him and his outstretched hand. She walked away, between the laden shelves of dusty tomes, down towards the huge, deep-set window at the far end of the room. As on the previous day the weather was dull; cloudy and grey. Nothing moved in the grounds outside. Beneath the table Bess sighed heavily.

'I was intending to seek an interview with you.'

She paused, then proceeded stiffly, her hands clasped together before her, 'I know you will agree with me that yesterday we were both somewhat overwrought by the extraordinary events and mishaps of the day. Things were said and done that I am certain we both regret.' She bent her head, frowning. 'I was intending to come to tell you that I am ready to forget, have indeed already forgotten, those unfortunate...unfortunate...*lapses*, and trust that we can continue the friendly truce we had established in our relationship. We *should* make the effort, if only for the sake of your parents, and my brothers.'

She drew breath, and turned slowly to face him, feeling just a little proud that she was handling this in a mature and sensible way.

'Balderdash!' said Alladay.

'I beg your pardon?'

'Beg all you like, Isabella,' he responded crossly, 'But stop prosing like a ninnyhammer! What you are saying is nonsensical! It is balderdash! Poppycock! Humbug! I kissed you because I wanted to. It was *not* an unfortunate lapse! I would dearly like to do it again.' She tilted up her chin angrily, her colour high. 'And I defy you to look me in the eye and tell me you regret the experience!'

'I...' she began, but her eye met his sardonic look, his raised eyebrow, and she faltered, and looked away. 'Of course I regret it! I have to regret it!' she burst out. 'Consider my circumstances! Consider yours! Consider the history of our acquaintance! You should be regretting it too!'

'Why? I see nothing to regret! Oh! Why is it, Isabella,' Alladay exclaimed hotly, 'that you can reduce me to a heartfelt desire to resort to violence and *shake* sense into you, within five minutes of beginning any conversation? Do you realise,' he continued furiously, 'that I entered this room intent upon telling you how much I love you?'

She glanced, startled, at his face, and looked quickly away, twisting her fingers together.

'Oh, no! That is absurd! We have thoroughly disliked each other for years! Years! You know we have! We cannot even speak without an argument!'

She paced up and down in front of the window, annoyed to find that she was shaking, tapping sharp staccatoes with her fingers on the deep wooden sill. He stood, both hands gripping the edge of the library table, leaning a little forwards, watching her over the great orrery that dominated the table-top. Bess, disturbed by the emotions, peered out anxiously round his boots.

'And I believe you are overlooking the fact,' Isabella burst out again, 'that I am already engaged to be married!'

He immediately made as if to speak, but she cut him short.

'I know! You are going to say that I dislike Lord Carlton Crue. That is true. And in the circumstances, and in confidence, I will tell you that I have written to my father telling him that I wish to be released from the engagement. And I will also tell you,' here the colour rose in her cheeks, and she clasped her hands to her breast, 'that I love someone else. I have done for months. I doubt my father will release me from the engagement. But even if he does my heart will not be free. In the world's eyes I may belong to Lord Carlton. In my heart I belong to another!'

Alladay's hands smacked hard down on to the table top.

'Lord Carlton Crue is a damned unsavoury libertine, and you will marry him over my dead body!'

'Don't be ridiculous, sir. You sound like a cheap, east-end melodrama!'

'And you sound like a penny romance! Believing your heart belongs to that posturing milksop Harry Exton!'

She gasped.

'How did you know?'

'I am neither blind nor stupid, Isabella. Have you forgotten how you paraded over half London with that apology for a man, myself and your brothers in tow? We the reluctant chaperons, while you hung on his arm and listened as he declaimed his abominable verses in honour of assorted parts of your anatomy. Retiring behind the shrubs for furtive embraces! You should be ashamed of yourself! The man is a conceited nincompoop. Married to him you would be bored within a month!'

'How dare you talk so? How dare you? What business has it ever been of yours what I do? None! None at all! Why...' here she paused, and her eyes widened '...why, you talk as if you were jealous!'

Alladay's face darkened.

'Far from experiencing jealousy,' he said, coldly, 'I spent those interminable walks in struggling to overcome an almost irresistible urge to box your ears!'

'Oh!' she said furiously. 'You are impossibly insolent! I will not remain here and listen to this.'

She stormed to the library door, ignoring Bess there waiting, shivering. She paused, speaking angrily back down the room to where he remained by the table, his face oddly bleak.

'Why must you stay here bothering me? You should be out visiting some of these heiresses! One misguided kiss has changed *neither* of our circumstances. To marry a fortune is your duty to the estate and your tenants. Though Lord have pity on the poor girl you choose!'

She swept out and shut the door sharply behind her, trapping Bess, who yelped pathetically. Exasperated, Isabella flung the door wide, hauled the dog through, and slammed it shut behind them.

Ruth was in Isabella's room when she stormed in there a few minutes later. The maid was sitting laboriously mending a torn flounce on the blue silk afternoon dress, spreading the skirts over her lap so she could imagine she was wearing the rustling fabric, and daydreaming of Stoat. She regarded her mistress's raised colour and rapid breathing with interest, cocked her eyebrows, but made no comment. Isabella irritably ignored her and picked up *Clarissa* to read, although she had already lost all patience with the heroine.

After some minutes Isabella impatiently flung *Clarissa* on to the counterpane and went to gaze moodily out of the window.

If only Harry would write! She felt guilty at the surge of anger she felt against him. She refused to believe that he had accepted her father's ban on communication. He was not so weak, so easily deterred. She *would* not believe it. She forced herself to remember his voice, the promises he had made. It was becoming frighteningly hard to recall. If only she had an address for him in Jamaica...

Lord Alladay was striding rapidly over the gravel beneath her bedroom window. Anger and frustration were plain in every step. Both a spade and a pickaxe rested on his shoulder, steadied lightly with one hand. He had changed from his smart jacket and waistcoat into old clothes, old boots. He set off up the fields, past the copse and his father's folly, never once glancing back at the house.

'Off after his treasure again!'

The laconic, disparaging tones were Ruth's. She had come up beside Isabella to look out, chewing through the sewing thread with her yellow teeth, scattering cards of thread from her lap on to the floor.

'What do you mean?' Isabella asked, startled.

'Him!' Ruth gestured with her head. 'Lord Alladay. After the family treasure! Didn't you know?'

Delighted at having the story to tell, Ruth watched Alladay vanish over the brow of the hill, then resumed her seat.

'It's the old legend of the family treasure, see! Though to my mind it has about as much truth as that tale about the dogs! It has always been known there was a treasure. Somewhere! No one knows for sure who buried it. Some say it was from before the Romans came, some king, or chief, was buried here. Others say it was during some trouble, a battle or such like, that the lady of the house buried all her silver plate, and her jewels, meaning to reclaim them later, then she was burned alive in this very house and they were never found. They do say that when the Kintrove need is greatest, then treasure will be discovered. Nurse Pusey, of course,' scoffingly, 'she believes every word of it!'

'Surely,' Isabella said incredulously, 'Lord Alladay does not take such a story seriously?'

'You wouldn't think so, would you? But that is where he goes! Truly! Digging for treasure! Would you believe it? But I haven't seen him come home laden with jewels yet, have you?'

She laughed. Ruth had not been pleased by Isabella's increased friendliness towards the formerly despised tutor, who was not at all what the maid imagined a future earl should be; or by her offhand references to Lord Carlton Crue. All Ruth's hopes and ambitions were entwined in more frequent visits from Worthing, not fewer. It was good to be able to show up Lord Alladay's folly.

'I would have expected you to show more loyalty to the Kintroves,' Isabella remarked coldly, obscurely annoyed by Ruth's sharp comments.

Ruth shrugged, unperturbed.

'We'll be moving on soon, won't we? As soon as your Pa gets back, and you marry Lord Carlton Crue. We'll be going to live in London. And won't I just like that! Stoat has told me all about London! He's promised to show me around. He rode over to visit me, on his afternoon off. All this way, special-like! Asked a lot about you and what you were doing.' She smirked. 'He thinks these old, poor families are finished. That's what Stoat says. The old Lord pushing wheelbarrows around, the Lady doing the vegetables, the Viscount burrowing for gold like a rabbit! Stoat laughs. Well, it's not how you expect real quality to behave, is it? Now, your Lord Carlton Crue! He's what you expect of *real* quality, isn't he? Isn't he just?'

'Oh, be quiet, Ruth.' Isabella lost patience with such gossip. 'You talk far too much. I won't have you chattering about me to that loose-tongued man of Lord Carlton Crue's. As for the way you speak of the family, I should have you laid off for saying such things.'

Ruth shrugged and pulled a face, hanging the blue silk back in the wardrobe, and going to the door.

'I don't know why Lord Alladay bothers with that treasure nonsense, anyway. He has only to marry one of these heiresses from hereabouts, and all his problems are over.'

She smirked again, and went out, banging the door.

'Ruth!'

It was a shout, and Isabella felt better for it.

The door re-opened.

'Lady's maids do *not* talk pertly, do *not* denigrate their employers, and, most especially, do *not* slam doors. If they do not give satisfaction they are dismissed. If I am not satisfied with you, I will be leaving you here when I marry, and employing a qualified maid in Town. Is that understood?'

Ruth dropped a sulky curtsy.

'Yes, miss.'

She went out again, quietly.

The following evening was the first entertainment offered by the Whyles. They promised a small dance for the young people; nothing formal, the girls' companion would provide the music on the piano, or possibly there would be a few musicians up from Brighton. There would be cards for the older guests, a light supper, just a pleasant meeting of friends and neighbours. So Mr Whyle had promised when he rode over to issue the invitation.

Isabella, Alladay and Lady Kintrove were to attend, Miss Pickering being employed in Brighton, and Lord Kintrove pleading forgetfulness.

'I don't enjoy such occasions as I used to,' he confided to Isabella, 'and I do so hate to distress people by forgetting who they are! I think I will stay quietly at home and take a glass of port in the library.'

He smiled a gentle, mischievous smile, and ran his hand over his fluff of white hair.

Isabella almost wished she could join him. She had learnt to enjoy evenings at Long Trovers now. She no longer retired early to her room to sulk, or shed self-pitying tears. She talked with Lady Kintrove, companionably helping repair the worn embroidery, or she joined with Alladay, and sometimes her brothers too, in games of cards, of spillikins, or even tiddly-winks. Sometimes Algie or the Beaumoyne boys stayed to dinner, and the games became raucously silly until Alladay dragged them all off to play billiards. Miss Pickering had been reading *Robinson Crusoe* aloud to the family each evening before she left to teach young ladies Italian, provoking much discussion on matters of survival, especially between Thomas and William. Now Alladay and Isabella took turn and turn about to carry on the story. That, of course, had been while they were on speaking terms!

It could not have been more unfortunate that now, while she was still angry towards Alladay, and confusedly refusing even to think of that extraordinary declaration that he had made, they should be going out together for an evening that had previously promised so well.

Isabella dressed for the evening in an atmosphere as frosty as that which was surrounding her conversations with Alladay. Ruth had not forgiven her mistress for the reproofs and threat, and her assistance was sullen and tight-lipped, despite the fact the Isabella was wearing one of her prettiest evening gowns for the first time since her arrival at Long Trovers. With silver-threaded crape over an underslip of butter-yellow satin, it was embellished with layered flouncing above the hem, and, about the low neck and tiny puffed sleeves, was decorated with hundreds of tiny white silk flowers, in scalloped lines, like dancing daisies in a meadow. The effect was charming. Her long evening gloves were white with a matching silver thread, and she wore little white satin slippers, strapped with satin ribbons above the ankle. Despite her sulks Ruth managed a respectable job on Isabella's hair. Threaded with silver ribbon, and a spray of tiny white silk flowers, it was piled into a knot high on top of her head, so that it tumbled down in loose curls. When all was done even Ruth's grumpiness faded.

'Now that's how a real lady *should* look,' she said with grudging appreciation. 'There'll not be another there to touch you! Ooh, but that dress is a picture!'

Thus fortified, Isabella went downstairs and found Alladay and his mother waiting for her in the hall, the carriage due at the door at any moment. Lady Kintrove was looking uncharacteristically elegant in green silk, with a soft white shawl, deeply fringed, hung about her shoulders.

Alladay, Isabella noticed with irritation, looked extremely well in evening dress. His cutaway tail-coat was dark brown, double-breasted, with neat covered buttons. His breeches of white kerseymere topped white stockings and black buckled shoes. He carried a *chapeau bras* beneath his arm and his cravat fell in folds of snowy precision.

'What an elegant pair you make, to be sure,' Lady Kintrove remarked cheerfully, rummaging in her reticule to see if she had remembered her handkerchief. She had noticed their reserve, but merely looked faintly amused, and continued to chatter with unconcerned amiability as they were ushered out to the carriage by Hopkins. Lady Kintrove enjoyed the occasional evening out.

For a family who had been in residence for such a short period of time, the Whyles were making their mark. Torches fluttered and glared by the gateposts and down the length of the drive to guide those unfamiliar with the grounds. It would have been hard, though, to miss the house, all ablaze with lights that had Lady Kintrove tutting darkly of extravagance. The glimpses they had of the interior rooms showed furnishings of the first elegance and every available luxury. The arrangements for the guests were lavish, far superior to the usual run of informal gatherings of friends and neighbours that took place in the locality.

'Well,' remarked Lady Kintrove, in an appreciative aside to Isabella, 'I guess his wife and daughters arranged a little more than Mr Whyle expected! This will start some social rivalry in the area. Won't that be fun?'

Several people they knew had already arrived. Lady Brockton was billowing ahead in a bright purple gown that set Isabella blinking, and had her daughter Gertrude trailing disconsolately in her wake, her white-frilled dress emphasising her pasty complexion.

Algie lounged over to greet them, resplendent in a blue tail-coat with silver-gilt buttons and breeches of a delicate sage-green. He raised his ornate silver eyeglass with exaggerated slowness to his eye, unable to look down because of the extra height of the folds of his cravat, and made his compliments to Isabella and Lady Kintrove. He drew his eyebrows together in pretended sympathy at Alladay.

'So conservative, dear boy!' he drawled, shaking his head carefully, and grinning. 'Plain white breeches! Now sage-green is all the go...' he put forward a leg to display it to advantage, and ignored Alladay's chafing aside on the struttings of peacocks '...or possibly canary! You will have to encourage him to something a little more daring, Isabella!'

'Me?' she said with raised eyebrows. 'Oh, I have nothing to say in the matter!'

She moved over to take her turn in greeting their host and hostess. Mr and Mrs Whyle were meeting all comers in the hall, and sending them through to a large room beyond that had been cleared for dancing. It was a pleasant room, surprisingly spacious, with two blazing chandeliers, and long windows giving out on to the dusky gardens. A piano stood in one corner, with an anxious lady in drab grey, who could only be the companion, hovering over a pile of music. A small raised podium had been provided for the visiting musicians, who had obviously arrived late. They were hurriedly taking off their greatcoats and unpacking their instruments.

Isabella was about to cross the floor to greet Chloe, Clytia and Julian when a hand rested gently on her arm. She paused, and looked up at Alladay's face. He gave her a slight, apologetic smile.

'A truce for this evening, Isabella?' he suggested quietly. 'I promise you can continue to hate me as much as you wish tomorrow. Let us be friends for tonight.'

She regarded him, head on one side. This dance might be more enjoyable if they were on friendly terms. She would have died rather than admit it to him after the way he had spoken of Harry—it annoyed her to admit it to herself—but she felt forlorn deprived of his easy conversation and company.

'If you wish,' she said carelessly. 'Without Harry here it is all the same to me whom I speak to or dance with. But I shall set a condition.'

'Oh, yes?'

He had frowned at her mention of Harry, and she smiled with exaggerated sweetness.

'Yes. You must undertake to pursue as many heiresses as may be here, regardless of whether they take your fancy. Not to spend the evening hanging around the card tables with Algie. You need to dance and display this reputed Kintrove charm!'

Despite his irritation, he laughed.

'Every heiress, Isabella? Are there so many? I had not realised! Your truce terms are such a model of generosity! To show my good faith I shall be as charming as I know how, and report to you at regular intervals on my progress, so that you may judge for yourself! But tell me, do they come with their moneybags strapped to their dresses so that I may know which they are?'

They were joined by Julian and Chloe, so she could not respond, although she glared, disdainful of such flippancy. They chatted against the scrapes and strains of the Brighton musicians tuning up their instruments. The Whyles had dressed to impress, Isabella thought, and was surprised and annoyed to find that she was forced to suppress an impolite urge to share her secret amusement with Alladay.

Chloe dazzled in a gown of lime-green satin, the skirts so burdened by folds, frills and flounces that were she to climb out of it, Isabella thought with amusement, it would stand independently and prove quite as interesting a companion as its owner. Across the room she could see Clytia in a singularly unbecoming confection of cerise sarsnet, simpering painfully, her squint more pronounced than ever.

Julian clearly intended to outshine all the rustic hopefuls of the area. His jacket was the brightest of blues, its silver buttons the size of coachwheels and shiny as full moons. The collar stood so high that it framed his head like blinkers on a nervous horse, the shoulders were massively padded, and the waist nipped in so tightly that Isabella wondered he could speak normally. Gold fobs dangled from his waist like a row of pigeons in the poulterers, above breeches of a yellow that almost glowed. Black shoes and stockings finished the ensemble, and he stood, shoulders back, hips forward, paying fulsome, unwanted compliments to Isabella, and taking sideways, admiring glances at himself as reflected in the long window.

Not long afterwards sets were called for the first dance. Julian asked a reluctant Isabella to join him in leading out the first set, and Alladay, with a meaning glance at Isabella, dutifully led Chloe on to the floor, labouring to engage her in light and witty conversation the while.

There was no doubt that Alladay kept his side of the bargain. He had not yet sat out a single set, and had honoured all the most eligible young ladies in the room with his attentions. He was obviously proving most popular. His partners laughed and blushed, and Isabella noticed with irritation that several of the young ladies gazed wistfully after him when he left them back with Mama. Oddly, his bad leg seemed very little of a handicap when he danced, and none at all to the admiration he was receiving. He even managed to bring a flush of colour into Gertrude Brockton's cheek. Every so often he caught Isabella's eye and raised an eyebrow, or smiled. Once, when he had reduced some young girl barely out of the schoolroom to an embarrassment of giggles, he dropped a furtive wink. She glared at him.

Isabella was likewise engaged for every set, and had a flattering queue of young men soliciting her hand, all eager to assure her that she was the most beautiful girl in the room. Only the knowledge that she was engaged to be married allowed the other young ladies to view her success with equanimity.

She enjoyed herself flirting a little with Algie, but found the insistent attentions of Julian Whyle a growing annoyance. He rudely cut out Arthur Beaumoyne who was awkwardly asking for his first dance, and whirled Isabella on to the floor before she had time to repress him, then hung about her after the dance had finished, noisily ordering unwanted lemonade and arrogantly cutting into her conversation with Chloe. It was on the tip of her tongue to pointedly remind *him* that she was an engaged woman, but she held back. Her feelings towards Crue gave her no wish to publicly remind herself or others of her connection with him. She all but ordered Whyle to go and invite poor Gertrude in to the next set. She needed to be rid of him. She wanted to talk with Chloe.

It was not until the dance before supper that Lord Alladay appeared by Isabella. She was sitting down, waving her painted chicken-skin fan idly by its mother-of-pearl handle, and talking to a pretty girl with mouse-brown hair. She had noticed him making his way across the room towards her; indeed, she had been oddly aware of his whereabouts throughout the evening, but she affected surprise, paused to deliberate, then accepted his invitation to dance gracefully.

'Note how well behaved and "truceful" I am being!' she said.

'And I. I trust you have noticed how obediently, if reluctantly, I have followed your instructions. Every heiress, known, probable, possible, or even potential, has been subjected to the reputed charm. Do you think they fell for it in droves? Shall I be inundated by heiresses fighting with each other to bequeath me their fortunes? What do you think?'

'I think you are being absurdly flippant, when it is obvious I have only your best interests at heart!'

'You are too kind, Isabella,' he said.

Whatever Isabella might have replied was cut short by the musicians striking up the chords once again, and conversation, especially upon such a subject, was impossible until the country dance had drawn to its energetic close, and supper was announced.

Alladay took Isabella's arm.

'Allow me to escort you in to supper,' he said. 'Then you can tell me at length how flippant I am!'

She would have liked to refuse him, but as Julian Whyle was hurrying towards her, his intentions plainly obvious, Isabella accepted Alladay's offer with alacrity. She firmly rejected Whyle's insistence that she abandon Alladay's prior claim with the assurance that they had already arranged to sit with a group of friends. That young man departed sulkily, looking daggers at Alladay, and strutted over to honour the pretty mousy-haired girl.

'Is he bothering you?' Alladay asked, with a frown.

'Only by his excessively persistent attention. I am sure I am intended to be flattered, but I am not.'

'If ever you wish me to hint him away...'

'Oh, good heavens, no. It is no more than a nuisance. But quickly, before we sit down, I shall tell you that I have made a cunning survey of the heiresses present on your behalf! I am assured by a most disgruntled Chloe that it is her sister Clytia who has the fortune! Whereas Chloe has a respectable portion of a thousand a year, Clytia is set to inherit *twenty* thousand a year from an aged bachelor godfather, which Chloe considers to be the grossest injustice. There! So now you know where to direct your charm. Do you wish us to join Clytia for supper?'

'No,' said Alladay firmly. 'We will join Algie over there with Abigail Wisbeach, and enjoy ourselves.'

In the event they were also joined by another friend of Alladay's, the Honourable John Whatton, or Hon-Jon, as Algie introduced him, and his sister Maria. They made a merry group, each capping the others' wild stories, and heads were turned their way, especially Julian's, glowering.

Isabella had not intended to mention the balloon flight. She was certain that her solo venture would be viewed with grave disapproval by the older, staider people present, and make her an unwilling object of gossip among the younger, even if her shocking choice of clothing was not revealed. But now she found she had no choice.

Algie, who had known the flight was due, and had been keen to be a part of it, begged to know every detail of the event. Despite attempting to give a dull, muted account, Isabella was instantly the object of awed admiration, particularly from the two girls, and had to recount her sensations on floating high above the countryside, and the drama of her landing, several times. By the end of supper she felt as if she must have flown halfway around the world, and hurtled into the ground with the force of a meteorite.

Alladay diverted some attention from Isabella as he enthusiastically continued what was obviously a long-standing flirtation with Maria, neither of them daunted by the fact that she was newly married and her husband was sitting at the next table. Isabella resumed her mild flirtation with Algie, but somehow her heart was not in the game.

The tired grey companion who had played throughout the supper break got up and left the piano as the musicians reassembled, refreshed. She rustled unnoticed away in her dull grey crêpe. People abandoned the supper tables and drifted back towards the dance floor.

'I am now ruthlessly to pursue the younger Miss Whyle, I suppose?'

Alladay had paused with Isabella by the supper table before following the others. He was looking down at her, his expression resigned.

'Naturally! If Chloe continues to tell her situation so readily there will be any number of keen suitors for Clytia's attention. You must make your mark now.'

She spoke earnestly, and was annoyed when Alladay sighed.

'Dearest Isabella,' he said, 'You must know this is utter absurdity. But no—don't argue—I am going! I would not renege on our bargain. I shall track her down hotfoot! And you?' he asked. 'Will you continue in you efforts to break poor Algie's heart?'

'I was doing nothing of the kind.' she began indignantly, but then she saw Julian scanning the room. He swivelled on his heel, unable to move his collar-blinkered head. She moved round to hide behind Alladay. 'Either lead me off to flirt with Algie, or take me,' she whispered hastily, 'and introduce me to any of your friends at all, but do not leave me to Julian Whyle!'

He frowned, but led her on to the dance-floor, where she was immediately accosted by Hon-Jon demanding his first dance.

'Thank you, sir,' she said to Alladay, and hurried to join the set.

It was well into the small hours before the carriage deposited its occupants back at the doors of Long Trovers. Lady Kintrove was yawning hugely, having indulged in a thoroughly enjoyable evening of gossip and cards. She wished them an immediate goodnight, muttering about unaccustomed town hours, and made her weary way aloft.

'Do you wish any refreshment before you go up?' Alladay asked.

'Oh, no,' said Isabella. 'We would only argue. You must remember that our truce only lasted while we were out. Now the clock has passed midnight, and you, my dear sir, have changed back into a pumpkin. Goodnight!'

She ran lightly upstairs.

CHAPTER THIRTEEN

ISABELLA was missing Miss Pickering. A fortnight ago, had anyone suggested that she might feel this, she would have laughed incredulously. Now, after their mutual confidences over the wine-bottle, she wished this eccentric new friend were here to share her uncertainties, instead of making elegant Italian utterances to bemused young ladies in Brighton. She was even prepared to risk another headache like that which had followed their previous talk! Isabella smiled to herself at the memory. It had been her first ever over-indulgence in alcohol, and Alladay had raised a very quizzical eyebrow when they had arrived at the dinner table arm in arm, laughing uproariously! Bess was no real substitute, and Alladay... She frowned.

Not that there would have been much time for confidences on that day after the Whyles' dance. There was no holding back Thomas and William and their feverish demands to be allowed their own balloon flight. Every day waiting seemed to them a day wasted. The weather continued cold and overcast, and Alladay, himself intrigued by the prospect of flying, had named today as the day for their venture into the skies. He had also, cunningly Isabella thought, avoided any chance of Isabella insisting on a second flight. He had agreed that Algie should accompany them, filling the fourth place in the basket.

This arrangement saw Isabella, looking cool, sophisticated and aloof in her brown riding habit and little beaver hat, abandon the smoke-bleared and sweating men fighting to fill the balloon, and trot neatly away up the hill slope. She intended to watch the ascent from near the copse at the top.

The balloon seemed to have developed a wilful temperament since its first flight, and Isabella could see it down below as she turned to look back from the top of the slope, heaving then sagging, belching smutty puffs of smoke over everyone nearby. She smiled, and allowed Marina to amble through the copse while she waited for the balloon to fill.

Lord Kintrove's monument to his sons was very much taller now than when she had first seen it. He had several ladders leaned up against the sides, each with a tidy stack of old stones at its base. He himself was not there. He had remained down by the house after luncheon, waiting with the rest of the household to watch the second flight. Isabella gazed sadly at the structure for a little while, then sighed, edged Marina carefully around the monument, and made her way back to her viewpoint.

The balloon was full, tugging and bobbing at its ties. She could see Algie examining in despair the state of his coat and buckskins, brushing at them ineffectually, while Alladay gestured impatiently to him to climb into the basket. The boys were already in, gripping the wickerwork tightly. The smoking trough was safely out of the way. Old Bill and three other of the men were holding down the stakes to avoid a repeat of the previous mishap. With a last check round the ropes, Alladay and Algie climbed up the platform, and slid down into the basket. Even at this distance Isabella could sense the tension and excitement.

'Let her go!'

The cry came up to her, followed by her brothers' echoing shouts, 'Let her go! Let her go!'

The men pulled at the ropes, and with a couple of awkward lurches the balloon pulled upwards, shaking off its last stake contemptuously, and soared steadily up into the cool skies. Heart in mouth, Isabella waved frantically, all her own surge of wild excitement flooding back as she watched. She nudged Marina well out of the trees to get a better view. The mare caught her thrill of emotion and danced impatiently. The balloon was drifting high over their heads.

'Goodbye, Izzie! Goodbye!'

Her brothers' shrill shouts wafted down to her. She waved again, and heaved a huge, quivering, envious sigh.

The group near the house was dispersing reluctantly after the excitement, turning again and again as they wandered back to their tasks to pause, point, remark and gain one last glimpse. Old Bill and one of his helpers had the pony already in the trap, and they could be heard shouting the direction they intended to take as they set off in pursuit of the aeronautical party. Isabella wondered whether to take up the pursuit as well. She hovered uncertainly, wanting to go, but knowing that she should not go out across country unattended, and, more daunting than the proprieties, that she could very quickly become lost. Despite her rides with Alladay many of the areas round about were still unknown to her.

It was probable that she would have returned dutifully to Long Trovers at this point, had she not suddenly espied an extraordinary figure in a bright yellow riding jacket, with huge glinting silver buttons, inadequately controlling a very showy chestnut horse as it minced and sidled up to the house. It could only be Julian Whyle who was peering arrogantly about from under the brim of his beaver hat. With a grimace of irritation, Isabella instantly turned her mare back into the copse, and, hoping sincerely that she had avoided detection, emerged on the other side to set off after the balloon at a smart trot.

It seemed that there was even less movement in the air today than there had been when Isabella flew. The huge striped shape hung in the sky across the valley from Isabella, and appeared quite motionless. She could even make out the tiny shapes that must be the occupants. Squinting her eyes against the light, she was almost certain which one was Alladay.

Unbidden, the thought she had been so fiercely suppressing leapt back into her mind. He had been going to say that he loved her. Absurd, of course. Ridiculous. Two people could hardly be less suited. Anyone could see that. Had he intended to tease her? Or had he been going to speak through some misguided sense of honour? What a fool the man was, she scowled. She knew he was deep in plans with Colwick to rebuild a row of cottages on the Witchbourne lane. She had been so pleased when Colwick told her. She knew the families who needed those homes. She also knew there was no money spare for such work. *He* had to marry money. And *she* was waiting for Harry.

She cut down the field towards the balloon, urging Marina into a gallop, making for an open gate that would take her through to the adjoining field that swelled up the opposite hill slope. With any luck she would keep them in sight as they drifted over the rise.

A band of trees stood along the skyline here, blocking her vision for a while until she pushed her way through to the clear slope of meadow that swept down into the next valley. She recognised where she was here. Along the bottom of the valley, beside a small brook, ran the lane that eventually reached the drive to Long Trovers. The balloon was hovering perhaps half a mile ahead of her, almost above the lane.

It was at this point that Isabella heard the smart rap of hoofs and became aware that some sort of vehicle was approaching down the lane. She could make out the heads of the driver and his man over the hedge-tops. At the same time she heard raucous halloos issuing from the balloon.

Looking up, startled, she saw that the occupants of the basket had also spotted the travellers, and her brothers were waving, and shouting jeering greetings. Perplexed, she looked back at the carriage.

She was just in time to see it suddenly lurch forward. The tiger on the back, who had been distracted, gazing up at the balloon, tumbled abruptly backwards and vanished from view. Meanwhile the carriage, the horses obviously crazed with fright at the sight and sounds of this monstrous thing in the sky above them, bolted into full view, and lurched drunkenly along the grass bank beside the track for some yards, reeling and bucking. The driver fell sharply backwards off his seat so Isabella had a clear vision of polished top boots waving skywards, then the entire contraption turned in an almost graceful curve, and tumbled into the brook.

Even as she urged Marina on down the slope Isabella was laughing. In that brief glimpse before the carriage turned, she had been almost certain she recognised it, and its occupant!

Before she reached the road she knew she was right. Lord Carlton Crue's most vicious tones cut saw-toothed through the air, blaspheming indiscriminately at balloons, balloonists, maniacs, criminal lunatics, assorted types of horseflesh, and Stoat. Isabella reined in Marina before she had been noticed, and stood quietly on the edge of the meadow surveying the scene, and laughing gently to herself.

One wheel had buckled under and broken in the accident, and the shaft nearest to it had snapped, so that the curricle lay on its side, tipping its contents, including Crue, into the ditch. The horses stood shivering in the mess of traces and snapped wood, mercifully unhurt, it seemed, while Crue struggled to heave himself up out of the glutinous mud and dense weeds that choked the brook at this point.

His stream of invective continued as unbroken as the flow of muddy water over his boots, increasingly now aimed at Stoat, who had yet to appear, and the varied possibilities of Stoat's parentage. Isabella listened to this unreined outburst with mixed interest and disgust. She wondered what Ruth would do if any harm had come to her new-found hero. Certainly it would do nothing to improve the atmosphere while Isabella was dressing!

It was with mixed feelings then that Isabella saw Stoat's unprepossessing figure come hobbling down the lane, back miserably hunched, and one hand holding the back of his head. He blinked dizzily, and steadied himself on the side of the toppled curricle before endeavouring to go to his master's assistance.

'Where the devil have you been, god-damned good-for-nothing, ale-sodden wastrel? Leave off holding your head like an ailing milkmaid and get me out of this dammed ditch. I swear I'll take my death of an ague. Come here, damn you, and give me your hand.'

As Stoat staggered forward Isabella could see the blood running in a sluggish trickle down the back of the man's neck and into his cravat.

'For shame on you, Crue,' she called, edging the mare through the hedge to the road. 'The man is far worse hurt than you are. Sit down on the bank, Stoat, until you are recovered. Lord Carlton is not yet so utterly decrepit that he cannot climb out of a ditch unattended.'

She enjoyed the outraged astonishment on his face. He remained quite speechless as he pulled himself out from the mud, but his expression became furious. She turned coolly away to where Stoat had readily obeyed her order, and collapsed in a half-swoon on the grass. He had obviously tumbled straight back on to his head when he fell from the curricle, and was still partly concussed. Isabella dismounted, hitched Marina to a branch, produced a handkerchief and soaked it carefully at the edge of the brook. Then she took it to Stoat.

'Hold this to the back of your head,' she said. 'It is all I have.'

She had no intention at all of nobly tearing bandages from her petticoats for Lord Carlton Crue or Stoat. Stoat took the wet linen with a wan, perplexed look.

'Leave mollycoddling that maundering milksop, and give me a hand to your horse, Isabella,' Crue demanded angrily. He was leaning heavily against the curricle, resting an obviously painful foot. 'I'll get back to the last village and order some men out here to clear the road and bring the horses back. Come here, damn you!'

This last as Isabella skipped smartly back to Marina and, using a sagging five-bar gate as mounting block, was back in the saddle in an instant. Crue, as he tried to catch her, stumbled heavily. He leaned back against the side of the curricle, his face mottled purple with fury.

'Damn you, Isabella. Give me that horse.'

'No! First, sir, I will not, as a matter of principle, respond to any man who speaks to me as you just have.' She had caught her breath now and had her response more controlled. Her tones were icily sarcastic. 'Secondly, I could hardly believe, if it were not *you* who spoke, that I *heard* your suggestion of abandoning me here on the road with no more escort than a man concussed! *Not* your most chivalrous idea, sir. Now, *my* proposal I find far more attractive.'

She was edging Marina back into the field as she spoke, keeping a wary watch on Crue, who appeared to be hoping for a chance to grab at the reins.

'I will ride back to Long Trovers, and send out a wagon and some of the men. You wait here and care for poor Stoat. I am sure you are all tender solicitude for the unfortunate man's welfare. If you wish for anything else, Widow Samson's cottage is no more than half a mile up the road. It is a poor place but she is a kindly soul. Do mention my name if you call. That will ensure her help!'

She shifted further into the meadow.

'Naturally I shall make all possible speed.'

She smiled sweetly, and set off up the field at a leisurely trot before Crue had gathered his wits to respond.

She looked back from the trees at the top of the slope. The balloon had disappeared from view. It had not been very high at any stage of the flight, hanging close over the tree tops, and Isabella suspected that the weight of three extra people to carry would almost certainly ensure a shorter flight. With a sudden surge of anxiety she wondered if they had yet landed, and if they had landed safely.

She was almost ready then to leave Lord Carlton Crue to his fate, and follow the course of the balloon, but she did not. She cantered steadily back to Long Trovers and, having organised some of the remaining men to go round with a pony and gig to collect the wounded, lead back the horses and arrange for the collection of the broken curricle, she went indoors to seek out Lady Kintrove and warn her of the imminent arrival of the two wounded.

That lady was not keen to hear that she was to entertain Carlton Crue, but she was interested.

'He was on his way to visit you?'

'Presumably. I didn't care to ask.'

'How do you feel about his staying here? Won't you find it very awkward?'

Isabella shrugged.

'Possibly. But he can hardly drag me screaming to the church door, can he? If nothing else, Bess would trip him up! No. I have an increased disgust for Lord Carlton Crue, but I no longer fear him. I will not marry him. That is a fact both he and my father will have to learn to accept. I will seek an interview with him tomorrow, and tell him as much.'

She tossed her head.

Lady Kintrove regarded her, head on one side.

'Hmm. Well, I will have a room made up down in the west wing, well out of your way. And we had better send out for Dr Millthorpe. *And* warn Mrs Stoke. Excuse me, will you, dear? Thank heavens that affected Whyle boy didn't stay. He would have been the final straw this afternoon. I hope those balloonists are safe!'

She hurried away in the direction of the kitchens, and Isabella retired to her room, curling up with a book in the window seat, where she could watch for any arrivals.

As the afternoon drew on towards early evening she watched the gig arrive back carrying an irate Lord Carlton beside his white-faced man. They were met by Ruth running frantically out to the stable yard, wringing her hands in anguish. Isabella glimpsed her supporting Stoat as he made his way indoors. Crue made his way in at the main door with the aid of two silver-topped walking-sticks, solemnly carried out to him by Hopkins. He hobbled indoors, face thunderous. Isabella remained in her room.

A little later a smart trap arrived, and a thin, gaunt cadaver of a man climbed ominously down carrying a large black bag. Obviously the doctor. Isabella did not stir.

It was much later, when she was chewing anxiously on her knuckles and making not even a pretence of reading, that Old Bill nursed the burdened trap down the drive towards the house. A glance told Isabella that they were all alive, cramped into the trap and steadying the basket between them. With a huge sigh of more relief than she had known she could feel, she picked up her skirts and ran down the corridors, down the great staircase, and outside to meet them.

Old Bill pulled the trap up before her and she stared up at them, anxiety dissolving into impatience.

'Well, don't keep me in suspense! What happened? Where have you been? Is anyone hurt? And did you see what you did to Lord Carlton Crue?'

Her brothers leapt down, both laughing and trying to out-talk each other, shouting to be heard. They were filthy, covered in mud, and smears of green lichen. The men, too, now she came to look at them. She caught Alladay's eye, and, without thinking, she smiled.

'Boys! Inside, and report to Nurse Pusey for baths. Now!'

There were groans, but he had his tutorish look in his eye, and they went.

'Algie is our only casualty,' Alladay said. He jumped down and took her hand briefly. 'I am sorry if you were concerned. We had the misfortune to descend in a tree at some distance from the nearest lane. Is that Dr Millthorpe's trap? I thought so! Surely you were not *that* concerned yet? But it is just as well. Algie has a badly sprained ankle. He was less than nimble descending the oak, though what he lacked in agility he made up for in speed! I never saw anyone come down a tree so fast since I did my trick down that walnut!'

'If you have quite finished amusing Miss Larkham with my misfortunes, Tony,' came Algie's aggrieved tones from the trap, 'I would appreciate a little assistance in hobbling my way to the saw-bones.'

Alladay grinned.

'You'll have to soothe his savage breast, Isabella. I think he is going to need it.'

'Wait until you see who else is hobbling around Long Trovers,' Isabella replied with grim amusement. 'We might all need our savage breasts soothed before long!'

He raised an eyebrow.

'Even a pumpkin?'

'Even a pumpkin,' she said.

Dinner was not an easy meal that night. Algie and Lord Carlton Crue both insisted on hobbling down to eat, despite offers to send their meals to their rooms, pressing offers in the case of Crue. Dr Millthorpe had pronounced Algie to be suffering from a serious sprain, and had recommended complete rest, a recommendation Algie had no intention of obeying. Crue, in the doctor's opinion, had suffered only severe bruising, and had left the outraged Crue with more instructions on the care of Stoat than on the care of himself. Stoat, of course, was enjoying the tender attentions of Ruth, who probably made up in good intentions what she lacked in nursing skill.

The realisation that the balloon which had caused the accident had originated from Long Trovers did nothing to improve Lord Carlton Crue's uncertain temper. Perversely, this did not encourage him to remain aloof from the family he had professed to despise, and he regarded Alladay with such open hostility throughout the meal that it was only through some skilful verbal manoeuvering by Lady Kintrove, who was, Isabella rightly suspected, enjoying the whole situation, that an outright clash was avoided.

Isabella was not enjoying it. She could only be thankful that she was seated as far as possible from Crue, and almost as far from Alladay.

She concentrated on eliciting from Algie all his feelings about the balloon flight, from the exhilaration of flying to the unhappy landing when they had dragged and tangled in a tall oak that grew in a field full of frisky young bullocks. He made a good story of the jolting tumble into the branches, himself flung clear of the basket and only saving himself by hanging on to the ropes of the balloon. He described how he had managed to descend much of the way down clinging to the ropes like a monkey, then had fallen, sliding and bouncing over the last branches into the clustered bullocks beneath, which had scattered, stampeding wildly over the field, leaving only their typical, odorous reminders for him to land in!

The other aeronauts had managed to climb from the basket into the stronger branches, and make a safe way down, but Alladay had apparently freed the basket and flung it tumbling down before coming to earth himself.

Isabella gave the story all the attention it merited, and more. She could hear in the background Crue's silky sarcasms and subtle, hinted insults. So disdainful was he of his rescuers that he could not even afford the Kintroves civility for an evening. Isabella blushed to hear him, with his arrogant assumptions that they were too stupid to understand. She wondered how long Alladay, who under his mother's quizzical eye was responding with arctic politeness, would contain his temper, and she longed fervently for the time when she could insist to Crue that she would have nothing more to do with him.

To her immediate relief he did retire to his room after the meal, replying, to her chilly request for an interview with him on the morrow, that he had every intention of speaking to her at length in the morning.

Everyone relaxed as he departed.

'Well,' said Lady Kintrove briskly, 'if you will excuse us both, Wilfred wishes me to help him in the library.'

Later, Alladay and Algie joined Isabella in the drawing-room. The evening was chilly after the succession of cool days, and a welcome fire had been lit. Isabella had been sitting alone, idly turning over cards in a game of patience.

They came over and sat down by her. Their conversation seemed oddly interrupted, and Alladay was glowering furiously, his hazel eyes shadowed dark in the candlelight. He sat, aggressively silent, staring at his fists clenched between his knees. Algie caught Isabella's querying look, and shrugged, a touch shame-faced. Isabella was suddenly certain that they had been sitting long over the port and discussing, in no favourable terms, Lord Carlton Crue. Algie shook his head slightly, warningly, then pointed helpfully to a card she might wish to move.

'Just tell me, Isabella,' Alladay burst out after some minutes, looking fiercely up at her, 'what in God's name possessed you to accept an offer of marriage from that man?'

Algie looked up, horrified.

'No, Tony, really, old man! It's not on. You can't ask a lady a question like that. Lady's privilege! Choose whom she likes.'

Alladay waved him aside.

'Be quiet, Algie.' He turned angrily back to Isabella. 'Well, Isabella? What was it? Money? Title? His irresistible charm? Convince me!'

Algie looked, agonised, at Isabella.

'You don't have to answer,' he said, with a wary glance at his friend. 'Over-generous with the port! A long and anxious day. Worried about those brothers of yours. Tiresome meal. He's not himself, you know!'

'For God's sake, Carstairs, will you be quiet?'

Alladay looked ready to vent the rage he could not expend on Crue upon radically re-arranging Algie's features.

'It is all right, Algie,' Isabella said, patting his arm reassuringly. 'I don't mind telling you. Either of you.' She gave Alladay a cool look. 'Because I never did!'

'What on earth do you mean?'

She ignored Alladay's outburst and continued to talk to Algie, who looked acutely embarrassed. 'I have never accepted an offer of marriage. Lord Carlton Crue has never asked me to marry him!'

'Then why...? How are you engaged?'

Algie's tones were tentative. He still could not feel that this was a proper subject for discussion.

She sighed, and gave a brief résumé of that early summer morning's meeting with her father. She glared defiantly at Alladay when she mentioned Harry's name, but he seemed uninterested.

'What you are saying,' Alladay concluded slowly, his rage seeming to drain away as his interest grew, 'is that Crue never asked you to marry him! You never accepted, and,' he glanced down at her hand, 'he has never given you, and you have never accepted, a ring or other token as a symbol of your betrothal!'

'That is right,' Isabella said bitterly. 'He has never even bothered to give me a ring.'

'Then you are not engaged!'

He sat back as if he had just stated a fact so obvious that it needed no further discussion. Isabella blinked.

'What?'

He turned to her with exaggerated patience.

'How can you be? You have undertaken no commitment, nor been asked to do so. No commitment has been made. You are not engaged!'

A huge grin spread across his face.

Algie was frowning, perplexed.

'But,' Isabella began, 'my father arranged the engagement. He announced it. It must exist!'

'*He* may feel bound by it,' Alladay said, 'but you don't. And you can tell Crue as much when you see him tomorrow. No need to wait for any letter from your father. Do you realise,' he continued, with a dreamy, happy look, 'that I could send a notice to the *Morning Post* tomorrow announcing Algie's engagement to... to Clorette, and it would be just as binding as the notice your father sent in.'

'Clorette? *I've* no intention of getting spliced. Not yet awhile.' Algie frowned. 'Whoever has a name like Clorette? Doesn't sound quite the thing.'

Algie was bemused, and could see no reason why Alladay and Isabella should both be laughing at his expense.

'Oh, no,' Isabella quibbled to Alladay. 'At least *Crue* had agreed to the announcement, even if I had not. It would not be the same!'

'Perhaps,' Alladay responded solemnly. 'But it's even money old Algie wouldn't fight about it once he saw her!'

'Especially not if she winked!' Isabella added, and to Algie's indignation they both began to laugh again.

'If you have all had your fun,' he said, resigned, 'I'll be taking my ankle up to bed. Some of us were wounded in this foolhardy expedition, you know!'

Instantly Isabella was all sympathy.

'I will give you a hand on the stairs,' she said quickly. 'I was about to retire myself.'

For some reason she was reluctant to analyse she did not wish to remain with Lord Alladay. He was looking far too cheerful.

CHAPTER FOURTEEN

'AND to think of dragging him off when he still looks so poorly! I was shocked at Lord Carlton Crue. I tell you truly, it's not what I expected of him. But, "leaving this morning," he says. Poor Stoat! You should see the size of the lump on his head. And all the fault of that wicked, unnatural contraption. I knew no good would come of it! You in those clothes! Now this accident! If the good Lord had meant us to fly he would have given us wings.'

Isabella hid further under the covers to escape the tirade. She had been given a detailed account of every bump, cut and bruise suffered by Stoat while she was undressing the previous evening. She wished to hear no more of him. Ruth was becoming altogether too opinionated. The only welcome news was that Crue was truly leaving. She pushed her head out, stopped Ruth in mid-sentence, and asked her to convey a request to Lord Carlton that she would see him in the green room at ten o'clock.

She let him wait until a quarter past before going down. She was busy finishing two letters which appeared to give her a grim pleasure.

She had taken especial trouble over dressing, selecting a cool, unadorned cream muslin with a long, slender line, and piling her hair up high on her head. Ruth looked pleased and hopeful as her mistress completed her preparations, and for opposite reasons Isabella also surveyed her reflection with satisfaction. She had aimed to look tall, aloof and sophisticated. She wanted all possible courage for this interview.

He turned towards her as she entered. He had been standing by the window, staring moodily out, his heavy black hair falling on to his forehead, his swarthy face sombre.

'Good morning, Lord Carlton.'

He raised his eyebrows, and stared at her appraisingly.

'Very nice, Isabella,' he drawled. 'You have been studying the fashion plates I left with you, I see. And to great benefit. The result is charming. Far more what I expect of my wife.'

Crue had arrived in the green room determined to reach a definite agreement with Isabella. He was irritably aware that the course of his engagement was not running as smoothly as he had expected, that he would need to make an unwelcome effort to retrieve the effects of the disastrous encounter in Worthing, and that Isabella was showing surprising tendencies to resist being either cajoled or bullied into unquestioning acquiescence. She was far removed from the pretty, obedient little doll he had been led to expect. He felt aggrieved. Horatio Larkham had already been abroad longer than he had expected, and Crue had his own reasons for wishing the marriage to go ahead as soon as possible. Waving a dismissive hand to quell Isabella as she drew a deep breath to speak, he began again, keeping his voice low, understanding, seductive.

'I am glad we have at last a chance to speak privately, Isabella. Our engagement has, I am sure you will agree, gone on long enough. Too long. Your father is away longer than I expected. Why should we wait? We have his consent. Dearest Isabella! I would like to continue with our wedding in his absence. Our relationship has suffered from a regrettable misunderstanding, and I am quite certain...' he forced a slow and intimate smile, usually a slayer of ladies' hearts, then frowned as Isabella recoiled '...that our marital delights would reduce this to no more than a distant memory. It would give me very great pleasure if the ceremony could take place as soon as possible.'

He paused, and moved towards her, one hand outstretched, while the other leant heavily on a malacca cane. He limped awkwardly, and gave a self-deprecating smile, certain of its appeal.

Isabella regarded him coldly. It seemed quite extraordinary now that she should ever have been so confused as to think this ageing libertine attractive. She noted the pocked cheeks, the sagging skin under his eyes and chin, the cynical look. She took an involuntary step backwards before standing firm to say her piece. The words she must say had been running in her head for half the night, but still it was not easy.

She tilted up her chin and looked him in the eye.

'You are right, Lord Carlton, and I agree absolutely, that our engagement has gone on long enough.'

A satisfied smile lit his face, and she frowned and shook her head slightly as she continued.

'However, I see a different end to our relationship. I wish to terminate this mockery of an engagement as from this morning!'

'Good God, Isabella——'

'Let me finish, if you please, sir.' Her voice rose as she pressed on, determined. 'I would like to point out for your notice that at no point in our regrettable association have you asked me to marry you. Not only have you not asked this, but I have not replied. I have never, at any time, accepted an offer from you. Furthermore, you have never given me a ring to confirm our relationship, a fact that I only regret because it now deprives me of the opportunity of flinging it back at you.'

His unguarded face was murderous as he glared at her with narrowed eyes, but she carried on, desperate to finish this once and for all.

'In view of these facts you will not, perhaps, be surprised to hear that I do not now, and truly never have, considered myself engaged to you. Whatever arrangement you made with my father omitted any consultation with me. I will not marry you, Lord Carlton, not now, or ever. I have written to inform my father of that fact. I have also written a letter to the *Morning Post* announcing that our engagement is terminated.'

He was rigid with rage, his face twisted and ugly.

'You have gone too far, Isabella. You cannot do this.'

He stamped his foot, and winced. He drew breath and made an effort to control himself. When he spoke again he was calmer.

'You are in no position to defy your father's wishes. He can dispose of you as he sees fit. That is his right. Only think of what this connection means to him. And it was unforgivable to send an announcement to the *Post* before we had even spoken.'

'Isn't it odd?' Isabella remarked. 'That is precisely what I felt when my father announced the engagement in just such a way. What a pity he is the other side of Europe. Now he cannot make his views known. And as for what the connection means to him, or to you for that matter, no one has ever informed me, so I am unlikely to concern myself over the issue!'

Crue looked at her sharply.

'So he *still* hasn't told you.'

'Told me what?'

He suddenly appeared more relaxed.

'How typical of Horatio. Couldn't let even word of it slip away from him! Well, well.'

'I don't know what you are talking about!'

'No, Isabella. I don't believe you do. Amusing, in the circumstances.' He glanced around the room. 'Ah, well. You have not, I think, seen the last of me, dear girl. Engagements have been interrupted before. Lovers' tiffs are common, after all, and you cannot marry where you please, without your family's consent. Once your father returns we shall speak again.' He smiled at her. 'Shall we have a parting kiss, until that time?'

Isabella hastened to the bell pull, and tugged it hard, hoping Hopkins was close by. She was astounded by Crue's reaction. He hardly seemed to take her announcement seriously. Like her father, he appeared to treat her views as utterly unimportant.

'I am quite serious, Lord Carlton,' she said. 'I will never marry you. I would rather die.'

Hopkins, opening the door immediately, for he had been loitering anxiously in the corridor, allowed his discreetly bland expression to mask his whole-hearted approval of this melodramatic pronouncement.

'You rang, Miss Larkham?'

'Lord Carlton Crue is leaving now, Hopkins.'

'Thank you, miss. His Lordship's hired coach has arrived and is awaiting his convenience.'

Hopkins eyed Crue, and stood stolidly holding open the door, waiting for him to leave, denying him the chance of a final, private word.

'When your father returns, make no mistake, we will speak again.'

Delivered in a confident undertone, this was all he could content himself with, and he limped out.

Isabella, deflated and puzzled, stood by the door watching him make his slow progress down the corridor to the main hall. With a little lurch of her heart she saw Alladay beyond him, waiting to see him off the premises. She heard them speak, and ducked back into the green room, where she could not hear. Alladay, she knew, would have seen her letters, to her father and to the *Morning Post*, waiting to be franked. He would know what she had done.

Suddenly confused, she felt she had to get away. She slipped quietly up to her room, collected Bess, her cushion and her sketching equipment, and made her way out of a side door into the gardens, and down to a quiet, secluded spot on the lakeside among the shrubs, with a tree-framed vista of the water and the hills beyond. She remained there sketching until it was time to take luncheon, and convinced herself that she was pleased she had not been interrupted. She had wanted the time alone.

She was surprised when only Lady Kintrove and herself appeared to sample Mrs Stoke's midday offerings.

'Your brothers have taken a picnic out on their ponies, and Wilfred asked for his meal to be taken up to the copse, as the weather is so much better today,' Lady

Kintrove replied in answer to Isabella's query. 'Anthony offered to take it up to him, and took a meal for himself as well.' She glanced at Isabella, who was concentrating on demolishing a chicken leg. 'He seemed...' she paused '...perturbed, perhaps?'

She waited but Isabella made no response.

'Lord Carlton Crue left us this morning, I notice,' she said, neutrally.

'Yes.' Isabella looked up at Lady Kintrove. 'I told him I would not marry him.' She gave a small, bewildered shrug. 'He was not pleased...but he hardly seemed to take what I said seriously! Just said I could do nothing without my family's permission. That he would speak to my father when he returned.'

'How odd. Do you have any other family besides your father?' Lady Kintrove asked, curiously.

'I know of none but the most distant cousins on my mother's side. She was an only child, and both her parents are long dead. We have cut all contact with my father's family.'

She looked up into Lady Kintrove's kindly face, then took a deep breath and spoke hurriedly.

'My father is bitterly ashamed of them because they are a working family who made a sudden fortune in cotton manufacturing in Lancashire. His parents wanted the best for him, and paid for expensive schooling. Now he is making his way in the diplomatic service, and pretends none of them exist. But I believe my grandmother is still alive, and my uncle who now manages the factories. I have never been told whether there are cousins.'

She paused, half expecting, and dreading, the look of disdain that crossed Lady Kintrove's aristocratic features. She flushed uncomfortably. Had her father been right to keep the connection hidden? Would these people now despise her?

'What a fool your father must be,' Lady Kintrove was saying briskly. 'Family is so important. It is a dreadful thing to set yourself apart from them. No social advancement can be worth such a rift, and no true friend would judge on ancestry alone. One of these unforgivable social conventions. I really do not hold with people who take such things seriously. What a shame for you, my dear. I should write to your grandmother, if I were you. If you leave it too long it may be too late, and you would always regret it, I am sure.'

Isabella managed a shaky laugh of relief. She should have known!

'I believe you are right,' she said. 'I would like to do that. I have always been curious.'

'Of course you have. It's only natural. Now, I have so much to do in the garden, I'm afraid that you must excuse me.'

'In which direction did Lord Alladay go?' Isabella asked casually.

'Anthony? Oh, he took my spade again! Over to the old quarry beyond the copse, I should guess, though he didn't say. It makes a pleasant walk,' she said.

'Thank you,' said Isabella.

Alladay had managed to see Crue out with the same arctic politeness that had carried him through the previous night's meal.

'I trust your leg will soon be recovered,' he said, as he walked with Crue to the main door.

Crue paused, leaning on his cane, and gave a deliberate, contemptuous look at Alladay.

'A pity I can't say the same to you,' he said with a small smile.

Alladay's fists clenched, knowing as well as Crue that he could not allow himself the pleasure of hitting his antagonist, injured as he was.

'I do not believe,' Alladay said coldly, 'that we will have any occasion to renew our acquaintance. Nor do I pretend that you will ever be welcome at Long Trovers. Goodbye, Crue. Your carriage is waiting.'

'Oh, the game is not over yet, young D'Estine. And don't forget, you are only a convenient pawn. When Horatio Larkham comes back Isabella will return to London, and you will be moved right off the board. *You* may not see me again. But Isabella will! As for returning here, who would wish to? Goodbye, sir.'

He made his way out to his hired carriage, where Stoat, pale and bandaged, sat at the back, and swung himself up. Alladay turned away, too angry and disturbed to watch him go. He very much wanted to talk to Isabella.

Alladay went directly to the green room, expecting to find Isabella waiting for him there. He had seen the letters she had written, and had guessed at their contents. He knew she had had an interview with Crue. Surely she would wish to talk with him now? The depth of his disappointment when she was not there, eagerly awaiting him, startled him. He stared about the room in bewilderment, uncertain what to do.

'I believe Miss Larkham went up to her room,' Hopkins quietly offered from behind him.

Alladay swung round, feeling foolish.

'Thank you, Hopkins,' he said with a smile.

Of course she would want to retire to the privacy of her room after the strain of such an interview. He wondered whether she would want him to intrude immediately, but he knew he could not wait. The sight of those letters had seemed decisive. The knowledge that she must have taken so drastic a decision, in addition to another announcement he had seen in the *Morning Post*, had sent all his hopes leaping up like the balloon released from its moorings. He hoped she had not seen that other announcement yet, however. He wanted to speak to her first.

He hurried up to her room, and knocked. There was no reply. He knocked again, waiting impatiently, then looked in. The room was empty. He wandered inside, and walked up and down, lightly touching things that were hers. He picked up her delicate silver-backed hairbrush from among the things on her dressing-table, tapping it thoughtfully in the palm of his hand. Then, with a bleak look around the deserted room he put it slowly down again. Realisation swept over him, and a great depression seized him, deflating all his hopes.

She had gone. She was not looking for him, and she was not waiting for him. He had been thinking like a fool. She was avoiding him. Whatever message those letters held, it seemed he had been wrong. It was not a message for him. He had thought that so much had grown between them that now even she could no longer deny it. Obviously, he had been wrong, and the pain of that realisation shook him. But he did not want her hurt. He went downstairs, took the most recent copy of the *Morning Post* and placed it under a pile of papers in his office, then went to change into his old clothes. He had no wish to remain any longer in the house.

He ate his bread and ham leaning against a bank at the top of the small quarry. Throughout the day the weather had been brightening, and now the sun was warm. He took off his jacket, loosened his cravat, and leaned back to get the sun on his face. The spade was beside him, but he felt no incentive to take it up. He knew himself for a fool.

Each time he closed his eyes his thoughts returned to Isabella. Isabella as a gauche fifteen-year-old, lonely and unhappy, when he had first taken up his post and had tried to befriend her. She had been so jealous of his closeness with her brothers that she had resisted all offers of friendship, arrogantly scorning him, pitting her wits against him, arguing, and contradicting.

But he remembered her fiercely supporting a school-friend wrongly accused of stealing, a spitfire of loyalty regardless of her own reputation, and later disobeying her father to visit another friend who had left the school when her family faced financial ruin. He had forgotten that determined streak in her. He should not have been so surprised when she began to champion his poorer tenants!

He remembered Isabella discovering her beauty, attempting, maddeningly, to flirt with him, then scorning him and spreading her wings as she tasted social success. For years now she had always absorbed some corner of his mind. She had enraged him, irritated him, amused him, worried him, infuriated him. But always fascinated him. She had ignored him, tormented him, despised him. And he had never allowed her to read any expression beyond cool amusement on his face. He had never believed it possible that their paths should be permanently entangled, but he had never managed to disentangle her from his thoughts.

It was not that he had always known he loved her. Far from it! But he had always known she was, by some quirk of fate, inextricably involved in his life. That morning's interview, when he had been summoned by Mr Larkham and told he was to take Miss Larkham as well as her brothers to his home for the summer, had left him reluctant, but unsurprised. It was a trick of the inevitable.

Now, he knew he loved her, and she did not care. Could she truly still believe that her infatuation with Harry Exton was true love? Probably she could not shake off the vision of Mr D'Estine, the despised, crippled tutor. And what had he ever offered her but honesty and arguments? He could not manage the seductive talk of a man like Crue, or Exton's ungainly poetry. Alladay's confidence in his new position, his new self, was still fragile. He did not assume himself to be attractive. He gave a small groan and sat forward, elbows resting on his knees, face buried in his hands. He had made such a foolish, unforgivable mess of kissing her, then blundered absurdly over telling her that he loved her. He was enveloped in black despair.

It was Bess's cold damp nose nudging into his face that made him look up. Isabella was standing before him, regarding him uncertainly. He had heard nothing of their approach, and following the intensity of his thoughts it was almost as if he had conjured her there. He stared up at her, speechless. In her delicate cream dress, her hair piled up to show the long slender line of her neck, she seemed as ethereal and improbable as a dryad stepping out from one of the beech trees behind her.

'I am sorry,' she said doubtfully. 'I did not mean to intrude.'

With an uncertain glance back at him, she turned to go.

'Please, Isabella. Please wait. I am sorry. I was startled.'

He jumped to his feet and went over to where she stood.

'You were the last person I expected to see here.'

'I was looking for you,' she said. She looked up at him, and the tentative, hopeful, wide blue gaze caused his heart to somersault disconcertingly. 'I wanted to talk to you.'

He steadied himself.

'What about?' he asked quietly.

She walked over to the bank where he had been sitting, and sat down, gesturing to him to come and sit beside her. He settled himself carefully at a little distance from her. He found it difficult to breathe steadily, and took a deep breath.

'I spoke to Lord Carlton Crue this morning,' she began.

Isabella looked sideways at him. He was staring not at her, but down at his clasped hands. He had pushed back his shirt-sleeves, and she could see the sunlight glinting on the fine golden hairs of his forearm, the movement of the muscle as he shifted and interlaced his fingers. Long, strong, fine-boned fingers. His hair was ruffled into short curls of bright golden, the sunlight sifting them with shadow. She longed suddenly to reach out and touch him, but his eyes were hooded, and she could not read his expression. She forced herself to look away, and gaze across the open grass to the beech trees.

In neutral tones she gave him as faithful an account of the interview as she could recall, but turned towards him in impassioned bewilderment as she finished.

'He seemed so unconcerned at the end. As if he did not believe me, or that what I said was irrelevant. As if he believed that as soon as my father returns I will marry him anyway. I told him I would not. And that I have sent an announcement of the fact to both my father and the *Morning Post*. It was as if none of that really mattered.' She shivered, and reached a tentative hand towards him. 'I cannot marry him. Truly, I would rather die.'

He clenched his fists tight together, and gritted his teeth against the words, knowing he should not say them, but somehow they said themselves anyway.

'Marry me, Isabella.'

There was the awful silence he had expected, and he was drawing breath to utter a dreary, despairing apology, when she spoke in a hesitant, small voice, with a despair to match his own. 'But you have to marry a fortune!'

He knew he was going to make a mess of this. He had always had some vague romantic idea that he would declare his love in an elegant drawing-room, and on one knee. Now he glared at the ground between his feet and the words burst out impassioned, unthought.

'Yes, Isabella, I should marry a fortune. Have I not told myself often enough? Haven't you told me? Endlessly! I owe it to my family, and to the estate. I know! But I cannot do it. I cannot! Not marry some squint-eyed, chattering female for the sake of her bulging coffers. I could not marry where I do not love. And it is *you* that I love. You, Isabella! Don't ask me why! I don't know. I know it is not what you wanted. Good grief, you have told me what you think of me often enough! And, yes, it is true that you infuriate me, exasperate me, drive me to threats of violence even, but Isabella, I cannot live without you!'

He drew a long, shaking breath.

'Except for the certainty that you will treat this offer with the contempt you will doubtless feel it deserves, I would not be saying this. For your sake I should not. I know that. You deserve better than I can offer. You'd get no luxuries here. It is going to be a long hard struggle to get this estate productive. There is only the empty title. But if the alternative is Carlton Crue, then, by God, at least I offer you loyalty, sincerity and love.'

He stopped abruptly, and dropped his head into his hands. What an appalling mess he had made of it all. He waited for her scorn.

'Anthony?'

He quivered, and raised his head.

'You *truly* could not marry a fortune? Not even Sarah?'

'No one but you,' he said bleakly, staring out at the trees.

She reached a small, tentative hand across and laid it on his. Startled, he glanced at her face. It was lit by a reluctant smile.

'I didn't realise for weeks that I loved you,' she murmured. 'How *could* I believe such an absurdity? By the time I knew it I could not *allow* it to be true. *I* cannot bring you the fortune you need. I tried so hard to ignore you, to find you somebody else, to fix my thoughts on Harry, and to concentrate on hating you like I always have! But Harry has faded to less than a memory. I cannot even conjure his face in my mind!' She looked down. 'I know it is ridiculous after all those years of despising each other, but when I think of love, it is your face that I see.'

Alladay scrambled shakily to his feet, unable to remain still, and, taking her hand, pulled her up to stand before him. He rested his hands lightly on her shoulders as if he could not believe he was touching her.

'Isabella,' he said. 'We have agreed it is absurd but—will you marry me?'

'I shouldn't,' she hesitated.

'We have also agreed on that.' He gave a small smile. 'But will you anyway?'

'Yes,' she said.

And they stared at each other with such dazzled surprise that she did not know whether they were laughing or crying when he pulled her into his arms.

CHAPTER FIFTEEN

IT WAS Bess who eventually brought them back to earth, nudging between them with her nose, indignant at being so long ignored. They drew gently apart, staring at each other, still dizzy with startled delight.

Isabella leant to stroke the old dog's head. Nothing, she thought, nothing had prepared her for what she had felt. Not even her flight in the balloon! She flushed as she looked at him and smiled, wanting his kisses again.

'Anthony,' she said.

He was bending, picking a length of grass, and turned to look up at her with a smile that made her heart leap.

'Just practising,' she said demurely.

He laughed. He was twisting the grass into a tiny loop.

'Come,' he said. 'Give me your hand!'

He took her left hand, raised it to his lips with a hint of self-mockery, then pushed the ring of grass gently on to her third finger.

'There is a traditional family ring at the house that I will formally offer you,' he said. 'But I don't want you to ever be able to say that *I* do not plight my troth with a ring!'

Oh, Anthony!' she said, putting her face up to kiss him again, and Bess heaved a deep, reproachful sigh and collapsed on their feet.

It was later that Isabella drew his attention to the neglected spade, and the piles of soft earth that pocked the side of the bank.

'Is it true?' she asked. '*Do* you come searching for treasure?'

He gave a shame-faced shrug and smiled.

'You are free to mock,' he said. 'It is certainly half true.'

'What do you mean?'

He sighed.

'Do you want the story from the beginning?'

'But of course! I only know what Ruth has told me, and you know what she is like for gossip. Sit and tell me.'

She perched back on the bank. The grass was smooth-cropped and the mound behind them was dotted with rabbit holes. Beyond where she sat the edge of a small quarry tumbled down to a tangle of brambles at the bottom. The air was still and warm, and pigeons cooed softly in the beech trees. She patted the grass beside her, and this time he sat close, and she rested her head against his shoulder.

'Well, I expect she gave you an accurate enough idea of the stories they tell,' he began. 'About the ancient chieftain? And the poor woman who burned to death in the old tower? And how when the Kintroves are in real need then treasure will be found?'

Isabella nodded. 'Yes, she told me all that.'

'We boys grew up on those stories, of course, and Jasper was always coming up with new plans to discover the hidden hoard. The first real clue came when we were here rabbiting. This,' he gestured behind them at the bank, 'was always the best warren. We came here often. One day Bardolph's favourite ferret stayed down and started to gorge on a rabbit she had caught. Wouldn't come up at all. Jasper wanted to go home and leave her, but Bardolph insisted we stay and dig her out. He had called her Boudicea and he loved her!

'It took us hours until we found her, but by the time we did we were not digging for the ferret, we were digging for the coins we were finding in the burrows. They were old enough for us to believe we had found something important. Marked "Carolus" mostly, we assumed they were from the reign of King Charles I. They were scattered, as if somewhere there was a cache that the rabbits had dug into, thus spreading the money through the warren.

'We never found any hoard, and I don't suppose I will now. I doubt it was ever anything of importance. But this has become a place I come to when I want to escape, to think, to remember... Then things seem easier if I stop thinking and just throw my frustrations into digging, and of course—there is always that niggle of hope!'

He shrugged again, and grinned at her. 'There, now you can laugh. I told you it was foolish.'

'No! It is not foolish at all!' Her face was alight with interest as she raised her head from his shoulder and took his hand in hers. 'It is exciting! Maybe there really is a hoard here! Perhaps from the Civil War? It would be right, wouldn't it? Maybe that was the ancestor who was burned! Was it really in the tower? Is that how it became a ruin? Oh, Anthony! If only we could find the hoard all our problems would be solved. It would not matter that you want to marry me and not an heiress. And only think. The legend tells that the treasure will be found when the family are in most need. You can hardly be in greater need than you are. Now is the time to hunt our hardest. Why don't we dig?'

She jumped to her feet and pulled at his hand, impatient to begin, as if this was an afternoon for miracles and she could not be disappointed.

'Where did you find the coins? Show me!'

'Could it be, Bess,' Alladay murmured in a deliberate aside, 'that I am shackling myself to a slave-driver? Wouldn't you think she might be content to sit and listen as I whisper sweet nothings in her ear? But no! She is only after my fortune!'

'Idiot,' she responded, her mind already engrossed in the problem of where best to dig. She heaved up the heavy spade and began to shovel at a pile of soil.

'Stop, Isabella! I surrender! I will dig! Don't spoil that dress, I love to see you wearing it. Anyway, that is a pile of waste I have already sifted through. Look. Over there is an old garden sieve that I keep for examining what I have dug. I'll dig, you sift!'

She laughed, gave him the spade, and ran to fetch the old wooden sieve.

They worked contentedly for some time, digging, sifting, pouncing on likely shapes in the earth, and groaning disappointedly when they were revealed as pebbles. Occasionally as they stood close together to study their finds they would find themselves distracted, and the unrewarding stones would be dropped forgotten to the ground as they discovered more rewarding things about each other.

The clouds had rolled back over the blue skies before they found their first coin. Isabella was shivering as she excitedly rubbed the earth from it. A sharp, cold wind had sprung up.

'We should get back,' Alladay said.

'Wait! I want to see what it says. This is the first treasure I have ever discovered!'

'Use my handkerchief to clean it,' he said resignedly, and watched her face with amusement and delight as she unselfconsciously spat on his handkerchief and rubbed eagerly at her find.

'I do believe it is from the time of King Charles,' she said, turning the coin to catch the best of the light. 'Look, CAROLUS. A round this side of the head, and CAROLO on the other. But the date is 1674. That is the second Charles. Too late for our idea of a hoard hidden during the Civil War. It is not gold. See how thin it is. Oh, look! I do believe it is only a farthing!'

She turned to hold it out to him, laughing and shivering, as the first heavy drops of rain began to fall, and in the distance they heard a full rumble of thunder.

'Bring it with you,' he said, 'and run! We are going to get drenched!'

He grabbed the spade in one hand, and clasped her hand tightly in his other, as they ran for the path through the beech trees towards the house.

'Do you want to stop and find shelter?' he shouted, pulling her along. There was another, louder, burst of thunder.

'Where?'

They skidded to a halt at the edge of the trees, and he swung her, laughing, into his arms, and looked down at her. She was panting, her face smeared with mud, and as she gazed up at him a great drip of rain rolled off the leaves above them and landed on her nose. She giggled, licking at the splashes, and he had to kiss her.

'We are getting exceedingly wet,' she remarked in surprise, some time later. 'If we ran along in the lee of this hedge, we might find some shelter beside your father's monument.'

He flung his jacket over her head to protect her, but she laughed and pushed it back on to her shoulders, shaking her hair out of her eyes. By the time they reached the copse they were both soaked, hair plastered to their heads, raindrops in streaming tears down their faces. Alladay's white linen shirt clung against his skin.

They rounded the side of the monument breathless, seeking shelter, and had leant gasping back against the stones of the wall before they realised they were not alone. Lord Kintrove was sitting disconsolately in his wheelbarrow, rain washing over him, rubbing at his arm. A simultaneous burst of lightning and thunder ripped aside the shadows and stunned them with clamour, leaving the picture of the old man sharp printed on their minds in the moments of deaf blindness that followed.

Then he was nodding at them through the rain.

'I fell from my ladder,' he said sadly. 'Only bruises, I think, but I believe I ought to get back. Clara will be wondering where I've got to. She does worry so. She won't be pleased that I was caught in this storm.'

Isabella ran over to him.

'Can you walk? We can help you. We are all so wet there can be no further harm from walking down the field, but much from waiting here in the cold. Will you walk down with us?'

Alladay half lifted his father to his feet, and with one of them on either side of the old man they ventured to the edge of the copse. The rain beyond was falling as solid as a wall. Alladay looked across at Isabella. He raised a querying eyebrow and, at her resigned nod, he smiled. After his smile no amount of cold or rain seemed important.

'Come on,' she said.

They plunged down towards the house, fighting through the battering of the water as if it were a live enemy snatching at their slipping feet, blinding their eyes and pouring into their open mouths. The old man did his best, but for much of the time it felt to Isabella as if they carried him between them.

Suddenly it was clear they had been spotted from the house. The great front door swung wide and men hurried out into the storm with umbrellas up. Someone took Lord Kintrove from Isabella's grip and helped him onwards. Alladay held a vast black umbrella over the two of them and they ran together for the glowing haven of the hall.

They stood in the hall, arms linked, clothes sodden, hair slicked to the skull, and dripped vast pools, their faces radiant.

'We are unhurt,' Isabella assured anxious questioners. 'Please see to Lord Kintrove. He had a fall.'

And they took her at her word, hurrying anxiously away to boil water, heat bricks and help the old man to his bed.

'A fine welcome to your new home!' Alladay said, smoothing the wet hair back from her cheek. 'Romantic moments are just not my forte!'

'But dramatic!' Isabella suggested. 'And who wants just romance when they can have high drama too? But we had better get changed into something dry, or we will both succumb to an inflammation of the lungs and the last act will become a tragedy!'

She touched a finger lightly to his cheek, and ran up the stairs to her room.

Fires were lit, hot baths provided for all three of them, and bowls of warming soup sent up on trays. Isabella had been thoroughly bullied by Nurse Pusey, and was huddled before the blaze in her bedroom grate, bundled into warm blankets, her feet in a mustard bath and obediently swallowing her soup, when a knock on the door announced Lord Alladay. He was changed, clean and dry, glowing from the vigorous use of a coarse towel, his hair drying into a tangle of candle-bright curls. Ruth, who had been towelling her mistress's hair, regarded his entry with suspicion.

'I wanted to bring you the ring,' he said at once, coming forward into the firelight. In the palm of his hand he held an exquisite gold ring, with a large, plain diamond surrounded by tiny pearls. 'I had to ask my mother for it.' He grinned. 'She appeared unsurprised, and extremely pleased, so I suspect she guessed my intentions.'

Isabella turned to Ruth.

'You may leave us now, Ruth.'

The maid left the room with an outraged glare and a furious flounce. Alladay watched the door close.

'Now for your dose of romance!' he said, very solemn, and lowered himself on to one knee. 'You see?' he pointed out helpfully. 'I have read all the best manuals of advice for young gentlemen. I know how this should be done.' He drew a deep breath, and placed one hand on his heart. 'Miss Larkham. Will you do me the very great honour of becoming my wife?'

She giggled.

'Did the manual never mention that one does not usually propose to young ladies who are wrapped in blankets, sipping soup, with their feet in a mustard bath?'

'Never a word,' he said, scratching his head, affecting an idiotic, perplexed frown. 'I must have bought the abridged version! Lawks a'mussy! Have I done it wrong? Will I get the wrong answer?'

She had to laugh.

'No, sir. It doesn't affect the answer. Miss Larkham is resigned to her fate—er—is much obliged to Viscount Alladay for his kind offer, and is most honoured to accept—provided he doesn't spill her soup,' she added hastily, as he advanced upon her.

When Lady Kintrove looked in later to reassure herself that Isabella had taken no harm from her drenching, she found her son and hopeful daughter-in-law embroiled in a heated argument over a game of spillikins, set up on the table between them.

'Come in!' Isabella called, thinking it to be Ruth, then continued her haranguing of her beloved. 'You knocked the table!' she was saying indignantly.

'Me? How can you make such an unjust accusation? It must have been Bess!'

'It was not! She is fast asleep behind me. And that's the second time! Just because this is the only game where I always beat you hollow you are resorting to low stratagems! I insist on taking another turn!'

Lady Kintrove coughed gently behind them, and they swung round to face her.

'Mama!' Alladay exclaimed. 'I hope you have come to wish me happy! Isabella has agreed to become something you always wanted—a daughter for you!'

'My dear!' Lady Kintrove's lined face was all smiles. 'I so much hoped for this to happen. The more I came to know you the more it seemed right. I am so pleased for you both; you are exactly what Anthony needed!'

'Are you sure of what you are saying, Mama? Don't you want to rush to save me by banning the connection? You must have been listening when you came in. I have consigned myself to a terrible fate! I am now irrevocably linked to an opinionated nag!'

Isabella threatened dire injury to him with a spillikin, and his mother smiled.

'Precisely, Anthony! It is just what you need!'

'I was afraid you might be disappointed,' Isabella confided, anxiously. 'Knowing how much more convenient it would be if Anthony would only marry a fortune. And I promise you, I did my very best to persuade him to!'

'My dear Isabella. Never, ever feel that we would wish a son of ours to marry where he could not love. My husband and I could never judge wealth to be of greater importance than happiness.'

'But,' Isabella said wistfully, 'it would have been convenient if they had coincided!'

Lady Kintrove laughed.

'I have never spent my life in crying for the moon, my dear, and nor should you. With sensible management the estate will come about. Of greater concern should be notifying your family of your intentions, and ensuring you are once and for all rid of that dreadful man, Crue! Why not write a letter to your father tonight, and one to your grandmother as well? I must go back to Wilfred now.'

'How is Lord Kintrove, ma'am?' Isabella asked.

'Not too well. The shock of the fall followed by such a chilling has done him no good. But we have him warm in bed now. We hope for the best.'

Later that evening Isabella wrote the two letters. She wondered, as she penned her news to her father, what his reaction might be. She had blithely accepted Lord Alladay's offer, and his ring. But she was too young to marry without her family's consent, and her father was more likely to greet her news with an apoplexy than with joy. She thought back to his past attitudes towards his tutor, or his other paid staff, and she shuddered. The realities of life with her father had seemed a long way behind her when she had rashly opted for happiness and accepted Alladay's offer. Life at Long Trovers had a disconnected, dream-like quality, having slipped from tormenting nightmare to ecstatic idyll. Could her father be persuaded to let the idyll last?

The letter to her grandmother was easier. Knowing nothing of the old lady, Isabella found herself writing frankly of her life, her hopes and her present circumstances. In case she had seen the announcements in the newspapers, she explained about her relationship with Lord Carlton Crue, and her feelings for the man. She ended with a hope that she would meet her grandmother soon, and sealed it down, curiously relieved.

After that she went to her diary and took out the letters, verses, and the lock of dark hair that had been treasured there for so long. She looked for a long, embarrassed moment at one of the poems, then fervently flung everything on to the fire.

That night the only thing treasured in her diary was a twisted ring of grass.

When Ruth came to her room at bed-time, Isabella knew she could no longer postpone telling the girl of what had occurred that afternoon. She broached the task with an inwardly amused apprehension which proved to be well justified.

'No, miss!' Ruth wailed, stepping back, her hands clasped to her flat bosom. 'No, no, you can't mean it! What of Lord Carlton Crue? So handsome, so kind, so elegant! What of the house in London, and all the fine life? What of all Stoat's promises? You don't mean it! You can't want to stay here forever? Here in Long Trovers. No one could. You hate it, you always used to say so. And think of what Nurse Pusey will be saying! About those horrible dogs! She will believe it is all true. You don't want that, do you, miss?'

Ruth paused, and gazed at Isabella with a stricken glimmer of hope. Her mistress dashed it immediately.

'The dogs were right, Ruth, and I no longer care if Nurse Pusey says so. She was wiser about my own feelings than I was myself! I am sorry, but I will never marry Lord Carlton Crue. You must simply accustom yourself to the fact, and try to forget about Stoat.'

Ruth stared at her, eyes wide and hand pressed over her mouth. She began to gulp and gasp, her face turned brilliant red, and she backed towards the door. Flinging the door wide she retreated into the corridor where her gasps became wavering screams, and by the time she had reached the stairs to her attic bedroom, she was indulging in a full-blown bout of hysterics.

Isabella watched as Nurse Pusey came out of her room, and stumped ominously after the retreating screeches, then sighed, and prepared for bed on her own.

CHAPTER SIXTEEN

IT WAS not Ruth who appeared with the little silver tray carrying a jug of hot chocolate drink and a plate of toast the following morning. The girl, with a long, gloomy, spot-pocked face and her dull brown hair dragged back and caught with a broken comb, lingered apprehensively in the doorway before bringing the tray to the bed. Isabella raised herself on one elbow.

'Who are you?' she asked.

The girl placed the tray awkwardly on the table beside the bed. Her hands looked huge, chapped red and sore. She went over to pull back the curtains.

'Me name's Agnes, miss. I'm kitchen maid for Mrs Stoke.'

She stood, rubbing her hands together, and blinking uncertainly.

'And Ruth?' Isabella persevered.

'She 'ad the 'ystericals all the night. Kept all us girls awake. Went on somethink chronic! Worked 'erself into a fever, Nurse Pusey says, but I think it's all temper meself. She's stopping in 'er bed today.' The girl began to edge over to the door. 'I've to get yer 'ot water, miss.'

She sidled out, leaving Isabella to her breakfast. Moments later all peace was lost as her brothers burst into her room after a cursory knock.

'Is it true, Izzie? Are you going to marry Anthony? Are you, really?'

They stood at the end of her bed, bouncing like acrobats on the rosewood tailboard so that the bed groaned and juddered. She hastily replaced her bowl of chocolate on the tray, smiled, and regally held out her hand. There was a moment of awe as they gazed at the magnificent diamond that graced her finger, before bedlam broke loose.

'Hooray, hooray, hooray! Can we stay here for ever? Papa won't care! He won't even notice, he's never at home. We don't want to go back to London. Anthony really will be our brother now, won't he? Just think, we'll never see horrible old Lord Carlton Crue again. I'm glad. Nurse Pusey was right about the dogs knowing best, wasn't she? When is the wedding to be? Soon?'

'Enough!'

Isabella shouted to break into the voluble enthusiasm. Her brothers paused, hurt, balanced precariously on the bed end.

'Jump down, so I can drink my chocolate without spilling it all over the counterpane.'

She waited until they had withdrawn to a safe distance, then picked up the bowl. William absent-mindedly helped himself to a slice of her toast.

'It's funny,' he said, looking at her over the slice with a puzzled frown. 'We always thought you hated Anthony. Right from when he was Mr D'Estine. You were always so rude to him.' He spoke with a slight awe at these memories of his intrepid sister. 'I'd never have dared say half the things you did. What I don't understand is why he now wants to marry you? Or why you want to marry him. I'm pleased,' he added hastily, 'very pleased, but I am surprised.'

Isabella gave a slow smile.

'So am I,' was all she said, taking the last piece of toast before it went the way of the first. She ate before she spoke again.

'I don't know when the wedding will be. I have to have permission from Papa.'

Their faces fell.

'Will he give it?'

Their tones suggested that they doubted he would.

'I don't know. I hope so. And as for what happens to you two, that has to be for Papa to decide. All I can say is, for myself I would love to have you stay here, but I expect Lord Alladay can't wait to post you back to town!'

'Oh, pooh!'

They dismissed such poor-spirited thoughts as impossible in their esteemed ex-tutor, and went on to tell Isabella about their proposed morning's fishing at the lake, their hopes for some good-sized perch, and dreams of a monstrous, vast-jawed pike. They were bidding her farewell, off to dig worms, when Agnes returned with the ewer of hot water.

'If Ruth is unavailable, will you stay to assist me this morning?' Isabella asked the gauche, lanky girl.

A raw flush of disbelieving pleasure poured over the girl's face.

'Mrs Stoke told me to do that,' she said gruffly. 'But I didn't think you would want me.'

She hopefully stood a little straighter, and smoothed down her coarse, grey apron.

'What shall I do, miss?'

Isabella swallowed her misgivings and smiled at the girl encouragingly.

'I would like your help for all of the time that Ruth is indisposed, please, Agnes. I am sure we will learn to get on together. If you could pour the hot water into the bowl, please, and then find my sprigged muslin dress from the closet.'

Agnes nodded like an anxious bloodhound, willing but without a scent to follow.

It took rather longer than usual, but Isabella was not displeased with the results when she made her way downstairs. Agnes's appearance was not promising, but Isabella had been surprised. She listened attentively, those great red hands were gentler than expected, and at least she did not gossip.

Hopkins moved over as she reached the bottom of the staircase.

'May I take this opportunity to offer you my sincerest congratulations, Miss Larkham?' he said, in a low voice, with a discreet but heartfelt smile. 'Lord Alladay and Mr Carstairs are in the library.'

With a twinge of guilt Isabella realised that for the whole of yesterday she had entirely forgotten poor Algie and his sprained ankle. She hurried down to the library.

Algie was sitting by the table near the window, his bandaged ankle propped before him on a chair. Alladay was sitting on the table-top, swinging legs clad in smooth buff pantaloons and polished Hessians, and idly twirling the planets in the orrery. The tassels on his boots tapped rhythmically against the leather. His face lit up when he saw Isabella.

'I have been keeping Algie abreast of events!' he said. 'He is disgruntled!'

'Oh, Algie,' said Isabella. 'Why?'

'Just a trivial discontent with the injustices of life! Nothing to blight your lasting happiness. Merely my reflections on a fate that can allow me to languish in my bed for one day, one short, fatal day. During that time, a mere, unconsidered twenty-four hours, this man, one who professes to be my true friend, contrives to rescue the most beautiful maiden who ever crossed our paths. A maiden who might have made any man's heart glad, even mine! In one casual stroke he saves her from the clutches of the world's foulest cad, and thereby gains from her a promise of eternal happiness! Meanwhile I, all unsuspecting, arise from my feather mattress, hobble plaintively down to breakfast, and there he stands, begging congratulations for the deed! Him I spurn! But to you, Isabella, I must wish every happiness. And if at any time this wastrel puts a foot out of line, come to me! I'll know how to deal with him!'

Isabella laughed, and lightly kissed Algie's cheek.

'Thank you, sir. I shall remember your offer! And thank you for your compliments. High praise from one who not forty-eight hours ago sat in the drawing-room here and declared he had no intention of getting spliced!'

Algie looked sheepish.

'It must seem odd.' Isabella continued, musing. 'When you retired injured I was engaged to one man; you recover, and I am engaged to another. I am afraid it denotes a shocking fickleness of character. What do you think, Lord Alladay? Do you feel you should reconsider your offer?'

Her fiancé paused to give her a thoughtful look, head on one side, before speaking. Her hair tumbled in a cascade of gold from a single ribbon. Her cheeks were lightly flushed, her lips apart, almost smiling. Her blue eyes were very wide, a hint of amusement behind the limpid innocence.

'Oh, doubtless I should. Who knows whom you might be engaged to when I wake up tomorrow? But I won't. I have a rash and trusting nature.' He smiled at her, looking up through his dark lashes, then remembered Algie, sat straighter and spoke briskly. 'But in the meantime I have drawn up this announcement. What do you think?'

He handed Isabella a piece of paper on which he had penned an announcement, to be sent to the *Morning Post* newspaper, declaring an engagement of marriage between Miss Isabella Larkham, daughter of Mr Horatio Larkham of Union Street, London, and Viscount Alladay, only surviving son of the Earl and Countess of Kintrove. A proud smile spread across Isabella's face as she read it.

'Do you approve?' Alladay asked. 'I thought we should take the initiative in this game of newspaper bluff. Make it more difficult for your father and Crue to revive any hopes of that association.'

'Oh, yes!' Isabella approved whole-heartedly. 'Post it off without delay. The sooner the better!'

'There is another newspaper announcement I wanted to show you,' her beloved said, with a quick frown. 'I left the paper in the office. If you will excuse us, Algie?'

'Oh, don't mind me! I can see it will be any flimsy excuse to escape away together. "Come to see my newspaper announcements", indeed! I ought to appoint myself chaperon, obviously. You only make good your escape on account of my incapacitating injuries.'

Laughing, but puzzled, Isabella followed Alladay. He led the way to the estate office. She had not ventured there before. There were shelves of directories, notebooks and ledgers. A large oak desk supported a huge inkwell, a tray of quills, a penknife, and a jar of fine sand for blotting. There was also a neat pile of correspondence. Alladay leant against the desk and took her gently into his arms.

'No regrets?' he asked. He was not teasing now.

'No,' she replied, equally earnest. 'No regrets.'

He drew a deep contented breath, and reached behind him, pulling the previous day's paper from beneath the pile of letters. He silently pointed to an entry, handed her the paper, and stood back to let her read it. She walked slowly over to the window, murmuring the words.

'Mr and Mrs Frederick Exton take pleasure in announcing the marriage of their younger son, Henry Charles Bablock Exton, to Miss Anne Clumbers, only child of Captain and Mrs Lynton Clumbers, of Kingston, Jamaica. The couple will continue to reside in Jamaica.'

She stared at the paper in silence for so long that Alladay was worried. Had she not recovered from her feelings for Exton? Then she turned towards him and smiled.

'Isn't it strange,' she said, 'I stand here and try to visualise Harry, and although I know the colour of his eyes, the colour of his hair, the face remains a blank. Poor Anne! Do you think she too has had to listen to his abominable verses? I sincerely wish her happy. I am glad, also, to know that Harry is not going to eventually erupt back into our lives. No doubt she is in line to inherit a vast sugar plantation. I wish him joy of it.'

She strolled back to the desk and dropped the paper down. She glanced more closely at his face.

'Were you worried? Did you think I might still care?'

He shrugged, and turned away, twisting the inkwell round and round on its stand.

'Perhaps. You were most insistent over your love for him.'

'Stupid!' She set the inkwell straight and looked up into his eyes. 'How else could I have blinded myself to my feelings for you? Forget Harry! I have. Let's go and challenge Algie to a game of cards.'

They had known that Lord Kintrove had kept to his bed that morning. No one had been surprised, after his ordeal of the previous evening. After a quiet night, and a good breakfast, a steady recovery from his shock seemed under way. It was only after luncheon that Lady Kintrove came downstairs looking drawn and anxious and asked Alladay to send a man for Dr Millthorpe immediately. The old Lord's fever had begun to rise. He would take no food, and tossed fretfully on the pillows.

Alladay insisted he would go himself, on Captain, to make best possible speed, and Isabella remained in the library with Algie. He, however, on hearing the news, sent to have his belongings packed, and requested a carriage brought round to drive him home.

'Don't want to outstay my welcome. Not with Lord Kintrove ill,' he said earnestly. 'Dashed inconvenient to have visitors to worry about when there is sickness in the house. Make my apologies to Tony, my dear.'

He took his leave of Lady Kintrove in one of her brief ventures out of the sick-room, before hobbling out to the barouche that Old Bill brought to the door. Giving Isabella an affectionate farewell kiss, he was on his way long before Alladay returned with the doctor.

'The man was attending a delivery beyond Witchbourne,' Alladay explained, frustrated, when at last he returned. 'I went to fetch him, but there was nothing to be done but wait. The wretched woman produced twins!'

He sighed and tossed himself down into a deep leather chair. 'How is Papa? Have you heard?'

Isabella had not heard, having occupied the rest of her afternoon in playing games with her brothers in an attempt to keep them quietly out of the way, then encouraging them to return to their essays on the lake's elusive fish. Alladay and Isabella waited for Dr Millthorpe to conclude his examination. His face was solemn when eventually he came down.

'As I have explained to your mother, the signs are not good. The Earl has a very high fever. He has been cupped, and the symptoms are somewhat reduced, but...'

The doctor sucked in his cheeks as he shook his head, and Isabella thought with a shudder that his always hollow features took on the aspect of a death's head as he gave his ominous message.

Alladay's face was pale with shock.

'What hope is there?'

The doctor pursed his thin lips.

'We can only wait and see how the fever progresses. But you must remember that your father is already old and frail. If he has indeed taken an inflammation of the lung, we must all pray he has the strength to fight. Now, if you will excuse me, I will return to his lordship.'

There were tears welling on to Isabella's cheeks as he left.

No one except the boys and Dr Millthorpe had an appetite for dinner that night. The boys made self-conscious inroads into the roast pigeons, haunch of boiled mutton and assorted vegetable dishes that Mrs Stoke had managed to prepare in addition to thin gruels and calf's-foot jelly to tempt the Earl. The others picked half-heartedly at the meats then pushed their plates aside. Lady Kintrove bravely attempted conversation, but her thoughts, like those of Alladay and Isabella, kept straying upstairs. Only the doctor worked steadily through the dishes, appetite unimpaired by the emotions around him. He excused himself after a single glass of port, and retired back to his patient.

'I have sent word to Mary in Brighton,' Lady Kintrove said, after he had gone. 'I thought she would want to come back before...in case...' Her voice cracked as it tailed off. She twisted her fluted sherry glass unhappily between finger and thumb.

Usually so brisk and decisive, anyone would have thought she was the strength of the partnership, supporting the Earl's frail confusion. But the possibility of losing him left her bewildered and unsure.

'I am glad, Mama,' Alladay said gently. 'Miss Pickering will be a great comfort to you, whatever the outcome.'

'Will you visit him this evening? You and Isabella. Tell him your news. It will make him so happy. I want him to know, in case it becomes too late.'

'Of course we will, Mama. As soon as Dr Millthorpe thinks it advisable.'

They waited through the evening in the drawing-room, sitting close, to give each other comfort, but their love was overlaid and constrained by thought of the white-haired old man, so recently hale and cheerful, now fighting for his life upstairs. For Isabella the situation held the horror of disbelief. It could not be true that this should be happening, so suddenly and unexpectedly, after the delights of yesterday.

It was eleven o'clock before Hopkins knocked at the door and asked them to go up.

The great bedroom was wreathed in gloom. Candles stood on the dressing-table, reflecting in the polished leather of the doctor's black bag, and wavering over his portable medicine chest. It stood open, and the rows of tiny labelled jars, and the little brass knobs of the shallow wooden drawers for powders and instruments, all glinted brightly. A small candelabrum flickered on a table beside the vast bed. Beyond was shadow. Shadow cast by the heavy black bedposts, by the looped blue velvet curtains, and the scalloped pelmet that hung around the canopy overhead. The shadows spread out, black and foreboding, reaching across the ceiling and down into the hidden corners of the room. Isabella took Alladay's hand.

'Your son and Miss Larkham to visit you, my lord.'

Dr Millthorpe's gruff voice came from beyond the curtains on the far side of the bed, and Isabella jumped.

She had not noticed him there. He came over, his face more gaunt and funereal than ever in the shadows, and spoke quietly to Alladay before slipping out.

'He is awake and aware now. But it may not be for long. Endeavour not to tire him. I shall wait just outside the door, should you need me.'

Alladay moved over to the bed and looked down at the frail old man propped on the pillows. He gently took the thin, veined hand that lay on the covers.

'Papa?'

Isabella hung back. She felt she had no place here.

'Shall I leave you alone together?' she whispered, but Alladay shook his head.

The old man opened his eyes, and smiled.

'Anthony,' he said, then, peering beyond, 'and the charming young lady who visits me as I pile my stones. I have forgotten your name again, my dear!'

She moved up to the edge of the bed.

'Isabella, my lord,' she said.

He had already drifted on in his mind, frowning over something else.

'Now Clara told me you had some news. Good news, she said. Is that right?'

'With your approval and blessing, sir, it will be very good news indeed,' Anthony replied. Isabella could sense the effort it cost him to keep his voice steady. He held forward her hand, clasped in his own. 'Isabella has consented to be my wife.'

His head motionless on the mounds of white-laced linen, the old man slewed his eyes to study their joined hands. The family diamond glinted as it caught the light from the candelabra. His face crinkled into a huge smile as he raised his eyes to his son's face.

'A wedding!' he creaked. 'I do so enjoy a wedding! Clara has hoped for so long that one of you boys would bring her a daughter, and some grandchildren. Congratulations, my boy. A splendid choice. So pretty, and always interested in my monument. And you, my dear. I wish you very happy. My blessing on you both.'

His voice was becoming fainter, wheezing softly in his throat.

'I think we should leave you now, sir, and call Dr Millthorpe back.'

'Wait.' It was only a whisper now, but they could not ignore him. 'He is gloomy, the doctor. Very gloomy. I don't think he gives a lot for my chances. If he is right, and doctors often are, y'know, don't wait. Don't let me spoil the wedding. Get me safe in the churchyard first, then let Clara have a wedding to think about. No long, fussy mourning. Hate you all to be dreary. And give her those grandchildren. Can't have her lonely. Look after your mother, my boy. She's a wonderful woman. Been a wonderful wife.'

His voice trailed off, leaving his words, uttered in short, whispered gasps, hanging on the air. Isabella was gripping Alladay's hand, the tears flowing unchecked down her cheeks. He led her to the door, and called the doctor and his mother to come in.

She left them, wandering alone through the dark, creaking corridors to her room, her candle flame fluttering in the draughts like a soul tugging to be free, knowing that Alladay wished to support his mother in her attendance on the old man through the night.

Ruth was waiting in the bedroom. Her face was still red and blotched, her expression sullen. The sulky silence in which she performed her tasks was welcome to Isabella, as was her speedy departure once her jobs were done. Nothing could have been less welcome now than the girl's customary spiteful gossip about the family which she served.

CHAPTER SEVENTEEN

IT WAS three days more before the old Earl died, but he was never again capable of coherent speech. He lay trapped in some distant world apart. The household limped through each day, mute with anxiety and grief.

Isabella spent much of her daylight hours greeting the many callers who visited Long Trovers, burdened with gifts and good wishes, all hoping for cheering news.

The general and his wife called, closely followed by Lady Brockton and the long-suffering Gertrude. The Beaumoyne brothers stood looking ill at ease, putting their queries gruffly as they twisted their riding crops around in their broad hands. The Honourable John Whatton and the Lady Maria stopped briefly, unwilling to intrude. Lord Alnstrop came with baskets of fruit from the Alnstrop hothouses.

Isabella became hardened to responding to their hopeful quest for good tidings, and replied as honestly as she could, finding her relief in knowing that she was sparing Lady Kintrove an ordeal she would have been unable to support. Sometimes Alladay stayed with her, but he also found the visits difficult, and he was much occupied in the estate office.

It was with relief that Isabella recognised Sarah Grice-Hewson as one of the occupants of a neat canary-painted whisky that pulled up on the third day of the Earl's illness. It was not until Julian Whyle cantered up beside them on his showy chestnut, and reined to an abrupt halt in a spray of gravel, that Isabella realised that her companions must be Chloe and Clytia. Instead of bringing them inside, Isabella, keen to get out of the house, took them to walk down through the gardens to the lake.

After the proper exchanges the three Whyles wandered apart to fully appreciate the garden design, and Isabella was left to talk with Sarah in peace.

'It seems terrible to talk of anything else when he is so ill,' Sarah said guiltily, taking Isabella's arm. She had dressed for the visit in a sober dark brown which made her look older, but she carried a cream silk parasol which she rested back on her shoulder, twirling it absent-mindedly as she talked, a perfect background to her bouncing red curls. 'But I know he wouldn't mind. Dear Lord Kintrove.'

She smiled and squeezed Isabella's arm, then could no longer resist the questions that were bubbling up in her mind.

'Come now. Confess and tell all. Algie Carstairs is spreading such rumours—no, I must be fair, he told me an amazing thing, and I am spreading rumours!—about you and Anthony! You sly thing! You have done it, haven't you? Stolen him from under my nose. Tell instantly! How did it happen? And what have you done with Lord Carlton Crue? For I must tell you that the rumours about you are as nothing to the rumours I have heard in Worthing about Lord Carlton. Nothing!'

'What have you heard?'

'No, no! Unfair! You shall tell first.'

Bowing to the unavoidable, Isabella shyly displayed her ring, then gave a detailed account of the deterioration of her relationship with Crue, with a concise epilogue on her sudden engagement to Viscount Alladay. As she finished Sarah subjected her to a sharp scrutiny.

'You imply your feelings for Anthony are new. What a minx! I never realised just how sly you are. Letting me think you would allow him to me! I do believe you loved him all along. Those arguments and haughty looks, they were all a pretence!'

'It was not as simple as that,' Isabella attempted, but Sarah was convinced she was right, and set up an enjoyable tease. It took mention of the Whyles to distract her.

'Now, there,' she said, preening herself and twirling the parasol cheekily, 'I do believe *I* have stolen an admirer from *you*. I hope you are properly desolated. Mr Julian Whyle could not speak of you highly enough when we met at the Lockes' card party after arriving back from Worthing. Every other sentence held your name. So tedious! You had made a certain conquest. Truly!

'This afternoon they called, knowing I was planning to be out—to come here—and they asked to accompany me. I couldn't help but wonder why!' She giggled. 'Then, just after I had *happened* to make mention of your engagement to Anthony, Mr Julian looked exceedingly peeved, then began to pay the most outrageous compliments, to *me*! Wasn't that extraordinary! You must know that he has invited me to go out riding with his sisters and himself tomorrow, and talks of organising a small evening party for me to attend, because I suffered the *unspeakable* misfortune of missing their ball! Well! What would you make of that? I trust you are devastated by jealousy and desolate at all you have cast aside!'

Isabella grinned, looking over the low box hedges to where the Whyles were grouped, pointing out the views across the lake. Julian was striking a casual pose, running his hand nonchalantly through his lank brown curls, and glancing hopefully their way to see if he was being observed.

'Those were not precisely the words that sprang to mind!' she remarked, drily.

Sarah giggled again.

'Ah, well. He may not be the Romeo he thinks he is, but his attentions will keep me amused. Life here is very tedious after the excitements of Worthing. But now! Let me tell you all about Lord Carlton Crue! You don't know what you have escaped!'

Knowing what she did, Isabella was not surprised by Sarah's gleefully imparted gossip. She had not realised, though, the extent of his heavy drinking, which, with his blatant flaunting of Clorette, had disgusted many friends and acquaintances. He was reputed to be heavily in debt, and, so said the gossip which the indefatigable Sarah had gleaned, was unlikely to be again considered for the diplomatic work through which he had first met Horatio Larkham, despite his standing and connections. He had come to be considered unreliable. All this could only serve to strengthen Isabella's determination to escape Crue at all costs.

She went to discuss the news with Anthony once the visitors had gone, but, as on much of the previous day, he was in the estate office with Colwick and Mr Bagshot, the solicitor. Mr Bagshot and the Reverend Mr Bailey, from the small stone church, filled with memorials to the D'Estines, which stood in Trovers village, and which the family had attended every Sunday for countless generations, were always at the house now.

She was delighted when a hired gig pulled up outside, and, instead of another visitor to entertain, Isabella saw Mary Pickering, her eccentric garments flapping in the sunshine. She tumbled down from the gig, bags and bundles clutched all about her, and hurried in to the hall.

'I am not too late? No? Thank God for that.'

Scattering parcels all over the floor, she gave Isabella a great hug. 'And as for your news, my dear, wonderful! Just wonderful. Dear, oh, dear! Such a mix of emotions!' And she wiped her eyes on an emerald-green handkerchief before running upstairs to see 'poor Wilfred', leaving her luggage where it lay. Isabella helped Hopkins pick it up.

When eventually he went, the Seventh Earl of Kintrove, Third Viscount of Neame, Baron D'Estine of Nore, Alladay and Kifford died quietly and without fuss. A little after dawn he simply stopped breathing, and his beloved Countess, dozing in a chair beside him, her hand on his, never noticed, until the bright sun cut through a gap in the heavy curtains and its sharp blade of golden light reached her face and pierced her exhaustion.

The funeral took place on another day of sunshine. Late summer sun now, and the harvesters, who were labouring in all the fields along the route to the church, unasked laid down their scythes and joined the cortège, holding their sweat drenched hats in hands rubbed hastily clean on their breeches. All the household servants were there, and the estate tenants, stiff in Sunday clothes, even down to old Widow Samson, as wizened as a raisin, and all the neighbouring gentry for miles around had come to pay their last respects. The road outside the church was cluttered with carriages, far more than could use the long row of iron rings set into the churchyard wall for the purpose.

Isabella and her brothers climbed stiffly down from the barouche with Miss Pickering. Anthony and his mother had travelled in the first coach, and now she could see him, sombre and absorbed in his black tail-coat and breeches, and severe black hat, organising the carriage of his father's coffin from the lych-gate into the church. He and Lord Alnstrop, the Beaumoynes, Colwick and Mr Grice-Hewson were to act as pall-bearers. Moving up behind Lady Kintrove, Isabella followed the slow procession into the church.

It was a simple and moving service, both in the church and outside, when the polished oak coffin with the heavy brass handles was carried into the elaborately carved stone family vault, all twined about with ivy, to rest with his ancestors, and his son Jasper. Looking around the assembled mourners, Isabella thought the quiet, self-effacing man to whom they were bidding farewell would have been astonished at the simple sadness so widely generated by his passing.

There were inevitably many faces unfamiliar to Isabella in that gathering, and it was not surprising that she did not notice the sharp looks she and her brothers were being subjected to by one little old lady. Oddly it was Anthony who noticed her, struck by the amount of jet that decorated her black poke bonnet, her bead-fringed black wool shawl, her glittering black reticule, and even the beaded tassels of her black parasol. At first glance she looked an amiable little lady, short, plump, with wisps of curling white hair framing her rosy-cheeked face beneath her bonnet. But the eyes were a sharp, considering, hard steel-grey. He frowned, unable to place her among their friends or neighbours.

She was there at the house for the cold meats also, he noticed, but in the crush of arrivals he had missed her name, and now his attention was taken by one person after another who was eager to stop and offer condolences.

He kept seeing the old lady from the corner of his eye, walking about with an assessing and critical gaze, summing up the house, the people in it, but particularly, he thought, the Larkhams. He frowned as yet another well-intentioned mourner came to claim his attention. The old lady, glinting with black beads, had not, from his observations, spoken to anybody. She quelled any approach with a cool smile and nod, and moved away. He was intrigued.

It was not until the guests were all reluctantly departing that Anthony's curiosity was to be satisfied. The old lady, her cascades of jet quivering, sat down upon an upholstered mahogany settee, and made no move whatsoever to leave. Isabella had vanished with her brothers, and Lady Kintrove, with a pleading look at her son, slipped away. She was exhausted, and Anthony would cope.

He went over to the old lady, and stood looking down at her. She was cosily rounded, her cheeks soft and pink. Her hands were folded neatly over the reticule that lay in her lap. Her mouth was folded shut, tight as a trap. She stared back with a critical eye.

'I am sorry, madam. I seem to have missed your name in the crush of people. I am——' he broke off, with a small shock of surprise. He had not yet spoken his new title, although it had been necessary to sign a sheaf of documents for Bagshot. He was reluctant.

'I am Lord Kintrove,' he said slowly. 'May I help you?'

'You would be the one who *was* Viscount Alladay?' she countered.

He bowed. 'The same, ma'am.'

'Hmm!' She was surveying him, head to one side. She seemed to make up her mind, and stood up, offering him her hand. 'Mrs Rose Larkham,' she said abruptly. 'I've come to have a look at the sort of man my granddaughter thinks she's going to marry. Bad time for you now, of course. I didn't realise that until I arrived down here. But despite that, matters will have to be discussed. I am putting up at the George in Witchbourne. When would be convenient to meet?'

She sounded sharp, shrewd and businesslike, but despite that he could detect a hint of aggression, perhaps defiance, in her tones.

He gave her a thoughtful look, and reluctantly smiled.

'I think,' he said slowly, 'and I certainly hope, that I am extremely pleased to see you. You came in response to Isabella's letter?'

'I did. I know my duty. I wouldn't let my husband down.'

'But you did not make yourself known to Isabella?'

She pursed her lips tight and shook her head. 'Never met my grandchildren. Funeral wake is not the place for introductions.'

'I would be very grateful,' Anthony said, hoping his mother would forgive him, 'if you would come to stay with us here.'

She thought for a few moments, and looked around the room. They were in one of the great staterooms, never normally opened in the day-to-day life of Long Trovers. A huge painting of a scantily clad Leda and the swan stared down at them from above the vast marble fireplace. An equally scanty Juno caressed a peacock at the other end of the room. She sniffed.

'Thank you, my lord,' she said, and he thought he detected a note of gratification and also of regret. 'But I won't intrude in a house of mourning. I know what's what.'

She heaved herself to her feet, and stood leaning heavily on the handle of her black silk parasol.

'But I need to speak with you and my granddaughter. Tomorrow I've a fancy to rest in my room. It was a long journey down from Lancashire, and, to tell truth, I've not recovered. I'd not be here now had it not seemed such a chance to satisfy my curiosity and have a look at you all. So, I'll call during the morning of the following day, Thursday, that'll be, in time for a bite of luncheon, if that will suit?'

'We will look forward to it, ma'am,' he said, almost truthfully, and escorted her out to her carriage, a solid, staid vehicle, expensive and respectable, with both coachman and footman. The footman leaped down to open the door for her.

'Until Thursday,' Anthony said.

She raised an oddly regal, plump white hand, and the equipage moved sedately away. The eighth Earl of Kintrove watched it depart, thoughtful.

They were all hovering, waiting to greet her, on Thursday morning, except Lady Kintrove and Miss Pickering, who had excused themselves and retired into the garden, intrigued, but still too emotionally exhausted to want involvement.

Isabella was twisted tight with nervous anticipation, furious with Anthony for having stolen the first encounter from her, relieved that he had paved a tentative way. Among so many, she had not even noticed the jet-beaded woman who was her grandmother.

'But *why* has she come hurrying down? Why did she say she knew her duty? What duty? To whom?'

She perched on the edge of her seat, taut, her brain seething with speculations.

Anthony raised his shoulders expressively. 'To defend you from my vile advances?' he hazarded. 'Don't fret. You will know soon enough.'

He continued reading his newspaper, maddeningly calm.

She sighed, and fingered her diamond ring, curving her right hand over it protectively.

The boys sighed in sympathy. Neat and scrubbed, they were seated opposite her on an ornate sofa. She had forbidden them to move until they had sufficiently impressed their newly found relative, and they were resigned, but still resentful, having planned to be out in the fields helping in the harvest. It was they who first heard the crunch of carriage wheels approaching, and they ran to look out, but a buttress of stone hid the view of the front door from the green room where they sat. It was left to Hopkins to announce the most startling surprise of all. He pushed the door to the Green Room open, and in stifled tones stated: 'Mr Horatio Larkham, Mrs Horatio Larkham, and Lord Carlton Crue.'

The visitors entered the room into the silence of utter bewilderment.

'Well, Isabella,' said her father crossly, ignoring everybody else and fixing her with a chilly eye. 'Fine capers you've been playing with these letters and newspaper announcements, and now of all times. Arriving back from France to find my name a point of gossip all over town.'

He surged pompously into the room, larger in girth than she remembered, fat-bellied and heavy-jowled, richly clad in a jacket of celestial blue broadcloth, over a satin waistcoat of striped cream and cherry pink. His pantaloons, of a delicate pale green, vanished into gleaming, chestnut-brown Hessian boots.

They were all standing, astonished. Isabella moved instinctively close to Anthony. She felt him lay a gentle, possessive arm around her, hand on her shoulder. Unable to reply, she blinked at the colourful vision that was her father, and then looked, bemused, at his companion. A small woman, perhaps in her late forties, her black hair was scraped uncompromisingly back and up, vanishing under her smart, round scrap of red hat with its impudently jutting feathers. Her black brows arched elegantly over very bright black eyes, her high cheekbones were exotically un-English, and her mouth was quirking into a small half-smile. Her creamy-beige pelisse betrayed a stylish, Parisian cut. She looked like a speculative robin.

'Hush now, Horatio!' she said, patting his arm. 'Let me greet my new family. Isabella, my dear, you *did* receive our letter?'

Mutely, Isabella shook her head. Little hands in bright red gloves flew to the lady's mouth as she laughed. Her eyes sparkled wickedly over the scarlet fingers.

'You have no idea who I am?'

Isabella shook her head. The small lady flung her arms wide.

'My dear! I'm your new stepmama!'

There was an audible gulp from Thomas, and Isabella quivered.

Anthony saved her from immediate reply. He stepped forward and walked briskly to the bell pull by the fire place.

'Please,' he said as he rang, 'sit down. I will order some refreshment.' He eyed Lord Carlton Crue, who had remained by the door, glowering at them all, and who now lounged over to a chair by the window without a word.

'Stepmama?' said Thomas, incredulously, and on the small interruption all the rest began to move, and arrange themselves to sit down.

'It seems I must congratulate you, Papa,' Isabella managed, and, drawing strength from the sound of her own voice, she continued a little more certainly, 'Where did you meet? And when did the wedding take place?'

Horatio Larkham was distracted from Isabella's affairs, and spoke with a warmth of proprietorial pride, and frequent interruptions from his wife, as he described their meeting in Vienna. She, it emerged, was the vivacious widow of an Italian count, a reknowned hostess, welcoming everyone who was anyone to her soirées, a popular and respected figure in the European world of diplomatic intrigue. She was also, Isabella surmised, wealthy. She watched her father, and part of her mind was curiously aloof, detached from her own relationship with him. She saw how proud he was of his new wife, how easily she managed him without denting his masculine assumption of superiority, and, strangely, how happy they were. It was like watching a man she had never realised she knew.

Then he returned abruptly to the news that had brought him hotfoot to Long Trovers.

'About your engagement, my girl. I leave you sensibly provided for, everything arranged. I come home to find your name in all the papers, gossip rife, jilting the man I chose for you. Well? Well? What explanation have you got for yourself?'

Anthony stepped forward.

'Perhaps I should explain, sir——' he began, but Horatio Larkham brushed him aside with an impatient wave of his hand.

'It is my daughter and this bungler Carlton I need to hear from. You keep out of this, D'Estine!'

Crue's angry response to this slander was never heard.

'Now that,' said a sharp little voice from the doorway, 'is no way to speak to an Earl, Horatio, and I'll thank you to remember it!'

The whole roomful was once again struck like gaping statues. Just like a display in Madame Tussaud's waxworks! The thought flashed into Isabella's whirling mind.

His mouth hanging ajar, his jowls joggling on to his cravat, Horatio Larkham wheeled slowly about and stared in horror.

'Mother!' he said, weakly.

The little old lady sailed magnificently into the room, ignoring Hopkins hovering behind her. She was royally resplendent in a gown of purple satin, worked in seed pearls at collar and cuffs, but in deference to the house of mourning she had retained her black bonnet and shawl. The jade beads swirled from her fringes.

Glancing around the assembled company, Anthony hastily suppressed a smile. Sidling dubiously in behind her, with a shame-faced shrug of helplessness, came Mr Bagshot, the solicitor.

The Earl smiled at him reassuringly, then spoke to his fiancée's grandmother.

'Good morning, Mrs Larkham. I am so glad you have arrived. May I undertake the unusual role of introducing you to your new daughter-in-law, Mrs Horatio Larkham,' Horatio could be heard making faint gobbling sounds, while his wife nodded cautiously, but he did not speak, and they all ignored him, 'your granddaughter, Isabella...' she curtseyed, dumbstruck '...your grandsons William and Thomas, and...' he hesitated, then finished coolly '...a visitor, Lord Carlton Crue. Please, madam, do sit down.'

Mrs Larkham regarded this pleasant young man with the halting step, the smile lurking behind his hazel eyes and a look of considerable intelligence, with approval.

'Thank you, my lord,' she said graciously. 'I will.'

There was an interruption as the tray of refreshments arrived, sherry and small spiced biscuits.

'Earl?' Horatio Larkham was muttering incredulously, as Hopkins reluctantly withdrew from this fascinating meeting, and quietly closed the door.

His mother accepted her glass of sherry with a dignified nod. 'Yes, Horatio, Earl! This young man,' she stated with satisfaction, and an air of having done her homework well, 'is Anthony Edward Oswald, Eighth Earl of Kintrove, and has a string more titles it would trouble a body to remember. Oh, I know, young man,' she eyed the Earl, without prejudice, 'there was no real inheritance but the estates. These are neglected but with potential. You need an urgent input of ready money.

'But...' she paused, then spoke decisively to Horatio, as if the matter were arranged and would be the solution to everything '...he is about to become my grandson!'

Carlton Crue, who had been fuming impatiently in his window seat, now leaped to his feet, his voice hoarse with anger.

'This is absurd! We have a bargain, Horatio, and documents signed to prove it. You made a deal, and she was to be mine. You can't renege on that bargain!'

'Well...' spluttered Horatio, with a warning frown, and an anxious glance at his mother '... well...'

'Made a deal, did he?' The little plump lady's mouth was opening and shutting as sharply as a rat trap. 'Thought to sign away his daughter's life and make a little something for himself? Yes? How very typical, Horatio. You haven't changed over the years, have you?'

Horatio's face purpled, and he cast an agonised and apologetic look at his new wife. His sons stared in open astonishment, looking from face to face, eager for more.

'As for you, Lord Carlton Crue,' the steely little voice continued, 'I've made some enquiries about you, too. Make no mistake. I don't waste my time. I've made enquiries about everyone involved. I won't dirty the air of this room with the smut that sticks to your name. Oh, yes, you were well enough respected in the past, I'll not deny that. But your days are long done, and I'll have none of you for a grandson. Never.

'Did Horatio never tell you that nothing can be done without my signature? Never thought that worth a mention, hey? And I suppose you had signed over to him a portion of the money as a condition of securing the engagement? I thought as much! Always greedy for more, aren't you, Horatio! Well, it's too bad. You should have known it would be a mistake to try to pass me over as a fool. Or my granddaughter, come to that.

'That one hundred thousand pounds,' she said portentously, 'will come here!'

She pointed one pudgy forefinger at the floor between her feet. 'I have a real *fancy* to have a grandson who's an Earl!'

She sat back, seed pearls stretching across her ample bosom, and looked well satisfied.

Crue was standing, white-faced, glaring at Horatio Larkham.

'One hundred thousand!' he croaked. 'You never said it was half that much! My God! My God!'

He stared wildly about the faces in the room. Mrs Rose Larkham watched him with a smug smile.

'And it's to go to him? A snivelling, money-grubbing cripple of a tutor!'

Crue's pointing hand shook uncontrollably.

'I never knew it was anything like so much,' Horatio was mumbling, to no one in particular, when his mother's words cut ruthlessly across his.

'I will have you know, Lord Carlton, that I *like* a man to know what work is!' The pudgy finger stabbed at the air towards the new Earl. 'He don't live by gambling and womanising. He don't hang on his parents and bleed them dry. This young man made shift for himself. He wasn't ashamed to take employment, *and*...' she shot a nasty look at Horatio '...send money back to his family! That's the sort of man that should get this money, and you, with that nasty tongue in your head, you can take yourself off.'

She gave an unpleasant smile.

'Your carriage will be at the door. I asked whose it was, and ordered it round myself when I arrived. I knew *you* would have no cause to stay!'

Crue shot a last furious plea towards Horatio, but that man was staring into the polish of his Hessians. With a shaking oath, Crue departed.

Mrs Rose Larkham took a ladylike sip of her sherry.

Isabella leaned towards her grandmother.

'Please, ma'am? Please explain. What do you mean, one hundred thousand pounds?'

'So he never told you?'

Isabella shook her head, and Horatio shook his.

'No point word getting about,' he said gruffly. 'Only cause the girl to be the butt of every fortune-hunter. Just protecting her. Anyway,' he looked accusingly at his mother, 'I never knew it was so much. That is unbelievable!'

'That is what happens when it is untapped and shrewdly managed, Horatio,' she said sharply. 'I know what's due to your father's wishes.'

'But, ma'am,' Isabella persisted, in an agony of uncertainty, 'what is this money?'

'Why, it's yours, my dear! Or it will be, on your wedding-day. That's why I brought the solicitor along. So your father and I can sign all the documents. That one hundred thousand pounds was left you by your grandfather, the *first* fortune he made in his factory, and it's to be your dowry.'

CHAPTER EIGHTEEN

WHEN Isabella eventually retired to her room that night she felt there could not be any further shocks.

Since that afternoon by the quarry when she and Anthony had finally acknowledged their feelings and all her world had been turned upside-down—no, all her upside-down world had at last landed the right way about—since that moment there had been unending emotional buffeting. It was almost more than she could comprehend.

Anxiety and grief, delight and relief, astonishment and disbelief, all had rocked her in the last few days.

Lord Carlton Crue had finally gone, exposed as the uncaring fortune-hunter he was. Her father had an exotic new wife, and henceforth would split his time between London and Vienna, agreeing to send the boys away to school and let them holiday at Long Trovers. He had docilely agreed to her marriage to Anthony, *and* signed all the relevant documents under his mother's steely eye, before journeying on with his beloved to spend a few weeks in Brighton. He had appeared reconciled to the loss of the share he had negotiated with Crue to extract from his daughter's fortune. He had heard much of Crue that he did not care for recently. His new wife had brought him wealth and all the diplomatic contacts he could need. Crue had become expendable.

More extraordinary even than an amenable father and a new stepmother, the Larkhams had acquired a grandmother. A little old lady whom one might have thought as round, soft and fragile as an overblown rose at the end of summer, until she fixed you with a gimlet eye and opened her mouth. She was shrewd, sharp, determined, decisive, opinionated, businesslike and thoroughly ambitious! Regarding her with horrified awe, nevertheless Isabella thought she was wonderful. More wonderful yet, Horatio was terrified of her, yet she and Anthony were going great guns, forming a fast friendship! Mrs Rose Larkham fancied being friends with an Earl!

Then the fortune. The figures still rang in Isabella's ears. Her incredulous delight still flooded her face whenever she caught Anthony's eye. She thought of all her scheming to find him an heiress—then with astonished satisfaction began dreaming new schemes.

'Those cottages,' she had said to Anthony at dinner, her eyes sparkling, 'you can tell Colwick to go ahead immediately. And order all the new farm equipment you need. And draw up plans for that extra barn. Also, I think we should build a school in the village. There is nothing for the children, and the Reverend Mr Bailey has often spoken of it. Lady Kintrove is keen. What do you think? May I plan it with him?'

He had laughed and told her to wait. The only money they had as yet was from a sale he was arranging, of an odd folly of a house on a far corner of the estate, that the old Earl had at last agreed to sell to finance the new cottages, and which Lord Alnstrop showed interest in acquiring on generous terms, probably for his sister.

But the wedding date had been fixed. In one month's time they would hold a quiet ceremony in the same secluded church where the funeral had taken place, surrounded by long generations of D'Estines, and all the Earls of Kintrove. Mr and Mrs Horatio Larkham would drive up from Brighton for the occasion.

Mrs Rose Larkham was staying for another week, and had been persuaded by a tired-eyed but amused Lady Kintrove that she was welcome to remain at Long Trovers and get to know her new-found family. Then she intended to take Isabella, travel up to Town, put up at Grillon's hotel, and spend the remaining three weeks in buying all of Isabella's trousseau as her wedding gift to her granddaughter, before bringing her back for the ceremony. It seemed as improbable as a fairy-tale.

But despite the shocks and joys they were all still desolate at the loss of that gentlest of men, whose absence left such a gaping rent in the fabric of their lives. If only, she thought, they could have told him the good news.

No, Isabella reflected, as she opened her bedroom door. There can be no more shocks. Life has delivered enough.

Agnes stood before her, a clean white mob-cap on her head, and a starched white apron about her waist. She was twisting her chapped fingers into an agony of contortions, her doleful face enlivened by wide, amazed eyes, and a half-smile hovering over her crooked teeth. It was evident she had big news to impart.

'Where is Ruth?' asked Isabella, apprehensively.

'Gone! Gone away, miss! She ran off with that Stoat, she did, this morning, the brazen 'ussy. To think! She 'id, she did, in Lord Carlton Crue's carriage, in among the baggage with a rug over the top! Old Bill's youngest's lad, little Adam, what 'elps with the 'orses on occasion, 'e watched! Saw 'er go! An' you know what she said? She said she wouldn't stay another minute in a place where she was cruelly betrayed, an' told to desert her true love! Honest! Imagine!'

Isabella imagined, and she imagined Crue's face when he arrived in Worthing and discovered what he had brought. She began to laugh, shaking helplessly as she gazed at Agnes. Agnes put a huge coy hand over her mouth and began to whoop in sympathy. It was some time before they stopped.

'Oh, dear,' Isabella gasped. 'Poor Ruth! I do hope she feels it is worth it. I hope that Stoat makes her happy.' She shook her head. She was still chuckling, but she had her doubts about Stoat. 'Well,' she said, resignedly, then gave a sudden carefree grin. 'You take over, Agnes! Six weeks, and I'll have trained you to be the perfect lady's maid. And you'll get three weeks in London. What do you say?'

Agnes's wide eyes and hanging jaw were answer enough.

It was two days before she left for London that Thomas and William sheepishly approached their sister and their erstwhile tutor, and broke the news of their intended wedding gift.

'We had no money to buy anything,' William explained earnestly.

'And there is nothing here to buy,' Thomas added.

'We thought we would make you something——'

'But we couldn't think of anything to make——'

'So we had a different idea,' William concluded. 'We are not giving you a *thing*. We are giving you a happening!'

He beamed at their puzzled faces.

'We are giving you a balloon flight! Together! Not us going up at all! Just the two of you, floating into the sunset. We thought it would be romantic!'

The Eighth Earl of Kintrove could feel his fiancée beginning to shake with laughter.

'It is!' he said earnestly. 'It is extremely romantic. But the balloon was ripped when I threw it down from that tree. I don't think it is usable.'

'It is, it is,' Thomas babbled, agog with their generosity. 'That is the present. We have stitched it all up. We have mended it. We meant to fly it ourselves, but then we thought we would give the flight to you.' He beamed at them angelically. 'And *we'll* have the next flight after that,' he added, firmly.

Isabella's laughter bubbled over, and she embarrassed her brothers horribly by hugging them.

'I think it is a wonderful—no, a perfect—wedding present. And truly romantic! When can we fly?'

'It must be cool to get the height,' frowned William, with professional consideration, 'and to be truly romantic you do need a sunset. We thought you would prefer to go before you get married, because afterwards you may be too respectable?' He turned the last sentence into faintly worried query, but he was already being interrupted by his brother.

'Anyway,' said Thomas. 'We want you to go soon, so that we can go afterwards.'

'Hush,' William frowned, kicking him, then turned an innocent face to Anthony and Isabella. 'Would you care to fly tomorrow evening?'

'Thank you. We would,' they replied, solemnly.

Algie, his ankle recovered, had been recruited by the boys to help with the ascent. The three of them, with Old Bill, were filling the balloon. The evenings were closing in, and the heat had gone out of the sun, but Mrs Larkham, Miss Pickering and Lady Kintrove were seated out, on the upholstered settee from the green room, which had been set for them on the gravel. They had a rug spread over their knees, and were much excited at the prospect of watching the ascent. The household staff stood in a gaggle behind them.

Isabella had been uncertain what her grandmother would think of her adoption of breeches, and she advanced to greet the three with some trepidation, but she need not have worried.

'I can see you're not one to let any little thing stand in the way of what you want. A chip off the old block, you are. Your grandfather would have been horrified, but he'd have been proud of you! Enjoy your flight, and come back safe, my girl.'

Isabella gave her a dutiful kiss. Perhaps the knowledge that Lady Kintrove had first suggested the breeches might have had some effect on this equanimity! She and Anthony walked over to the old store, and stood back, leaning against the flint wall, waiting for the wallowing, swaying balloon to fill. Anthony put his arms around Isabella, and held her, leaning her back against his chest.

'We never did dig up your treasure,' she said. 'Only a farthing. I shall keep it always as a good luck charm!'

'I don't know,' said Anthony, his chin just touching the top of her head. 'Who wants wealth? I found all the treasure I'll ever want up by that quarry.'

She laughed softly.

'It takes me by surprise nowadays when you say these beautiful things! So out of character! But the money will help. We are going to be disgustingly rich.'

'I know. It will make life considerably easier, and I feel less guilty at having persuaded you to share yours with me. But it is true. It is not the money that matters.'

'No.' She snuggled a little closer in his arms. 'I would have liked to find that treasure, though. Just for fun. We must set the boys to hunt it. It is just what they would like, and think how happy Nurse Pusey would be if another old legend came true!'

'She believes it already has! She is thoroughly satisfied. According to her, the tradition only alleges that when the Kintrove need is greatest, "treasure" will be found. And I found you. You found your grandmother and a fortune. *Ergo*, the legend is proved!'

Isabella laughed, and turned to face her love, her hands resting on his chest. The cloth of his coat was rough, a coarse country woollen mix.

'That woman is amazing,' she said. 'She used to make me *so* angry, happily assuming I would marry you! Just because of a few dogs. The impertinence!'

'Was the prospect so very bad?'

'Quite unthinkable!' She leaned back a little in his arms, frowning up at him earnestly. 'How could I even contemplate marriage to a man who had never made the slightest response to any of my advances, whether I flirted, or scorned him, or flaunted my charms to others to make him jealous? He would only look faintly amused, as if at the capering of a delinquent child, then deliberately hunch his back and affect ugliness to repulse me. Such a man deserves only punishment!'

'Oh, I can assure you, he got it! They weren't easy, those years in London.'

'Was is so very bad?' she asked in her turn.

'Quite unbearable,' he said with a slow smile. 'But I was astoundingly brave, and gained my just reward.'

'It may be more just than you care for! You realise we shall argue incessantly?'

'No! It is as William said. We shall be married, and therefore too respectable!'

'Poor William. He is going to be horribly disillusioned. We will never become entirely respectable, and will fight like cat and dog!'

'Life would be tedious if we did not. And besides...'

She was looking up at him with that edge of provocative defiance. Her lips were parted ready to laugh, her eyes teasing, hair pushed back. Her absurd boy's garb made her look about fourteen.

'Besides, what?' she asked.

'Besides,' he said huskily, pulling her closer, 'we can always stop the arguments like this.'

And he showed her what he meant.

It was Algie who brought them back to the moment.

'Hate to intrude! Hate to spoil the show for all your staff, come to that, but the old airship won't wait. She's raring to go, tugging at the guy ropes. Can't disappoint the boys. Time for you to do your bit. Leading roles, you know!'

Isabella and Anthony looked about them, brought back to their surroundings with a jolt of surprise. The entire household staff, and the three formidable ladies on the upholstered settee, were all watching with interest, many with foolish smiles on their faces. The balloon hung huge and vivid in the air, with William and Thomas hanging on to ropes and expectantly looking their way.

'Well?' Anthony said, with a faint smile, as Isabella blushed apologetically at Algie, 'we seem to have given our audience a satisfactory romantic interlude. Come on. Now for the grand finale!'

It was with the same bubbling of excitement as on her previous flight that Isabella climbed up on to the platform and slid down into the wicker basket. Anthony jumped lightly down beside her. It was not yet sunset, but the sun hung low over the trees, spilling long saffron ribbons of light through the branches and down the fields to the house. Outstretched shadows strode from bushes and hedges. A light breeze tickled through their hair, and wafted trails of autumnal woodsmoke from the smouldering trough.

Anthony surveyed the gathering of people, his people, and the vast sprawling house, a jumbled patchwork of shadows and glowing pinks and golden in the evening sun. Beyond, in every direction, spread his acres. Together they would restore these lands to prosperity. He looked down at her.

His hazel eyes seemed to her darker than usual, the lashes thick and long against the sun-browned skin. She watched him draw a deep breath.

'This is the moment, Isabella. Too late for regrets. It is just us, setting off into the blue.'

'There is nothing,' she stated simply, 'that could be better,' and leant up to kiss him.

There was an involuntary cheer from the eager spectators, cries of 'Good luck', *'Bon voyage'*, 'God speed', filled the air, and 'Let her go!' shouted William.

They were away, in a breathtaking upward climb, high over the roof-tops, over the woods, over the village and the Church, floating joyous and free as the summer air.

Algie and Old Bill had already set off in the gig in speedy pursuit, when William spoke. He was standing with his brother on the platform and watching the balloon drifting steadily westwards, a dark shape against the flaming red, silver-pink, golds and turquoise that spread gloriously over the evening sky.

'Now *that*,' said William, with deep satisfaction, '*that* is romantic!'

The other exciting

MASQUERADE
Historical

available this month is:

A PASSING FANCY

Deborah Miles

For the sake of his health, Cleo Montague and her father embarked from Plymouth for warmer climes. But the journey to Australia in 1858 proved too much for his strength, and Cleo found herself travelling on alone. Determined not to abandon her father's dream, and with superb millinery skills to earn her living, Cleo found herself setting up business in the goldrush town of Nugget Gully.

But this was only possible at the cost of accepting Jacob Raines as a silent partner. A decent respectable woman, Cleo knew that any hint about black sheep Jake would ruin her reputation in the community . . .